CONGRATULATIONS
ON EVERYTHING

CONGRATULATIONS
ON EVERYTHING

Nathan Whitlock

MISFIT

For Meaghan Strimas

"SAY, IS MY KINGDOM LOST?"
– *Richard II*, William Shakespeare

**"WINNERS FOCUS ON WINNING;
LOSING TAKES CARE OF ITSELF."**
– *The Risk Illusion*, Theo Hendra

Jeremy wore a skirt of keys. They shimmered on his waist like small fish living in the safety of his belly's shadow and grew wild at the back in schools of five and six. They balanced him out – with his skinny legs and dumb gut, they steadied him and helped correct his walk. On the edge of 50, he moved as if pushed hard from behind, falling forward, about to drop out of his life's frame like a character in a self-aware cartoon. He stumbled through days, weeks, years.

There were keys for every job, every lock. He could have laid them out in reverse chronological order and gone back through every door over which he'd ever had authority, until he reached his 19-year-old self: the busboy at a resort in the Muskokas, all panting and horny and chubby, hauling cases of beer and dumping ashtrays, working his way up to a coveted spot behind the bar. One of his very first bosses, while handing him his very first key, told him the house rule was *liquor in the front, poker in the rear*. Jeremy said he didn't know the place hosted card games, then quickly tried to find a way out of his mistake, which was pointless: every bar and restaurant has its own grammar, its own language, and it pleases the native speakers to laugh at struggling newcomers.

Years later, when he'd fought his way out from behind the bar and was starting his first managing position, there were more rules.

"Don't let the staff go Christmas shopping. You know what I'm talking about?"

Christmas shopping? He thought it was another joke.

"Not really."

It was simple: every December, a bunch of high-end whiskeys and scotches disappeared from the storeroom, along with a lot of the good wine. Everybody's mom and dad got a nice bottle for Christmas, and the bar absorbed the losses. No big deal, right? Like the bartender who pours out a whole bottle of good bourbon for himself and the rest of the staff over the course of a night and writes it off as *spillage*, laughing as he underlines the word, daring management to call him a liar. Jeremy had done it himself, before he was put in charge. For his mother's birthday he'd swiped a bottle of sparkling wine, which she thought was champagne. He didn't tell her otherwise, since that's what he'd thought it was when he grabbed it, and only realized the truth after she pulled off the dollar-store wrapping paper. His mother cried, "Champagne!" as she turned the bottle round and round in front of her face, reading each word on the label, delighted. She paused at *Niagara-on-the-Lake*. "This must've been *expensive*."

He accepted a pat on the back from his father.

Jeremy started counting the liquor stock every morning instead of once a week, and would confront staff when the counts were off. All that shit had to stop: the Christmas shopping, the spillage, throwing some bottles in a bag on the way to an after-work party. It was theft, pure and simple. He was management now; he had crossed over. He could fire them. He occasionally did – some people couldn't be told.

Jeremy kept every key. One day, a day filled with light and music, he would turn them all over as proof he'd worked hard, that he hadn't been a complete asshole when he'd had every chance to be, every right to be. That he'd overseen hirings and firings, and done so as fairly as he could. That when he got his own place, when the Ice Shack was finally up and running, he had tried to make it good, a decent place to work, an oasis. He'd tried to make it the exception. In an industry filled with assholes and psychotics, he was the rare good guy. He'd done some shitty things – sure, fine, he was the last person to deny it – but that was only because he worked in an industry filled with assholes and psychotics.

He'd been better than he had to be, put it that way.

Some bars and restaurants were lawless zones. People spent months or years working up the courage to quit; others simply walked away, like kids abandoning a game they suddenly realized they were unlikely to ever win. These escapees looked back in amazement that such things could go on without someone, some higher authority, stepping in to restore order. It took a long time for their bodies to unclench, for the dread to fully drain out of their systems. The wildest things happened, the absolute craziest, like in a prison yard when the guards have been bribed to look the other way. Sex in a staff bathroom or in a kitchen store-room on bags of rice the size of fat children. Wads of cash pocketed and "lost." Coke snorted off wooden cutting boards stained mahogany by years of raw beef and steak. And worse, really greasy stuff: a cook who worked with the tip of his cock poking out through his fly like a little helper elf with a squashy pink hat, so only the poor young woman who did the salads could see. An owner who asked his female staff to work in short skirts and no underwear. A bartender who told Jeremy he liked to piss on his fingers just before starting his shift, then again at some point during the night, and would rub them along the lip of every glass he filled. He didn't do it out of anger, but rather to keep clear in his own mind who, exactly, was in charge – and it sure as fuck wasn't the idiots crowding around and yelling at him about how long they'd been waiting for a beer.

Jeremy had seen it all, and hated it all, and tried as hard as he could to keep it out of the Shack. (He made the bartenders spritz disinfectant gel on their hands mid-shift, for one thing.) He sometimes felt he ought to get more credit for that. He didn't get sucked in by self-pity: even decades later, he retained the scorn of the run-ragged busboy for owners and managers who sat at the bar all night feeling sorry for themselves. But there were moments, when he had yet again managed to avert a disaster not of his making without receiving a single thank-you, that he wondered if he was being held to a different standard, a higher standard.

Someone, a customer, told Jeremy he was *Very Zen*.

Which was true, he thought. He didn't bite people's heads off for no reason, didn't walk around the place punching holes in walls or throwing chairs. He didn't fire people or give them shitty shifts to prove a point or exact some kind of petty revenge, or to humble someone he thought might be getting a little too high and mighty, or to cut off at the knees a potential threat to his own authority. He didn't freak out when things went wrong. He didn't sit in his office snorting up clouds of coke just to give all that anger a better focus, like chalking a pool cue. (That crap made his heart bang against his ribs like a wild animal, anyway.) A long time ago, while working for a pair of owners who hated each other and behaved like battling superpowers, with the staff as hapless proxies, Jeremy watched a cook get thrown through a glass door. Another time, a waitress got slapped – actually *slapped*, across the face, with an open hand – after messing up the order for a table of nine. That just wasn't him. He had never hit anyone, ever. Never even came close. How could he?

He saw so much, endured so much, and never flew into a rage. On a Friday night, right in the middle of a rush, he'd watched, helpless, as the bartender knocked to the floor a stack of pint glasses that were waiting to be slipped into the automatic washer. "Watch!" Jeremy shouted. Too late: glass went everywhere. He would have to run out the next day to buy a box of replacements. Add that chore to the list, which might as well have been on an endless scroll of paper that reached the floor and unfurled across the room like Santa's. He nearly threw his own glass down and stomped on it.

"That's the way," he said to the bartender, as condescending as a farmer moving cows out of a barn. "That's what we're paying you for. Keep it up, *dude*."

Later, when the broken glass had been cleared up and things were calmer, Jeremy called the bartender over and told him not to stack them that way. "You're just asking for trouble." He said it quietly, like a coach not wanting to break a player's concentration.

Another time, coming to collect the cash-out at the end of the night, he'd found the lights still on, the doors unlocked, and the bar completely empty. The zippered deposit bag with the evening's cash and credit card receipts was sitting out in the open on a table next to the door. He stood and stared at it, amazed that it had not been stolen, and almost ready to believe it was a mirage or a trick. The bar's stereo was blaring "Free Fallin'" by Tom Petty, which no one was allowed to play while the bar was open because it made one of the waitresses cry. In the kitchen he found the last dregs of the floor staff sitting around the open door of the walk-in fridge, laughing and complaining that the heat wave and the broken air conditioning had forced them in there. They were sharing tequila and could barely stand. It was somebody's birthday, they told him, as if to protect themselves from any curse or hex he might call down upon them. Jeremy laughed, because he could not fire them all, or at least not all at once, and would be forced to do so one by one, over the course of a few weeks as he was able to replace them. Not one of them got mad at him for doing so, and he let them go with more disappointment than anger. He wanted to ask each of them: *How could you be so stupid?* Instead, he said only, "Try not to do that at your next job." There was no point in yelling – the damage had been done, the lessons were already being learned. A few cried, though not the waitress who always broke down over Tom Petty: she spent their brief meeting looking out at the street through the large front windows. When she left, he gave her the CD with "Free Fallin'" to take with her.

Jeremy told people he was like a duck swimming: all calm on the surface, but underneath going a million miles an hour. Even when he stopped to scan the pages of the *Sun*, it was only to glean quick facts about sports, weather, and gas prices that could be used to spark conversations with customers in the bar that night. The only break he got was first thing in the morning, when he sat in his own kitchen at home and ate toast while listening to talk radio. He listened to the old men and women who called in just to have someone to go on and on at, airing the grievances that were their entire existences, the fears and resentments that alarmed them into staying alive a little longer.

I don't understand how the government can just keep spending money like it's nothing.

You walk into a store and nobody offers to help anymore.

When did saying 'Merry Christmas' become such a crime?

Everyone is so busy with their little phones, wasting their time on nonsense.

I can't even take the bus now, the kinds of people you see.

He recognized the type: lonely, needy. He'd worked in enough bars to know. He would sit there at his kitchen table with his mouth open, smiling slightly or shaking his head, taking everything in, every word spoken, every complaint made, accepting all of it. As if the people on the radio were in the room with him and more than willing to keep the conversation going while he ate his toast and nodded along.

Twenty minutes of that, followed by a shower and a quick shave, and he'd be moving. Keys tinkled as he stepped off the curb to get into his Jeep, fresh sunlight burning the street, bleaching it clean. The keys dug into his side as he drove and poked him as he reached for something in the clutter of invoices, parking tickets, and CDs on the passenger seat and on the floor. A heavy group of them hung from the steering column as he drove, shifting on the unpredictable tide of his thigh. Jeremy had worn the keys for so long he didn't even notice them anymore. It took him a few seconds to clue in when people pointed them out. He'd shrug. *You know me.* They usually did. When he bought a new lock for the garbage shed next to the bar, the woman at the hardware store smiled at him.

"You gonna have room?"

"Oh, you know – if I don't nail it down somebody steals it."

Now he was the one waiting for a laugh.

"No, it's the old one's fucked. Someone got at it with a crowbar or something. There's nothing in there but broken patio chairs and that kind of thing. You know. Anyways. Don't need the bag."

And he left, adding one more key to his belt.

The keys touched the walls of his narrow house as he walked and scratched at the back of his chair as he sat in his kitchen, that hot kitchen that collected all the heat from the back of the fridge, the stove, and even the basement furnace, which was relatively new and still eager to please. Every morning he put his coffee in the window to cool, and always forgot about it, always always always. So he would take a few sips then pour the rest out, feeling stupid. Bending over to pick up a penny only gave you a bad back – that's what he told his staff. It was something his father said, and his father was the cheapest fucker in the world, at least when it came to spending money on himself. His father always had new shoes sitting patiently in boxes at the bottom of his closet, waiting for the pair currently in use to wear out. His father still had a VCR connected to a TV in his basement, where he'd watch episodes of variety shows that had gone off the air before Jeremy was old enough to walk. Jeremy had spent more than a few nights sitting down there with his dad, watching Sammy Davis Jr. dance and sing in black and white. And yet: worry about the dollars, not the pennies.

"That doesn't mean I'm all into you wasting money," he always added, just to be crystal clear.

He touched his keys while chatting with whomever was on bar that night or with a group that had come in to watch the game or celebrate a birthday. He looked at the keys, picked through them to remind himself of something he needed to do or needed to ask someone else to do, something that needed fixing or replacing. "You look like you're about to eat it," a server said as Jeremy stared down at one broad key, trying to remember which lock it fit. He wore them for the entire day, unlocking tool boxes and breaker panels and the vanilla-coloured safe where he kept the day's receipts. They touched the wood of the bar as he leaned against it. They shook when he laughed – the hardest at his own jokes. At the end of the night, the keys fell with his pants when he finally got home, got undressed, and let himself drop into bed face-first like a little kid. In the morning, with his mouth full of moss and his mind inching toward surrender, he would carefully draw out the belt and attach the keys to whatever pants he planned to wear that day.

Jeremy's neighbourhood was a relatively new one, sitting at the fat end of a wedge created by the crossing of two highways that cut Toronto off at the forehead. The thin tip of the CN Tower and the jumble of downtown were only visible from third-floor windows. The neighbourhood had bubbled up around a cookie factory in the 1970s and '80s and then crowded over the bare ground left behind when the factory was shut down and flattened. Not long after he moved in, city workers came to chop down the trees, all up and down the block. Every tree was sick with the same thing, some little worm that got under the bark and embroidered the bare trunks with tunnels. Nothing to rake at least, he joked. Nothing to rake and nothing was going to fall on his Jeep in a storm. That had happened to people he knew who lived in areas full of old, untouchable trees: everything shakes, the rain hits the windows like silver wasps, the kids cry in their beds, the dog does a strange dance by the basement door. And then *crack!* – a branch goes, and they find it the next morning holding the crumpled roof of the car in the crook of its woody elbow. Still, Jeremy wouldn't have minded having one or two still standing in his backyard to keep the house cool and maybe make the area look a little less apocalyptic. People tried planting new ones, thin saplings that didn't make it much above shoulder-height before giving up the ghost. He didn't want saplings.

"I want to order them up full-grown," he said at the bar. "I don't have time to watch them go through puberty."

His house was semi-detached, and gripped its conjoined twin like the weaker partner in a three-legged race. It was in rough shape when he first moved in: full of scuffs and holes, the basement naked and unfinished and becoming animal with the grey fur of dust and mould. The backyard fence falling in on junk and thigh-high weeds, every room painted pale orange like an old motel. He had contractors in and out of the place for nearly six months to paint over everything and install new cabinets and fixtures before he decided it looked respectable enough. His yard, however, never got up to speed. Next door, the grass was green and welcoming, as soft as moss.

"I try sometimes, I honestly do. I run out and buy a whole shitload of things. I get the seed, the fertilizer, the little shovels. Nothing works."

"I seen you out there," his next-door neighbour said, as if confirming an alibi. His neighbour was as old as his father, somewhere in his mid-70s, and wore a baseball cap with the name of a naval ship on it – the *HMCS Something-or-Other* – and an arterial spray of red maple leaves. The man's daughter was in the navy out east, where she'd once spent a week pulling bodies out of the ocean after a passenger jet went down in sight of Peggy's Cove. His wife was dead: cancer – Jeremy had been told which kind, but could never remember, and it was too late to ask. He sometimes heard bagpipe music coming through their shared wall first thing in the morning, sounding like a Scottish regiment was on the march through the living room, about to burst through the walls in an explosion of kilts and broken plaster.

"The grass doesn't want to grow, but I get points for trying."

His neighbour said, "Gotta keep at it." Like a parent explaining to a child a burden shared by all the people in the world.

Another widower lived across the street with three kids. Two widowers on one block – must be bad luck, Jeremy thought. Something was killing the trees, the grass, the wives. Jeremy had spotted the motherless family right away when he was first looking to buy: the three boys and their father almost identical, but for their ages and sizes – all thin and healthy, with straight hair the colour of milk and blue, sinister eyes. They looked like a single member of an advanced race, caught in a time loop and thrust into simultaneous existence. He was cheerful, though, this Future Man surrounded by his past selves. The children were mute, but Nicolas, the father, always waved and shouted hello.

Nicolas admired Jeremy's Jeep, and Jeremy was only too happy to fill him in on the car's virtues. He still had an almost painful affection for it, and felt every new scratch and ding in his heart. "Look at you!" the salesman had said when he was first thinking of buying it. Jeremy was halfway across the lot, holding the ignition key in the air, locking and unlocking the car to measure the maximum distance. "Look how far you can go! You won't lose it!"

"I wouldn't anyway, you should see my memory," Jeremy said.

He made Nicolas stick his fingers into the deep ruts of the Jeep's tires.

"These suckers *laugh* at freezing rain."

Nicolas agreed. "You'll never get stuck."

It was as if this Future Man had let slip a fact about Things to Come: whatever Jeremy did, whatever he attempted, he would not get stuck. He would roll right over obstacles, stopping only to rescue others who'd gotten bogged down. It was what he always tried to keep in mind whenever he was neck-deep in some staffing problem, some stupid personal issue that had become septic and burst all over the floor, tripping people up and getting its smell on everything. He would wade in and start cutting away at the infected emotions, trying to determine what could be saved, what could be dealt with on another day, and what needed to be dealt with *now*. Even when the dispute at the heart of the whole thing was stupid and trivial, he could usually perform this cleanup job without completely losing it, because he never got stuck, because he was Very Zen.

When Jeremy went out in the morning, he often saw Nicolas and his three boys walking in single file, tallest to smallest, out to the minivan. The boys fought for space inside the van with their elbows. Jeremy once watched as the youngest tried to push the cat's face through the tiny squares of the living room window screen. The boy pushed hard, pulled the animal back into the darkness, then pushed again. The cat put up with this treatment for longer than Jeremy would've guessed, then both he and his tormentor disappeared in a flurry of fur and yelling. All of those people living in one house: it wasn't for him. Big families meant endless hysteria and the worst sadism – he'd known a boy in elementary school who'd gone after his three sisters with a flaming branch from a campfire, giving one of them a scar on her cheek the shape of a long division sign. For years after, the kid saw a counsellor who talked to him about his anger, his favourite hockey players, and whether or not he ever played with his thing. Jeremy remembered being amazed to discover grown-ups knew about playing with your thing. He'd assumed it was a kids-only activity, like climbing trees and writing swear words on the slide in the playground.

At home, he needed emptiness, silence, space. He needed to have the bathroom all to himself and to fart loudly when he came out of his bedroom in the morning. He needed to run out of the house first thing without a goodbye. He needed to come home long after midnight or, very occasionally, not at all. He needed to sit, undisturbed, on the stairs, pressing his hungover head between his thumbs until he could think clearly enough to seek out grapefruit juice and Tylenol. He needed to keep things simple. Work was the thing, the Shack was the thing. Neighbours who'd been awoken by the sound of his Jeep returning home long after midnight would see him on the move again while they were waiting for their coffee makers to make coffee or for their kids to find everything they needed for school. Neighbours who thought it wouldn't hurt him to pay a *little* more attention to the city's garbage and recycling pickup schedule and *maybe* not come flying up the street at three in the morning blasting Kim Mitchell's "Go For Soda" loud enough to wake children and disturb pets – even *they* acknowledged how hard he seemed to work.

So when things finally went all to hell for him, when everything fell apart with the Shack and everything else, most people saw it as something close to tragic. Jeremy was an arrow that had been bent and mangled many times but was always left pointing in what looked like the right direction. You had to be a truly awful person to want to see it snapped.

> "EVERYTHING YOU DO, EVERY EXPERIENCE – IT'S ALL EDUCATION.
> I DROPPED OUT OF HIGH SCHOOL."
> – *Burn to Learn*, Theo Hendra

The Ice Shack formed the short end of an L-shaped strip mall perched on the edge of a ravine. Its patio jutted out into space – the trees seemed to hold it aloft on thin, grey arms. Jeremy liked to go out there every morning before he started any serious work. Even in the winter, he'd slip the doors open and step out onto the crust of snow for a few quick breaths of air. When the branches began to crowd the deck in the summer, Jeremy would grab the machete he kept hidden in his office, not letting anyone out there with him as he moved shirtless along the railing and hacked at the creeping fingers of the trees. Afterward, he'd come in sweating, all speckled with green gore, and drink a quick pint of draft while the staff fought back laughter. Charlene, the young woman who handled most of the lunch shifts, would hand him a bar towel and the clean shirt he'd left hanging on the back of a stool.

"It has to be done," he'd tell her when he was halfway through his restorative pint.

She didn't dispute this.

He told her that when he'd first opened the Shack – she wasn't around back then – some of those trees were not nearly as intimidating as they now seemed.

"I'm the only one around here who keeps getting younger."

Charlene said she sometimes felt as though she were 70 years old, though she was barely 30 at the time.

"That's all up here," he replied, touching his temple with the tip of his finger.

In the spring, the river was angry and turbulent, but by the end of the summer, it shrank down and came alive with torn garbage bags that whipped against the bars of submerged shopping carts. Kids sometimes got the idea to wade in and collect the empty bottles lurking at the bottom. A few of those bottles were from the Shack, but most came from teenagers drinking beer and vodka under the bridge. When Jeremy was still a bartender and out of town one summer, a teenager tried jumping from the bridge. A dare had been issued, so the kid climbed up onto the railing and dropped down into the water. It was nearly two in the morning, Jeremy was told – his mother kept him up to date on that kind of thing while he was gone – and the ambulance attendants and cops were forced to carry the idiot up the steep bank to the road. The kid dislocated his shoulder and almost drowned, but worst of all, he'd been speared through the thigh by part of a metal bed frame. It filled Jeremy's legs with ice to think of that poor, stupid bastard sitting there, pinned and bleeding, probably blacking out from pain while the dark water moved past him, unimpressed.

From the Shack's patio doors, Jeremy could see the spot on the bridge where the kid must've jumped. He always wondered if his friends stuck around, or if they ran off the instant they knew he was hurt, the moment the dare turned foul. Jeremy liked to think he would've stuck around, had he been there, though he never would've been the one jumping. Don't be the first one in or the last one out, his dad used to tell him. Get in there once the going is good, and then get out before it all goes bad.

Jeremy said, "You have to know, though, don't you? You have to be sure when it's good. And you have to be able to predict when it's about to go bad. It's not simple."

Just don't ever be the dummy left holding the bag, his father told him.

Fair enough.

Once a month, Jeremy would grab some garbage bags and pick his way down the hill behind the bar to clean up all the things that had been flung down from above. He felt strangely calm down there. Ankle-deep in snow or brush, surrounded by bottles and trash, he would stand and let the shadow of the patio creep down the hill toward him.

"This ravine was made by retreating glaciers," he told the bar-back who volunteered to come down and help him clean up, and was taking the opportunity for a quick smoke. "Millions of years ago, everything around here was underwater. Millions of years from now – probably water again, who knows?"

Or a desert, the bar-back suggested.

"I doubt it," Jeremy said. "Not with the winters we've been getting. Indians used to use this river, too. They'd go all the way down to the lake in canoes."

"To do what?"

"I have no idea. Sell fur maybe? Beat the shit out of each other?"

The bar-back found a lighter in the grass and checked that it still had some life.

Jeremy looked up and said, "Look at the patio. Isn't that impressive? Can you take a picture on your phone? Never mind, finish your smoke."

"There's one of our big dinner plates," the bar-back said, pointing into the thick brush. "And a couple forks, look! Why do people chuck shit over the side?"

Jeremy didn't know why people threw things. He didn't know why they wrote nasty shit on the walls of the bathroom. He didn't know why they shoved napkins and food into the folds of the seats in a booth. He didn't know why they took off without leaving enough cash to cover the bill, never mind a tip. Inviting strangers into your place was an act of faith. He had never struggled with that faith, never had any real sense of doubt, until he got a place of his own. With the Shack, he'd been tested, but he'd also been rewarded.

"Just watch you don't slip into the water. It's faster than you think."

He let the kid scramble through weeds and dead branches retrieving lost cutlery and ruined menus, while he indulged a private vision of the Ice Shack as an ark that would float away safely with everyone inside when the waters rose again in the world. This, he decided, was why some owners burned out so fast, or became jaded and cynical: they never took the time to watch their places be quietly blessed by sunlight. He had taken a few courses in hotel and restaurant management early on, but those were entirely for show. His real education, as he'd told many people at the bar, staff and customers alike, had come from watching the owners for whom he'd worked over the decades, noting every successful strategy, every fruitful ritual, but also every fatal mistake.

And he'd worked: on his way up, he grabbed every shift, took on every project, volunteered to stay late, and came in on his days off to see if extra hands were needed. He stuffed every corner and every crack with work. Many of the work friends he made dropped away – they were only there until something less stressful and less nocturnal came along. Most couldn't understand why Jeremy stuck to it: after a certain point, didn't he wish he could work normal hours, sit at a desk, go out at night for fun, sleep? He'd once spent half a year working a desk job, he told them, and it had felt like being stranded inside a moon colony. He remembered constantly wandering down sterile hallways lit with fluorescent bulbs, nodding and smiling at co-workers he would never get to know better than he already did, laughing at jokes that stayed within strictly professional boundaries, wishing he could walk around with his shirt off and bare feet just to feel less constrained. He went home every night feeling like a failure for being unable to find his groove amid all those cubicles, coffee machines, and magnetized picture frames displaying photos of children. It wasn't until much later that he realized the problem lay not in him, but in the situation: he simply wasn't built for a place like that. It was a bad match. He was a beaver locked in with the turtles. He belonged in rooms that were full of energy and chatter, that saw tides of people wash in and out throughout the day, that shook with noise and threw everyone lucky enough to work there into the weeds. In the Shack, he had found his home.

"I'm out every night," he said. "I eat and drink for free, and I sleep like a baby."

He chided people for using the term *service industry*.

"That makes me feel like a butler," he said. "And it makes you sound like an accountant."

What he did, what his staff did, was more fluid than that term suggested, there was more art to it. It took more than mere business savvy to make it work, and though money was a large part of the motivation, it was not the only one, or even the most important one. There were easier ways to make money.

Christ, there had to be.

One of Jeremy's first managing jobs was at a bar called the Pour House, on a dead-end street a few blocks from a college campus. It did well – especially on weekends, when the rooms filled with enough drunken students so you could barely move.

The owner of the Pour House was an architect with hair as white as ice cream that was always pulled back in a ponytail. He smoked cigarettes with a long plastic filter like a femme fatale in an old movie. His name was Bruce, but he insisted on being called Big B. He had never owned a bar before, and never worked in one, and so immediately attributed the success of the place to his own innate abilities, his sense of things, his understanding of space. *Space* was everything – it was more important than the price of beer or the ratio of girls to boys. He would walk into the place during the afternoon when it was quiet and would stand with his hands on his hips in the middle of the room, his bright ponytail jutting out from the back of his head and curling around gently on his shoulder like an animal sidekick. He would stand in the spot he believed to be the exact centre of the bar, stretch out his arms straight in either direction, then slowly turn his body so that the tips of his fingers became like sensors analyzing and storing data from every corner. He would turn all the way around, and then lunge forward to rearrange a group of tables or move a plant to another part in the room.

"*Movement*," he said to Jeremy. If he were in the mood, he would expand upon the idea: "Movement. Action. Air. Space. *Life*."

Sometimes Big B questioned the bartender on the arrangement of the bottles behind the bar or wondered aloud if they should print the menu in reverse order, starting with desserts. That would be fun and unexpected, wouldn't it? Instead of the same old thing? It didn't really matter much what Big B did: the bar was perfectly located and always made money. After Jeremy had been there for a couple of years, a spot became available a few blocks away, an old coffee shop that had finally given up the ghost. Jeremy sometimes parked across the street before work and stared at the place, imagining how he could transform it, what it would look like with customers packed right to the door. He didn't know his boss had been thinking the same thing until the day Big B walked in, ponytail straight and proud, and announced he'd signed a lease for the location and was planning to open a wine bar called Big B's.

"It'll be an older crowd, more exclusive. More casual, more intimate, more intense."

At the time, Jeremy was dating one of the Pour House waitresses, a woman named Tracy who was always talking about becoming a teacher because she was so good with kids. That was what she kept saying to Jeremy when they lay together naked and sweating in his bed or hers, their hearts slowly calming down: "I've always been really good with kids. It's weird – I really like them."

Jeremy never agreed or disagreed with this. He hadn't had any experience with kids by that point, and felt that the urge to have one was deeply perverse, a kind of self-mutilation, like wanting to have a limb cut off or to be blinded in one eye. What he did do was offer to arrange her schedule so she'd be free to work at a daycare or take childhood education courses during the week, but she never seemed all that enthusiastic about the idea.

Jeremy liked Tracy. He liked her hair, which smelled like green apples from her shampoo. He liked her eyes, with their heavy lids. He found that erotic. Her breasts pointed out in different directions, like chameleon eyes. They were small, but Jeremy decided he preferred small, after so many years of preferring big. He felt this was a sign of his growing sophistication, the way he'd been drinking imported beers and eating more seafood. The way even something like heavy eyelids could make him horny now. He didn't like her laugh – loud and horsey, and on a hair trigger – or how much pot she smoked, or how she would tell other staffers intimate things about him, but he was able to overlook all that.

The wine bar finally collapsed, taking the Pour House down with it: the new place had been kept afloat by siphoning off money from the old. There was so much debt to settle, so many loans, so many unpaid invoices, that Jeremy didn't expect to get any kind of payout, but Big B met him outside the locked bar early on a Monday morning with an envelope filled with cash, the equivalent of three weeks' pay. His hair was completely ragged, the ponytail shredded and loose. He sighed and shrugged and said, "Money."

Jeremy nodded to show he understood.

The money wasn't enough to get Jeremy through the summer without work, so he took a bartending job at a golf course in Etobicoke where a manager who was younger than him told pussy jokes all day. Tracy couldn't find another job right away and had to move out of her apartment in the middle of the night and in with her older sister, who had a house and a husband. She hated being there, and would often stay with Jeremy at his apartment. They fought a lot. One night, they were lying in his bed with all the blankets off. It has a humid night. He lay there watching grotesque faces form in the shadows on the wall, just like when he was a kid. Tracy had smoked half a joint earlier in the night over his objections, and he wondered if he was second-hand high.

Quietly, he asked the dark: *"How is a pussy like a new car?"*

"What?"

He'd thought she was fast asleep.

"You heard me."

Once she was fully awake, they talked and talked until they were broken up. She lay in his bed and cried, and he went to sleep on the couch – it was her last night there, after all. His time at the Pour House was ancient wreckage, always floating just offshore in his mind. He considered himself lucky to have less of it in his past than a lot of people he knew. Some had wrecks piled up right to the beach, fouling the waters.

Jeremy's conception of the Shack had been vague at first. He'd carried it with him for years, tucked somewhere in the back of his mind as he moved through more than half a dozen bars, restaurants, and hotels. The best and clearest idea he had for the kind of place he wanted was actually an anti-idea, a vision born of opposition. It showed itself to him while he was in his 30s and managing a Crane's franchise. Crane's was the kind of place that had big walk-in freezers full of skids of frozen steaks, each hard shingle of meat as big as a shoe print and already crisscrossed with artificial charbroil lines. In the dining room, there were saddles on the walls, as well as doors from antique Coca-Cola fridges. The name Crane's was everywhere, printed on the cut-off bottoms of wooden barrels in bright red letters like wet licorice. Jeremy liked to say that you could stand in the middle of any Crane's location in the world and have no idea what country you were in, or even what continent. If there was a Crane's in China, its customers were eating under saddles and old-timey fridge doors.

At Crane's, they encouraged diners to time their meals, from the moment of ordering to when the plates arrived at their table. There were cards they could fill out with these times and leave on the platter with their bill or slip into a box by the front door. They were also encouraged to calculate their servers' Smile Points – literally, the number of times the poor kid taking their order managed to smile at them, and how big and bright the smiles had been. These, too, were to be handed in or dropped into the box. Part of Jeremy's job was to collect these cards at the end of each night, calculate wait times and Smile Points, then issue warnings or gold stars. Staffers were encouraged to rat each other out for petty theft, general laziness, and misconduct, under the guise of empowering them to help improve the business from within. This was done using cards, too, with another drop-box bolted to the wall just outside Jeremy's office. It had been bolted to the wall in the kitchen, but kept getting torn down or filled with hot coffee and worse.

After years of it, Jeremy felt as tight as the pristine maroon golf shirts he and every other employee had to wear whenever on Crane's property. Standing with the rest of the floor staff, singing "Happy Birthday" to some clueless child or clueless grandparent, he wanted to scream at them all to *run*. Slowly, the pictures and posters disappeared from his office, as though he were preparing for a prison break and wanted nothing to weigh him down. When he finally left, it was with the certainty that *his* place would be nothing like a Crane's.

Pretty much the only good thing to have ever come out of the Crane's job was a free trip to New York City for a big conference of owners and managers. At the airport, it was all darkness outside the floor-to-ceiling windows, and he could feel the cold through the accordioned walls of the walkway onto the plane. The jet had already noisily shed its connections to the terminal and begun a slow turn toward the runway when the whole thing went black and stopped dead. It was as if the thing had been knocked unconscious. It was soon enough after two planes had head-butted the World Trade Center towers that all the passengers froze, afraid of what would come next.

Over the PA system the captain said, "This is a new jet." She sounded amused, as though they were all children in her care. "It doesn't seem to like the cold," she said, meaning the plane. "We're going to take her back and reboot the computer and then everything should be fine. Very sorry for the inconvenience. Won't take too long."

"It's colder where we're going," Jeremy said to his seatmate, an Indian woman in a pantsuit the colour of a blood orange.

"In New York?" she asked, a little alarmed. She'd only lived in Canada for a year, and couldn't believe there might be any place colder.

"No, *up*." He pointed at the roof of the cabin. The woman looked to where he was pointing, then got the joke and smiled.

In New York Jeremy bought dozens of stickers, statuettes, and buttons to give to his staff, as well as a poster that showed the island of Manhattan as a slice of pizza, which, years later, had pride of place on the wall behind the bar at the Shack. He walked down to Ground Zero, which still smelled like someone was burning tires in the middle of the city. Everywhere he looked he saw American flags hanging from shuttered buildings, in the windshields of dump trucks and police cars, and pinned to jackets, as if the attack had come because the people there had forgotten what their flag looked like and were determined not to make the same mistake twice. Jeremy stood there at the site and tried to appear appropriately solemn, before admitting to himself that he was disappointed: it was just a big pit with some hoarding around it. The most famous city block in the world, and they weren't doing a thing with it, at least not yet. You couldn't even get anything to eat, other than a hot dog. He regretted not going down to see the Statue of Liberty when he had the chance. As he stood there shaking his head with disappointment, an elderly man who looked like Morgan Freeman patted him on the shoulder and told him America would stay strong, they'd get through this. On Jeremy's way back to the hotel, he stared at a woman in a red rubber dress who was at least six-feet tall, with thick arms that looked muscular and hard. Later, he realized it had been a man dressed as a woman. This pleased him, as it confirmed that he was in the middle of something unusual, something special.

The conference itself was mostly a waste of time: lots of presentations about ways to inspire staff. Most of them he already knew. There was a speech by a former bartender who had lost her right arm in a bus accident while travelling in Mexico. She told them how the company had helped her get through the hardest times right after the accident, how it was *so* amazing to know she had this huge family supporting her. She couldn't tend bar anymore, of course, but now worked in human resources. Jeremy cried at her story like everyone else.

The part he had looked forward to the most was a presentation by Theo Hendra, whom he'd never seen in the flesh. Hendra was the author of *Power Tools*, *The Yes Equation*, *More Yes Equations*, *Closing the Confidence Gap*, and more. (Plus a handful of semi-pornographic sword-and-sorcery novels he'd written in his 20s and mostly kept out of print ever since; Jeremy had tried to read a couple of those, but gave up a few pages in, feeling like an intruder.) Of all the books that Jeremy had ever read about building success strategies, self-actualization, and doing away with fear – and there were a lot – Hendra's were the only ones that made any kind of sense. What he gave were the facts of life, straight up: you do this, you avoid that, you keep on top of these other things, and you *might* have a fighting chance. If, on the other hand, you lose your focus, let your emotional life get too messy, and take the people around you for granted, or are simply not up to the task, you are almost guaranteed to find yourself scrambling around begging for help to delay the inevitable and fight off people who try to rob your dreams right out from under you. You'd have nothing left to do but lick your wounds and settle for second-best. Jeremy appreciated being told the road ahead tilted upward. No fish ever jumped into a boat because it was beautiful, no deer ever jumped in the way of a bullet because the hunter seemed worthy. Those were the lessons that stuck.

Jeremy constantly had to defend Hendra against the exact kind of corrosive negativity the books worked hard to neutralize.

"Isn't he a total scam artist?"

He'd heard this more than once.

"How many of his books have you actually read? How many?" Jeremy countered.

"None. He's got weird teeth."

"Oh, well, there you go: case closed."

Hendra, he told people, had given him something very valuable: a direction. He was lucky; he'd seen people hit a certain age and suddenly fight their way into the religion of their parents (or grandparents) as if forcing open the doors of a departing subway car. Or they would arm themselves against boredom with hobbies and crafts. Or they had more kids than they needed. Or they started running – at some point, it seemed as though just about everyone Jeremy knew was gobbling marathons and half-marathons, and bringing their special shoes to work. Jeremy's fragile knees would not allow him to join in, but he happily blessed their efforts and tried not to judge. He didn't need to run, he didn't need crafts or church. Every place he worked in, even Crane's, glowed like an arrow, pointing him toward his ultimate goal: a place of his own.

In the big convention hall in New York, Hendra came bounding out onto the stage in bicycle shorts and a tight T-shirt, clapping his hands over his head like a fitness instructor, with "Every 1's a Winner" playing loud enough to be felt through the floor, and the flashing lights bringing everyone to the edge of a seizure. Jeremy chanted along when Hendra called for the crowd to shout out the Three Principles of Personal Power. He stood in line to beat on a bright yellow punching bag with the word FEAR written across it in big black letters. A team of young assistants wearing headsets ran up and down the line, handing out free copies of a new, expanded edition of *Power Tools*.

Back in Toronto, in a taxi from the airport, Jeremy opened the book. On the very first page he turned to, he saw the word *Canada*, which seemed so unusual that he read the passage that surrounded it, right there in the taxi. And as he did, he began to sweat under his shirt. A massive jet glided down heavily above him, throwing a quick shadow over the entire road, and the relentless thunder got into his ears and his arms and almost made him drop the book with excitement. Even before the taxi joined the halting highway traffic, he decided it was time to make a move. It was time to open his own bar.

And he knew what he was going to call it.

"RELATIONSHIPS ARE NOT DISTRACTIONS; THEY ARE INSTRUCTIONS."
– *The Passion Play*, Theo Hendra

For weeks at a time, Jeremy would only go home from the Shack to sleep – and even then, for barely five or six hours at a time. He'd once thought seriously about installing a shower in his office and buying a decent pullout couch. He sometimes stood in his living room at home, or in the small hallway just inside his front door, and wondered if it was worth paying for those walls, those windows, and all the invisible streams of water and power and WiFi moving through the place, when he spent so little time among them. Even on quiet nights, he loved staying at the Shack to the bitter end, helping the servers cash out and messing sweatily with the stereo behind the bar. He felt it was important to be around as much as possible, if only to ward off, by his mere presence, the sudden and total panic he was certain would descend the moment he left.

He trusted his staff, but only to a certain extent. He knew that if things got too busy, if disaster struck, they would start to whirl and stumble. He put the palm of his hand on their backs – shifting it quickly if he accidentally touched the disapproving cross-strap of a bra – and told them to roll with it. Everything's cool, comp a few drinks, no one's in a hurry. With his hand he would draw out the hysteria that formed within each of them like a tiny storm. Even when he didn't seem to be doing much of anything – just talking and drinking and walking around – he was spreading calm, maintaining order, putting out fires. One time, he'd had to put out an actual fire when a busboy dumped an ashtray into the garbage without dousing the glowing cigarette butts it contained. Within a minute, the trash was flickering. Jeremy moved fast, throwing in a whole pitcher of flat beer and getting the windows open before the alarm went off and the sprinklers drenched them all with cold rain. There were cheers. Jeremy smiled and put his hands in the air as his chest heaved under his shirt.

"Crazy night," he said to the bartender. "Cheers!"

After he locked the doors for the night, the staff would slump in their chairs, and he would assure them he had no problem if they wanted to smoke a joint on the deck, as long as they were discreet about it. "After tonight, I don't blame you," he said. "It's cool." He lived for this kind of casual charity, this display of benevolent power.

Sometimes he didn't get home from the bar until sunlight was already showing in the sky. Once, as he walked from the Jeep to his back door, he heard a train, moving somewhere off in the distance, hoot *shave-and-a-haircut* as it rolled along the borders of his neighbourhood. Jeremy stood there for a moment, amazed. The train hooted again – *toot toot te-toot toot* – but by now it had rolled itself to another part of the city. Jeremy felt childishly privileged to have heard it, though he knew he would regret staying out so late. He waited for the train to sound again, but it didn't. Or else it was too far away when it did, off where it could only be heard by stray cats, raccoons, and the poor bastards who delivered newspapers before dawn.

It was the kind of thing he could never explain to people who could not understand why he did what he did: he would never have heard that train if he'd been stuffed in an office somewhere, keeping normal hours.

———————————

He had originally bought his house in the hopes that it would move forward his relationship with Terry, the woman he was seeing at the time. It didn't; they split up. Which had not come as a shock: throughout the whole time they were together, there seemed always to be an incongruity at the core of their relationship, as if they could never quite settle on a compelling motive for staying together beyond mutual loneliness. He thought of the house as something solid that could anchor them, and had visions of the two of them painting the place, of sitting out back with a beer when it was warm outside, and of her filling the rooms with the smell of home-baked bread and soups and desserts that he would happily come home from work in the middle of the day for. He had no idea if she could bake, but the visions persisted.

When he and Terry were first together, they went out on dinner dates and drank enough wine to become unselfconscious. Afterward, they would hold hands as they walked through the parking lot, and sometimes she would lean her head on his shoulder, and even though in that moment he would feel as though actual, lasting happiness were finally being dispensed, it never seemed to take, and the next time they saw each other, they'd have to start all over again. When they had sex, still in the glow of the wine, it was always at Jeremy's place. And she hardly ever stayed the night. When she did, they'd be watched closely the next morning by one of his neighbour's white-haired children as they walked to his Jeep or her car.

She would whisper, "Is that one of them?"

"The youngest."

"How can you tell?"

"I'm guessing."

Terry had a child from a brief earlier marriage, a little girl who refused to accept the fact of her mother's relationship with Jeremy, showing him less warmth than she would have an estranged uncle. She went away every other weekend to stay with her father in Guelph and would come back with a superior smirk on her face, as if she had, over the past three days, been given the chance to see the world as it really was, free of all blinders, filters, and lies. Her father let her watch movies full of swear words and naked kissing.

"Are you an alcoholic?" the girl asked Jeremy.

"No, sorry."

"All the people at your work are alcoholics."

The way she said it, it sounded like a religion.

That was her father talking, Terry told him. He should just ignore it.

"Why is he saying this shit to her?"

Terry gave him a look he had come to recognize, which said that the acts of minor emotional vandalism committed by divorced parents were outside his jurisdiction. He was, at best, an innocent bystander, collateral damage.

Jeremy spent more than a year trying to win the girl over. He sat through elementary school assemblies in which class after class marched onstage to berate the tight-smiled audience with Christmas carols while the young music teacher beat back their voices with the sound of an upright piano. He stared in growing incomprehension as Pokémon cards were laid out one by one before him, their individual strengths and weaknesses explained in exhaustive detail. He drove them both down to the shore of Lake Ontario, walked with them along the sand with the busy rumble of the expressway just behind them, and did his best to help when the girl cut her foot open on a piece of green glass the size and shape of a Dorito. He helped and commiserated, even though it was entirely her fault for running around on the sand with no shoes, which both he and her mother had warned against. "*Homeless* sleep down here," he explained again as Terry cleaned and bandaged the girl's foot. To make her feel better, he collected smooth, harmless beach glass for her to take home while she whimpered and bled through the bandages. The next time he came over, he brought her a big slice of cake from the bar, and even though she puked it all up in her sleep that night – forcing Terry to pick a thousand tiny slivers of coconut out of the dryer after putting the sheets through the wash – the moment when he'd unveiled the cake for the girl was the closest she ever came to expressing delight in his presence.

Mostly she tried to ignore him. Or worse, she would do little things to annoy him that he knew were deliberate, like sitting in the back of the Jeep and humming that weird synthesizer tune from *Beverly Hills Cop*. He had never known what it was called. The girl told him, but it didn't sound right. "Are you sure?" he asked her. She said yes, and rolled her eyes. Or *almost* but not quite rolled her eyes, since she knew rolling her eyes would get her in trouble with her mother. The tune used to be everywhere when Jeremy was younger, back when Eddie Murphy was hot shit and the funniest thing in the world. Then it was gone. Then it was back, and no one knew why. The tune had snuck back into the environment through young kids, like the flu, infecting whole schoolyards before spreading into homes. Terry thought it was cute. Her daughter was learning to play it on the piano, she told Jeremy, both resigned and proud. All the girls in her class were. It was a contest to see who could learn to play it all the way through first.

The girl hummed it in the back of the car, and Jeremy joked about a hundred times being enough, thanks. She always said sorry and gave the back of his head a look that he'd catch in the rear-view mirror. Within a minute, every time, the tune would start again, quietly.

"You're doing it again."

"I can't help it!"

"Sure you can."

He gave her mother a knowing look that wasn't returned.

The only common ground he ever found with the girl was animated movies, which Jeremy usually enjoyed even more than she did, unless the movie involved the gauzy, sexless, aggravatingly delayed coupling of princes and princesses. He'd get restless waiting for the big wedding scenes to end, for the team of fat horses to pull the carriage away into the rising line of credits. The girl *loved* princesses and aspired to be one when she was older. "Pretty sure you have to be born one," he told her, which confused the girl and angered the mother. For her eighth birthday he bought her a toy castle where all her doll princesses could live and entertain. Not a single princess ever set foot in the castle: it stayed in a closet, then came back to Jeremy's house when he and Terry broke up. He put it at the end of his driveway and it disappeared overnight. Someone's princesses were sleeping well in it, though they'd never know the whole story.

Terry always seemed to be looking at him as if through a two-way mirror, studying and observing him, never fully impressed with her findings. He could see it, and knew that look meant she found him inadequate in ways she wasn't yet fully able to articulate but would soon crystallize in her mind.

"We're doing alright, right?" He tried to make it sound like a statement. "You and me – it's good. Right?"

"It's good," she'd say, and would repeat it: "No, it's good."

"Good."

It wasn't, and the crack that had appeared in the relationship finally became too wide to ignore.

There had been nothing serious since. Just a few dates now and then, and the occasional lucky strike that ended with him and some relative stranger going at it at home or in his office at the bar. Nothing lasted very long, which he told himself and everyone else was because he was so busy all the time keeping the Ice Shack going.

"This place is 24-7. I'm lucky if I get a second to breathe."

Jeremy's parents had heard about the relationship with Terry, though they never asked him directly about it – they hadn't met any of the women he dated since he was in high school. His mother sometimes said things about how lucky it was he didn't have any children, given the kind of work he did and the kinds of hours he kept. "You'd never see them," she said. "But then, maybe we'd get to see them all the time!"

"We don't have enough room here for kids running around," his dad said.

It was his sister who had filled them in on the whole Terry situation. Marie was never convinced it could last, though she at least went so far as to call it a *relationship*, rather than a *fling*. She had a clearer perspective, she felt, living outside of the city with her husband and the three kids she carried around like trophies. Shortly before Terry, Jeremy had gone out with a waitress from Newfoundland who Marie thought was using him to get good shifts. Before that one, it was a travel agent who she predicted would drop him the minute she decided she wanted kids. She was right in both cases, but he was reluctant to give her the satisfaction. Marie was nearly a decade younger than Jeremy, but having kids had vaulted her over him, as far as she was concerned. And working in bars all the time was kind of childish to begin with. "You like it because it's one long party," Marie said.

"You don't know what I do all day. I barely sit down, ever."

Look: he showed her the scar on his wrist where it'd been sliced by a broken pint glass that had fallen into a sink full of ice. He'd reached to pluck it out, and it got him, turning the ice as pink as a snow cone. When that happened, you had to scoop out all the ice, then spray the sink down with hot water and bleach. It was a real operation – if you tried to just scoop out the bloody ice and leave the rest, someone would complain, and if the city ever heard about it, there'd be health inspectors coming in through the windows. Jeremy didn't allow for that kind of corner-cutting, anyway. It happened on a Saturday night, and the floor staff was in the weeds, so he refused to go to the hospital, opting instead for an oversized bandage from the first aid kit, held on with duct tape.

"I don't even want to know how much blood I lost that night."

"Do you know what my insides looked like after Logan was born?" Marie demanded. Logan was her oldest. He'd come out of her as easily as a suitcase, ramming his way through her pelvis with a head like a bloody cannonball. The next two slipped out as clean and quick as silverfish. She said it was because her first had paved the way, as if her reproductive apparatus were a highway that'd been blasted through a cliff.

He was indignant. "I never said having kids was easy. It's hard, I know! Terry was in labour for three whole days, she told me. The father had already fucked off by that point, too. Three days, all on her own. Can you imagine?"

"That's what women have had to do forever."

"Okay, but is that *my* fault?"

He got more sympathy from Charlene, the day waitress. She had the knack, he noticed, for taking care of her duties and seeing to whatever random customer was in the place while still looking engaged in the conversation. It was, frankly, a skill that some of his other staffers could've stood to work a little harder in developing. As Charlene listened to him, she would wipe silverware that had come back from the kitchen lightly braised with dirty water.

"I don't know if it was her kid or if it was her or me, or if it was all just bad timing," he told her. "It never seemed to gel, you know what I mean?"

"I think so."

"What really sucks is that now the girl is going to be wondering where I am."

He knew this wasn't true: if Terry's daughter did wonder about him, it was only out of a worry he might show up in her life again. He wasn't missing *her*, that's for certain.

"It must be awful to be a kid in that situation," he added. "I worry about her a bit. I hope she's okay with everything. Sorry to be dumping this all on you."

She told him it was okay, she was used to it. People always told her personal things.

"Obviously, I've had things where I just was in it for whatever, for fun, and didn't really try," Jeremy said. "I'm being totally honest here: I've been a shithead in my day. And I've been in things where I've been a total nice guy and *she* was the shithead. Or we were both shitheads. But with this, I don't know. I thought this one was it."

"It's cool that you tried, though. It sucks that it didn't work, but that just means maybe she wasn't the right person."

"But you never know until it's too late, do you? You never really know if someone's right or wrong until you're deep in there and it all goes to shit."

She said he was being too negative. He agreed, and was happy to be called on it.

"I'm usually the one telling people that. You'd make a good social worker."

"MORE IMPORTANT THAN WHO YOU KNOW IS WHO KNOWS *YOU*."
– *The Winning Heart*, Theo Hendra

Charlene occasionally stayed for dinner after her shift, and Jeremy would offer her a couple of drinks on the house. A reward, he said, for making it through the day, though most days were quiet, with only the slightest hint of a lunch rush – a lunch *crawl*, he called it – and few tips to be had. He rarely even scheduled a dishwasher. He sat with her while she ate. The other staff gave her sympathetic looks, but she didn't mind. It wasn't like she had better ways to spend her time. When Kyle, her husband, had to study for one of his veterinarian courses, he took over the entire living room, and usually the kitchen, too, so she would get into bed and watch TV or read the whole night. Or else she just lay there saying, "*You motherfucker, you fat fucking motherfucker*," over and over and very softly to their cat, Woody.

Jeremy liked to talk about the plans he had for the Shack's future.

"I want to nab the pharmacy next door and knock out the wall between us. Maybe make a little lounge over there, with couches and different music and that kind of thing."

"Like a chill room," she said.

"A what?"

"A chill room, like at a rave."

"You weren't into all that, were you?"

"When I was younger, a bit."

"Why, for God's sake?"

She tried to explain. She'd only been to two or three raves in her life – maybe four, if she counted the one that got raided less than an hour after she arrived – but each one glowed pink and friendly in her memory. She remembered walking through parking lots with her friends, the pills they'd all taken kicking in and obliterating whatever dark mood had been squatting on her all week. She'd feel cleansed and full of light. The music came through the walls like the heartbeat of a dragon, and right away it was as if anything could happen: she could walk through the doors of the building and into the mass of moving bodies, and her body would crumble into glittering dust that floated around the dancers' heads. Or she might grow, like Alice, until she was 50 feet tall and unable to get back out of the building. She kissed people she'd never met, boys and girls, and sweated through every layer of clothing she had on. On the dawn subway, bus, or taxi ride home, she and her friends huddled together like puppies and drifted in and out of sleep, and she would crawl into her bed without taking off her sweaty underwear. Her mother, annoyed with her for being out all night, would pick that exact moment to vacuum the apartment, and would make sure to bang the nose of the howling machine against Charlene's bedroom door over and over again.

All she could tell him was that the dancing was fun and she liked a lot of the music.

"Well, I'm not planning on building a *chill room*," Jeremy said. "But it'll be something. Anyway, that's just one idea. I have all kinds of plans in my head. Just waiting for the right moment to pull the trigger."

"I wouldn't know where to start," Charlene said. "To change things, I mean. If it was already working okay. I'd be afraid of wrecking something."

Jeremy was adamant that when he did finally expand the Shack, he would be smart about it. He'd worked at places that had tried too soon. Or too late. Or in all the wrong ways.

"That's the whole trick," he said. "Knowing when to make your move."

He asked her if Kyle had gone to raves with her, which made her laugh so hard she felt white wine shunt up into her sinuses. He held out a napkin while she coughed.

Jeremy had to be careful when it came to Charlene's husband. Kyle was the kind of person who gave too much weight to every little thing. It was impossible to joke around with him – he would demand that you back everything up with hard evidence, or clarify a position that you'd only taken for the sake of conversation or for the hell of it. *What did you mean by that? Where did you hear it? Were you making a joke?* He would stare at people's mouths while they spoke as if studying them for clues. He was fundamentally incapable of shooting the shit.

Kyle didn't know when to let things go. He got into stupid fights with people. He'd almost lost his job when the head of the animal shelter tried to shift some of his duties around. Kyle raised a stink about it, and was sent home for the afternoon. He later admitted to Charlene that he didn't mind doing different work, he just wanted it acknowledged that he was voluntarily agreeing to the changes, and was under no obligation to do so. She screamed in frustration. His nickname at work was *Stalin*, because of the fat biography of the Soviet leader he was often seen reading during his first year there. At home, they were stuck in a drawn-out, low-level war with their downstairs neighbours that had begun when Kyle demanded they quit parking their car so that it blocked the rusted Honda Civic behind the building. The Civic, which belonged to Kyle's mother, almost never got driven – as the neighbours pointed out, it had a grey coat of dust on it and was often feathered with dead leaves or snow – but he banged on the door downstairs every time he came home to find the laneway plugged by their plum-coloured minivan. That led to fights about the recycling bins, about bicycles in the hallway, about mail placement, about the use of the laundry room in the basement. Charlene, desperate to escape the hate coming up through the floor, begged Kyle to let them move, but he insisted they were in the right, so they stayed put. If anyone ought to leave, it was those assholes downstairs.

Jeremy had encountered all kinds of people like that in his day: guys who would fight it out over a dollar extra on their bill, who treated any mistake in their order as proof of contempt or total incompetence. It was almost always easier to just smile, comp the bill, get the pricks out of the place as quickly as possible, and hope they had a brain aneurysm on the drive home.

It was hard with Kyle, because you never knew what he might latch on to. The most innocent joke would ignite a long, tense argument. One summer the parking lot in front of the Shack was getting repaved. Jeremy had been assured the whole job would be done in a couple of weeks, but after a promising start, the work site began to resemble an elaborate funeral, with everyone moving slowly as if struck down by grief. Jeremy would watch them through the window of the bar, grinding his teeth in frustration. He was watching this slow spectacle when Kyle dropped Charlene off before her shift. It was pouring rain, and they were both soaked.

"You two look like drowned rats. Grab some of the clean bar towels. There's coffee – I just made it."

Charlene pulled off her raincoat and groaned at the sight of herself in the mirror.

"I look like such a *man* when my hair's wet."

As she struggled, Jeremy watched her with a benign smile, like a father watching his daughter walk down the aisle. "You look fine," he said quietly. Kyle stood just inside the doorway, dripping. He accepted the mug of hot coffee Charlene brought him, but did not thank her – or Jeremy, for that matter.

"Check this out," Jeremy said, nodding toward the men in hard hats standing under a tarp. "It's like they're afraid they're going to melt, the poor babies."

"You're obsessed with them," Charlene said. "Just don't look."

"There's probably not much they can do when it's this wet, is there?" Kyle asked.

"In China, they can throw a highway together in a month. A whole highway, with overpasses and underpasses and all the rest of it. For fuck's sake, there are army engineers who can build a bridge over a flooded river in less than an hour. These guys are just dog fuckers."

"Why don't you go ask what's going on?"

Jeremy gave a snort. "They'd use that as an excuse for taking twice as long."

"I don't understand, though. If you're angry at them . . ."

"I'm not angry!" Jeremy protested, still smiling. "It just pisses me off to see them waste all this time."

"Kyle, it doesn't matter." There was a note of warning in Charlene's voice. She could sense her husband was getting his teeth into something.

"They'll be here for another week, I know it."

"Well, how long was it supposed to take?"

"Who knows? However long they feel like taking."

"You could ask them. Ask the foreman or whoever it is."

"Getting a straight answer from these guys? I might as well talk to the chair."

"Well, look: if you're not even going to talk to them . . ."

"*Kyle* . . ." Charlene said.

He turned on her: "*He*'s the one who is so mad about it," he said. "*I'm* just saying it doesn't make sense to stand here and get angry if you're not going to even go out and ask what's going on."

Jeremy put his hands up in surrender and smiled. "You know what? Charlene's right: I shouldn't even be looking. It just makes me crazy. I know it will, so I shouldn't do it."

Charlene told Jeremy how long she and Kyle had been together, and it nearly made him dizzy, the idea of two people being in each other's pockets all that time.

"He lived right near me when I was in kindergarten, actually," she said, "though I don't really remember ever talking to him until we were in high school. I went out with this guy Matthew in Grade 11, my first real boyfriend, who was a friend of Kyle's and a complete asshole. He treated me like shit."

"What would he do? Give me an example. Or don't, if it's too personal."

"Oh God." She pretended to think about it. There were lots of things, and none of them had ever lost their power in her memory, or their sting. "He would forget to pick me up, and I'd be stuck at home all night. He'd say sorry, and I'd have to pretend it wasn't a big deal."

"That just means he was a teenage boy."

"He sometimes drove really fast, just to scare me. I'd be crying, and he still wouldn't stop. Racing along with me screaming."

"Same thing: teenage boy. That's like the dictionary definition."

"He wanted to do a threesome."

She said it quickly, getting it out before she could think twice. Jeremy's eyes widened, and he lifted a finger in the air as if assigning her a point in the game of Bad Boyfriend Tennis.

"How much wanted? Asked? Talked about? Brought someone along?"

"Brought someone along. Without asking."

His finger went up again: another point.

"And you were not into it."

"I hadn't done a real onesome, yet – or a twosome. You know what I mean."

She took a big drink of her wine, as if the things she was

telling him were nothing. Not even Kyle knew about that time Matthew brought Miranda Clapperton along. Black hair like oil. The first in their grade to get boobs. The first to go most of the way with a boy, then the first to go all the way. Miranda had probably done anal by the time Charlene finally winced her way through the loss of her virginity. So she felt outclassed, sitting in the back seat with a Coke bottle half-filled with stolen rye. The other two just *stinking* of booze.

Jeremy asked if she'd gone through with it.

"No. And he was pissed at me for a long time."

"So you dumped him."

She closed her eyes and flinched.

"Oh no . . ." He started laughing. Her expression fell apart and she laughed, too.

"Don't say that! I thought we were going to be married someday – I told you I was pathetic. I think I thought I deserved it."

Jeremy shook his head, though the few girlfriends he'd managed to get in high school he'd treated like shit, too. For a while he'd hung around with a bunch of guys – mostly jocks who'd hit the ceiling on their athletic abilities at 16 or 17 – who treated girls like game pieces. And not even pieces for a sophisticated game like Risk or Monopoly, but something more brutal, like Hungry Hungry Hippos. That's exactly what they were: hungry, hungry hippos. There was one guy who bragged about talking a girl into doing something the rest of them had only ever read about, something they'd always suspected was partly myth. It was never independently verified and the girl never said a word, but all the same they started calling him *Mr. Brown*.

"Kyle asked me out after Matthew dumped me," Charlene said. "I guess he had a crush on me the whole time. I was such a loser back then. I was miserable. Kyle was so sweet."

"I bet." Jeremy couldn't hide the slight curl of sarcasm.

"He was!" she said. "He totally was – he *is*. He can be so super sweet, he just has a hard time doing the things people expect you to do. He always has to be going the other way."

"I can respect that."

Kyle, she said, didn't like that she worked in a bar.

"What's wrong with working in a bar?"

She tried to condense all the things Kyle had said to her about it into a single sentence, one that wouldn't offend her boss. She couldn't. "He just doesn't like it," she said. "He thinks I'm surrounded by old drunks all the time. I tell him it's not like that, and he's been in here before, so he knows it's not like that, but whatever."

Jeremy shrugged. "He's just being a little overprotective, that's all."

"He thinks I should go back to school, and I know he's right, but I just can't make myself do it. What would I even go for at this point?"

"You're talking like your life is over. I'm older than you, and I'd go back to school in a second if there was something I wanted to go back for. *'School is proof we're an intelligent species, because it shows we know we're not as smart as we like to think we are'* – that's Theo Hendra, by the way. What are you interested in?"

"What I should really do," she said, "is go back to Grade 1, start over. I could be like a total cougar."

He thought about this. "Don't be so hard on Kyle. He's a good guy."

———————————

Kyle sometimes said things to Charlene about Jeremy. About all the keys he carried around with him, about the self-help books he swore by. About how he clearly believed the bar was the most important thing in the world. A film crew once came to the area to shoot an episode of a cop show called *Enforcement*, and there'd been talk about them shooting some scenes at the Shack. For a week, Jeremy went on and on about it. He even promised staff and some of the regulars parts as extras. Ultimately, the crew packed up and went on to the next location without getting in touch, leaving Jeremy to denounce the entire television industry as being filled with liars and vultures. He refused on principle to watch the show when it finally aired, even after some of the regulars said they had spotted the Shack in the background of scenes ostensibly taking place in Baltimore.

Or the time the mayor of Toronto came to the Shack for a business lunch with two other men. They sat in a booth – the mayor, a big guy, on the end – and Jeremy served them himself. He still had a photo from the occasion on the wall behind the bar: Jeremy and the mayor standing side by side, both smiling and giving the thumbs up. "He had the club sandwich special, drank two beers and a coffee, and paid with a *hundred dollar bill*," Jeremy said when he showed people the photo. "I tried to tell him it was on the house, but one of his assistants gave me the cash after he left and wouldn't take it back. I was going to frame it. He sat right there, the mayor of the entire city."

"*Of the entire city*," Kyle said to Charlene, in a voice that was nothing like Jeremy's.

She told him he was being unfair. What Kyle didn't get about Jeremy was that he was at least always trying to make things better. He always made an effort to keep people going, to brighten things up.

"Like one of those clowns who perform for sick kids in hospitals," Kyle suggested.

That was *really* unfair. But she laughed, anyway.

She could see how tired Jeremy was most of the time, how overburdened. She would never say it to his face, but he often looked as though he were about to collapse. He had dark smears beneath his eyes like smudged mascara. He sometimes disappeared into his office in the afternoon to take a nap, and would emerge an hour later looking even worse. But he rarely took it out on the staff or let his mood foul the air in the place. She had worked for people whose emotions were like unfixed pets, always being set free to torment the staff and cause havoc. Like Mr. Mathewson, the director of the library where she had worked weekends in school, whose wife was cheating on him with a cop, and who took it out on the volunteers. Or like Ron, the head counsellor at the camp where she'd worked for most of one summer. Ron got dumped by his girlfriend and spent most of the time in his cabin, filling it with heartache and pot smoke. The rest of the counsellors were forced to try and keep the place running. Charlene put together a disastrous overnight trip for the campers that resulted in a sprained ankle, two pairs of lost glasses, a few near-drownings, and something dangerously close to pre-teen gang rape. (She let the victim sleep in the counsellors' cabin for the rest of the week; the young perpetrators got sent home, complaining the whole time that it was no big deal since they'd only used their fingers.)

Jeremy, by contrast, seemed to Charlene to be carrying the whole bar uphill on his shoulders. He fought to keep everyone happy, to give everyone working there every-thing they needed. He remembered the smallest details: the birthdays tucked into the most miserable corners of the calendar, the ailing parents or pets, the vicious ex who was to be chased out the front doors on sight. The way he moved among the customers, doling out attention like soup, which Kyle found so pathetic and fraudulent – Jeremy lived for it. He could wade into a tableful of first-timers, or connect two strangers sitting at the bar and leave them chatting together happily. More than once, he had pointed out a couple whom he'd first introduced to each other, right there in the bar. In one case, the two were sitting, having a beer, and planning their wedding.

"One day their kids will be coming in here with fake ID. That's the circle of life, right?"

And yet, people had no trouble going after him. They did it behind his back, when he was out getting something for the bar, or on one of the rare nights when he would go home early. Or they did it openly, which was somehow worse, because he would laugh right along – sometimes genuinely, but Charlene could tell when he was only laughing to be a good sport, the joke having cut a little deep. One of the cooks, who was notorious for having had sex with his girlfriend in the walk-in fridge during a slow night, did an impression of Jeremy that consisted of tucking in his shirt, sticking out his gut, and slapping everybody on the back with one hand while spilling an imaginary drink with the other. He even nailed the stumbling walk. There'd been a plan to buy Jeremy vanity license plates that said *MR HAPPY* as a Christmas gift. They never went through with it. Charlene wished they'd had, just so he could've turned the tables on them: he would've put them on his car. Or else he would've nailed the plates up behind in the bar and pointed them out to everyone who came in for a beer, killing the joke with enthusiasm. She sometimes saw him walk around the bar, taking an obvious delight in the spread of tables and chairs, looking into every corner. He did the same behind the bar, staring at the draft taps and sinks with an expression on his face that was boyishly erotic. He was endlessly impressed by the shape of the Shack, by its twists and corners and hidden features. Every Monday morning, when the beer delivery arrived, Jeremy would walk out to meet the truck backing slowly across the lot, holding his hands up in the air and smiling, looking like a village chieftain greeting the white men on horses.

"A LOT OF SMART PEOPLE SAY THERE IS NO WAY NOAH COULD HAVE BUILT THE ARK. BUT HE BUILT IT ANYWAY, AND HERE WE ARE."
– *Big Ideas, Small Miracles*, Theo Hendra

The space that eventually became the Shack had originally been a Chinese restaurant, one in which an old couple served meals to a dozen or so senior citizens who didn't care about the ethnicity of the food, just as long as it came with lots of sauce. Jeremy used to go there with his parents when he was a kid, and always got sick from stuffing himself with chicken balls. What he'd loved most were the red plaster dragons sitting on their haunches in the entranceway. He would stand in front of the dragons, which he was only slightly taller than, and try to stare them down. He always gave up with a shiver after less than a minute. By the time he came to scout the location, the dragons were chipped and fading, their ferociousness softened by age and neglect. He toyed with the idea of keeping them there, then decided they'd just attract drunken vandals and jokers. Plus he didn't want anyone thinking the place was still Chinese.

Converting the old restaurant took a lot longer than Jeremy had planned for, and almost longer than he could afford. The work was done mostly by a group of young guys who had dirt and grease rubbed right into their skin, as if they'd been dipped in dark oil. At lunchtime, they would all sit on the bare wooded floor, eating submarine sandwiches and drinking big jugs of Pepsi. Jeremy felt soft around these young men. Soft and vulnerable, as if they might at any moment decide to pick him up, carry him to the edge of the unfinished deck, and hurl him down into the ravine.

When they were finally, miraculously, close to done, one of the guys told him he thought the place was turning out really well.

"Honestly? When we first started, I was like, *Whatever, buddy. Good luck*. But now it looks really fucking nice."

The other guys agreed: Totally. Really nice.

Jeremy, overwhelmed, had to look away.

In charge of the whole operation was Benny, whom Jeremy knew from way back, and who had worked on his parents' new house and on his sister's house – though she said she would never hire him again after coming out of the bathroom from an afternoon shower wearing a towel to find him standing and grinning in the hallway, holding a beer from her fridge and getting a good long look at her. He had skin like beef jerky, with white scars all down his arms. He told stories about falling off roofs and through windows, being shocked by bad wiring, and getting hit square in the back with a sledgehammer. He was missing a thumbnail on his right hand, taken decades ago by a stack of cinder blocks that had shifted suddenly and caught his fingers. Another time, some idiot dropped a whole cup of nails on his head from about four stories up. Some of the nails had stuck out from his scalp like lightning rods.

Before they did anything to the place, Jeremy and Benny had walked through it, worrying about the size of the kitchen, frowning at the state of the bathrooms. The fact that it had been a Chinese restaurant spurred Benny into long monologues about the fundamental dirtiness of Asians. As proof of his belief, Benny told Jeremy about a truck he'd bought from a Korean couple who owned a pet store: he spent an entire day pulling layer after layer of rotten, soggy cardboard out of the back of that thing, gagging the whole time. Just to top things off, the truck had the brass outline of a fish stuck to the back. He had left it there, thinking it had something to do with sport fishing, until someone finally told him it was a Jesus fish, the one people put on their cars to show they are born-again Christians. Soon as he heard that, he went out with a screwdriver and yanked the thing clean. "When Jesus starts advertising *my* business, I'll start advertising his."

"That's a good policy."

Jeremy indulged these rants because of the pile of cash he knew Benny had squirrelled away somewhere. There'd been a rough job, a long time ago, in a government building: Benny got hurt when a wall fell on him. He was offered a huge settlement, enough to let him sit on his ass for a few months while his body mended, and he took it. He spent two weeks on his couch watching TV and getting drunk, and then was right back at it, putting in furnaces and wheeling fridges up people's driveways with only a slight limp and the occasional wince as evidence that anything had happened.

Jeremy took Benny out for lunch while they were working on the Shack, away from all the sawdust and lumber. They grabbed a table in the corner of a noisy sports bar. He ordered a pitcher of beer, and they clinked glasses across the table. They talked about nothing for a while before Jeremy steered the conversation around to the Shack. "Here's the thing," he said. "You and me, we know how to watch and wait for the right moment. We see everyone else fucking up huge, and we learn from it."

"Sounds about right."

"We've been around enough of these places to know: the biggest mistake people make is trying to do it all on the cheap. You've got to be ready to lose it for a while before you start making it."

"I don't like losing it, that's for sure."

"Me neither. I'd rather be making it. Cheers to that."

Jeremy came to the point: he had enough money to get to the starting line and beyond, but once things were up and running it was always smart to have some extra cash on hand in case things got a little rough while people were still finding the place.

"You know how this shit works, how this business works. You know you can't just drop your line through a hole in the ice and expect a fish to come jumping out right away."

"I've never gone ice fishing in my goddamned life."

"I mean like how you have to wait and be patient."

"The people who freeze their nuts off trying to catch one goddamn fish, they're just asking for trouble. I seen trucks go right through the ice because some idiot didn't know when it was time to friggin pack up and go home."

"I'm totally with you on that. You have to know when it's time to get the fuck out of Dodge. What *I'm* talking about is this: what would you say to putting some money in the bar?"

Benny frowned harder than he already was, as if he'd found within himself a vein of displeasure even more deep and rich than the one he normally worked.

"What do you mean – put *my* money in *your* bar?"

"More like: *invest* your money in *our* bar. We can work out whatever terms work for you. I'm totally flexible on this. Think about it."

He put his glass down. "Don't need to. Not interested." He did the work, he got paid, and he went home, same as his guys. He would come in and buy a beer or two once the place was open, but that was as much money as he was willing to give. The stuff didn't grow on trees, and he didn't believe in handing over cash he wasn't sure he was going to get back.

"Obviously you'd get it back," Jeremy said. "And more."

"Oh sure. Free money – all I gotta do is pay for it first. No thanks. No such thing as a free lunch."

When Jeremy pointed out, with a little more heat than he intended, that he'd just had one, Benny pulled out a $20 bill and laid it flat on the table.

"I don't like to owe anybody anything,"

"Come on, I'm totally joking. Your money's no good here."

"Then how come you're after it?"

Benny sulked quietly for a few minutes before taking another gulp of beer. Slowly, as if confessing a crime, he began to tell Jeremy about a friend he'd had when he was a lot younger, back when he was just out of school. The two of them made money by painting houses together – they were good at it. At the end of the day, they'd get a few big bags of potato chips, take them back to Benny's little apartment, smear the chips with ketchup, and bake them in the oven. Sometimes they'd have a six of beer with it, and that was their dinner.

"Not really following your point here, Benny."

"Point is, we invented *ketchup chips* – there was no such thing before. Swear to God, you can look it up. So this so-called *friend* of mine starts talking about selling them, and asks me to give him some money to set things up. He kept talking about us being millionaires, so I gave him half my paycheque, three or four months in a row. Anyways, he ends up fucking off with the money. So I don't get involved in any of that nonsense anymore, thank you very much."

Jeremy told Benny that he respected his decision, then he poured out the last of the beer and made a toast: "To the Ice Shack, and to the inventor of ketchup chips."

"I broke that little prick's nose for it," Benny said.

"Point taken."

A few weeks later, Jeremy stood out on the deck of the Shack, which didn't yet have railings, and called his sister. Marie answered on the first ring, and told him right away that her pregnancy was giving her diarrhea, so he should not get upset if she had to hang up on him all of a sudden.

"So when is that place of yours going to be up and running?"

"A month. Month and a half, max." That was the soonest he could afford to hire staff.

"You've been talking about it for so long, I was starting to wonder."

"Wonder about what? That it would never happen?"

"Well, it wouldn't be the first time, would it? Lots of places go belly up before they open their doors."

"I was actually calling to maybe get some encouragement. It's been a rough week."

Jeremy picked up a length of unpainted wood, a slat for the railings. Pretty soon, there'd be tables and chairs where he was standing.

"When were ketchup chips invented, do you know?" he asked her.

"What's that?"

There was a squeal of voices on the other end, and Marie broke off to answer her husband, who was shouting something at her. It was already dark out – the bridge lights had come on, and Jeremy could see the glittering stripe of the river through the bare branches of the trees.

"Look, are you asking me to tell you everything will be fine with your bar, that you're a total winner?" she asked him, then the phone went dead. She must've dropped it or pushed the wrong button with her cheek.

"Couldn't hurt," Jeremy said into the sudden silence.

A framed photo from the Shack's opening-night party hung on the wall behind the bar. Smaller photos – of parties and birthdays and playoff nights, all curled slightly with age – were pinned casually around it. Staff and customers held up bottles and glasses, grabbing each other around the neck, their mouths open or smiling, the flash giving them the glowing red eyes of demons. One of the bartenders called it their Zombie Gallery, and the name stuck. Most were from the first few years of the Shack's existence. Jeremy kept saying they needed to start adding new ones – he had dozens of images waiting on his laptop, but couldn't figure out how to extract them and get them printed.

"Just as well, I guess. We don't need any more pictures of me looking all hammered up."

In the opening night photo, Jeremy stood on a bar stool and struck a bodybuilder's pose, his face red and his hair dripping with brightly coloured paper streamers. The staff got it framed for the bar's one-year anniversary, upon which Jeremy attempted to recreate the image, and almost fell sideways through a table covered in party snacks.

By the time the original picture was taken, Jeremy was oblivious to his surroundings. It was past midnight, and the party had been going officially since eight o'clock, though he'd been drinking on and off since noon, and only had a few bites of things as he ran through the kitchen throughout the day. He couldn't keep anything solid down, his stomach and his head were floating free like balloons tied together by a long string. As the sun went down outside and people started to pack the place, he had a vision of the bar filling with dark water. Everyone in there was like a sea plant, anchored to the floor and rooted, while Jeremy moved among them on invisible currents. He went out onto the patio a few times, where he had strung coloured lights through the railings, and the lights looked like incandescent candy. He got afraid of being washed over the edge and down into the ravine below, and tried to stay near the safety of the bar, with its heavy gravitational pull. The cold wood felt good. He smacked it hard a couple of times, claiming it, like it was the flank of an animal. *Mine*, he thought. People around him – friends, staff, drunken strangers – whooped and cheered. Everything in the place, every salt shaker and ashtray and fork, had been brought there by Jeremy. He could have touched any object in the room and said exactly how much it had cost him in money, trouble, and time.

Benny was there, walking around like a proud uncle. "This fucker wanted me as a partner!" he shouted at the young man standing next to him.

Jeremy, laughing, said, "I don't know about *partner*. Not too late, though!"

His parents showed up early in the evening, and he gave the two of them a quick tour. His dad, Gord, was especially impressed to see all the young men in whites working in the kitchen. Nothing else looked like *work* to him, none of the other staff acted like employees. His mom, Anne, offered to help clean up when someone dropped a full glass of vodka and cranberry juice behind the bar. Jeremy led her away, telling her it would be taken care of. Marie didn't come to the party, but sent a card with a photo of a vintage biplane flying upside down – Jeremy'd had a poster exactly like it on his wall when he was a teenager. She used to bug him by sneaking into his room and hanging the whole thing upside down, so that the ground was the sky and the plane appeared to be flying right side up. The card said: *You're flying high. Just don't look down!* Inside, there was a note apologizing for missing the party and congratulating him on getting the Shack open at last. There was only one X and one O at the end. One kiss, one hug. As if she didn't want to spoil him.

He bought a round of shots for a group of guys who all played hockey together in some beer league, then corralled into the group a woman who'd been walking by on her way to the bathroom. She had on a tight sweater-blouse with a glittering tiger on the front, and was with a group of other women who were all done up with hair teased high above their heads.

"One shot," Jeremy said. "One shot with all my new friends here." Like baby animals waiting to be fed, the hockey players standing with him watched the bartender's hands as he poured out the dark shots. "This is my bar and this is my party, so you have to. By law."

The players urged her to say.

Her name, he found out after the shots had been downed, was Julie. They shared three more rounds of shots, a plate of nachos, and had a long, rambling conversation about women soldiers serving on the front lines in Afghanistan – Jeremy had no strong feelings about the subject, but Julie, whose ex-boyfriend was in the military, convinced him that having women right in the middle of it all was a distraction for the male soldiers and a liability, given how Afghan men viewed women in general.

She shouted in his ear: "They're like cavemen over there!"

"They are over here, too!"

Which got her laughing.

The two of them ended up downstairs in his cramped office, up against his desk, there being no couch yet and no room to lie down amid all the boxes. She kissed like a big, friendly dog: wet and frantic with her mouth wide open and almost covering his completely. He realized, at some point, that he was enjoying himself, really enjoying himself. As she raised her jean skirt, he also realized he didn't have a condom anywhere. He figured he could probably get away with timing things just right, but then she produced one, flashing and crinkling, from her purse.

"That's lucky." He pulled at the wrapper with his teeth.

"Luck has nothing to do with it," she said, then laughed so loud he worried someone would hear them.

Afterward, she gave him a sympathetic, forgiving smile, kissing him on the forehead as he stared at the floor and tried to catch his breath. He felt he ought to have lasted longer, given everything he'd had to drink, but he came almost before he was aware he was about to. He wanted to stay there in the office for the rest of the night. Something had fallen out of him, like an engine falling out of a car. The humming that had been in his ears all night was gone, and it seemed as though the party upstairs had gone silent. Maybe everyone had gone home, sneaking out quietly while he was downstairs. They'd all just been humouring him.

"You need some pictures in here or something, or some plants – it's not very homey," Julie said, looking around his office. "You're standing on my purse." She pulled down her blouse, restoring the glittering tiger, which now looked as gentle and friendly as a house cat.

Later, after he'd locked the doors, Jeremy convinced himself that he ought to stay the night, to sleep in one of the booths. It seemed like something a new owner should do, to make sure everything was okay. The bartender persuaded him to go home, and called him a cab. When he woke up in his bed the next morning, he was still fully dressed, there were coloured streamers in his hair, and one of his pockets was gummed up with a used condom.

———————————

The bar fell into a deep hole early on, but Jeremy refused to worry, knowing this kind of thing was cyclical. How could it not be? The first few months had been a dream – the place was packed at least four nights a week. In fact, that whole first spring and summer were good, the patio was always jammed. Jeremy floated through the crowds like it was his birthday every night. But then business dropped off a little in the fall, and died out altogether the minute snow appeared in the air. People scattered. It stayed bad all winter.

He told his staff, "You just have to hold it together. We'll climb out of this. Just watch."

A couple of servers left, along with some of the kitchen guys, and he had to fire a busboy, who retaliated by stealing beer from the basement. They made the best of the really bad nights, like the time they pushed aside a bunch of tables for an impromptu staff dance party during a Tuesday that seemed to stretch on forever. A waiter who was taking lessons got everyone tangoing across the room.

A wine rep cornered him one night. "I don't know what your exact situation is, but maybe you need to bring some partners in." He could see the empty tables, the nervous wait staff, the lurking cook.

"Are you offering?"

"I don't have that kind of money, are you kidding?"

"Then what are you worried about? It's not as bad as it looks. I won't end up living in a cardboard box. Worst comes to worst, I'll sell the place off and go live in a cabin somewhere."

Brenda, a waitress who'd been there from the start, finally came to him on behalf of the rest of the floor staff. Everyone was pissed off about the scheduling and the lack of tips. Servers were coming in for shifts, only to be sent home after an hour with nothing in their pockets. A few people were already looking for something else – she thought he should know that. She wouldn't say who, only that they were people who probably wouldn't have trouble finding a spot elsewhere. "They don't want to leave. They like you, and they like working here, but they can't live on nothing."

"They like me, but they're fine with me taking all the risk, while they jump ship at the first sign of trouble. I sleep maybe four hours a night, Brenda. If I could snap my fingers and fill the place with millionaires, don't you think I would've done it already? Do you think I'm intentionally sabotaging my own business?"

"That's really stupid. Nobody thinks that."

"So why is everyone coming after me, like I have some magical key that will make people come and spend money?" He grabbed a handful of the keys hanging from his belt and jangled them at her. "Is there a magic one here that I don't know about? Just tell me and I'll use it."

"Oh, stop being such a baby, Jeremy. God, I can't stand it. You've got too many people on the schedule right now. If you need to, fire a few people. I can help decide who."

"Brenda is my rock," he told people. "If I could clone her, I would. I keep a lock of her hair in a vault, just in case I ever need to clone her."

"Remember that when you start handing out raises," she said.

"Isn't it enough that I remember you in my prayers?"

Early on, the two of them would find themselves alone in the bar at the end of the night, the rest of the staff sent home, the doors locked on the last of the drunks. While they drank, Jeremy would cue up "Superstition" by Stevie Wonder, which he insisted on playing at least once a night, just as he'd done way back in his bartending days. It seemed important to have something like that: a tradition, a good luck charm.

"Just listen to this. Blind as anything and listen to what he's doing." He paused to let the sound of massed electric pianos take over the room. The surface of the bar became a keyboard over which Jeremy's fingers moved effortlessly.

She finished her glass. "I'm so sick of this song."

"Then you are sick of life."

They would talk about some of the more difficult or memorable customers they'd dealt with, about awful jobs they'd had in the past, and then finally about funny or terrible things they could remember from their childhoods. She told him about her uncle, who used to babysit her, and who had a habit of sneaking into her room at night to masturbate while he watched her sleep. She'd planned to confront him about it one day, but he had his head taken off in a car accident before she had the chance. She laughed about it, and said she only wished he'd suffered a little more.

Jeremy had little to offer in response, and so he told her about a cousin of his who, at the age of 16, went running off the end of the dock at her family's cottage and landed headfirst on a rock just below the surface, snapping her neck and dying instantly. He told her how, at the funeral, the family discovered she had dozens of friends they hadn't known about. There was even a boyfriend no one had met before, who was invited to speak and who said something about how jealous he was that most of the people there had known her since she was a baby, while he'd only met her a few months earlier.

Brenda looked like she was about to cry. "Oh my God. Life can be so fucking shitty."

"That's not the only way of looking at it."

The dead cousin actually belonged to a bartender Jeremy had worked with one summer. He'd heard the whole story about the broken neck, the funeral, and the boyfriend while the two of them stayed up all night, sitting on a beach and drinking vodka. From then on, he always associated death with the way the water looked from where they were sitting: black and shifting, throwing off sparks of moonlight.

Jeremy told Brenda about his sister's miscarriage, which had happened the first time Marie and Brian tried to have kids. It was not long after the two of them got married. Marie named the unborn baby Gordon, after their father, though they had refused to let the doctor tell them the gender. She still talked about that lost baby sometimes, especially after Christmas dinner or whenever she'd had too much to drink. She'd get weepy and talk about how afraid she'd been that she was not fit to have children, that her own body was rejecting her claims to motherhood.

She'd had three kids since, so Jeremy figured it was a case of one step back, three steps forward.

He once asked Brenda if she ever wanted kids, and she looked at him as if he had just broken into song.

"Me neither," he said.

More than once they ended up naked in her bed with the smell of sex and wine and extinguished candles filling the small room. She always fell right asleep as soon as they were done, and he would lie there with her frog-green IKEA reading light on, looking through whatever she had next to the bed – usually a book about mental health or a bright magazine full of celebrities he didn't recognize. He liked both equally. When Brenda finally left the bar, lured away by a supervising job at a hotel company, they made a half-hearted attempt to keep dating, but it didn't last, and he gradually accepted that, as with so many things in his life, it was the Shack that had made whatever it was they'd had happen. On her last night there, he put on "Superstition," and insisted she dance with him in the middle of the bar. There was a photo of it somewhere.

Business at the Shack eventually climbed back up to a respectable level, thanks in part to the deal he'd made with the local slow-pitch league for discounted group dinners after practices and games. "Thank God for ladies and their friggin baseball," he said, surveying the tables full of women in uniform. "What'd I tell you!" he shouted happily at one of the waitresses as she flew past with four full plates on her arm. "She'll be complaining later about how busy it was," he said to whoever was standing next to him.

The other thing Jeremy did was convince his parents to put more of their money into the bar – money that they'd gotten from selling the house Jeremy and his sister had grown up in and moving into a tiny, cottage-style home. As he liked to point out to them, that money was only going to sit in a bank and do nothing. It took three successive dinners at their new house to get them to even consider the idea.

"We're not millionaires," his father declared while they ate ice cream out of small bowls.

His mother asked, "Do you maybe have too many people working for you? The times I've been in there, it looked like you had a waitress for every table."

"It's not anywhere near that, come on. Anyways, if you start cutting corners, it's not long before you might as well sell out to a Crane's or somebody."

His father asked if it would be so bad, making someone else take on all the risk.

"It'd still be your bar, essentially."

Jeremy put his bowl down. "No, it wouldn't. *Essentially*, it would belong to someone else. There'd be someone else's name on it. Essentially, I would be back working for someone that isn't me. That would be the *essence* of the situation."

"I'm only saying you need some help and money is an issue. You can't just stand there doing nothing."

"Who said I'm just standing here doing nothing?"

His father shrugged and kept eating. "Well, I don't see you doing any contests or anything."

"Contests? What do you mean? Like raffles?"

"What about that thing where the woman won that truck?"

Jeremy knew exactly what he was talking about, and nearly laughed at the absurdity of it. A car dealership in Barrie had held a contest in which they put a brand new truck in the middle of the lot and made people stand around holding on to it. The last person touching it got to drive the thing home. It took nearly three days to declare a winner.

"You're not serious, Gord, come on."

"Why not? Get a dealership to donate a car."

"Do you know what state she was in at the end of that thing, the lady who won the truck?" Jeremy asked him.

"I think we should talk about something else," his mother said, but Gord was angry enough to want to keep going. "I have no idea," he said. "Why don't you tell me?"

Jeremy leaned in. "People said she was cheating because she wore diapers, but diapers only last so long. After a while, it's the same thing as not having them."

His mother said, "Jeremy."

"Sorry, but it's true – she was a total mess by the time it was all over. So here's my question: if I'm going to have people standing around pissing their pants, how does that really help me?"

His father got up from the table and put his bowl in the sink with a clatter.

His mother talked to Jeremy in their small backyard after her husband went to bed. It was a beautiful night, with a slight glaze of clouds to soften the stars that were visible just beyond the glow of downtown.

"He's just worried about you getting into this so deep you'll never be able to climb back out."

"It's a little insulting that you don't even believe I know what I'm doing, after all this time."

"I'm sorry, dear."

Jeremy eventually convinced them to liquidate some of their retirement savings to put into the bar. "Does this mean we're co-owners now?" his father asked.

"More like silent partners, or guardian angels."

"As long as we see some of that money back before we die."

"Oh, you two aren't going to die. You'll just keep moving into smaller and smaller houses until you both disappear."

**"I DON'T CALL WHAT I DO A *JOB*, AND I DON'T CALL IT *WORK*.
I CALL IT *LIVING*."**
– *Powerful Positions*, Theo Hendra

Jeremy liked to get to the Shack in the morning before anyone else so he could sit at the bar with a fresh coffee and watch the morning light puddle on the floor, grow in intensity, and spread throughout the room. Then he would open up all the doors and windows to release the stale air and do his rounds. He sometimes found new things scrawled on the walls, or that another vinyl booth that had been slashed. There was the occasional illicit cigarette in the bathroom left to scorch the edge of the sink. He collected glasses and plates tucked into corners and undiscovered by staff. He *tsk-tsked* these as he would the carelessly discarded clothes of a child. If the staff had once again left greasy lemon wedges in the sink overnight, he'd attack the clouds of new fruit flies with a bar towel, shaking his head the whole time and wondering why – *why* – this kind of thing was so complicated for some people.

The next person to arrive was Tyler, the day cook. Tyler was not yet 20, and never said anything to Jeremy that didn't sound as though it were being spoken by a prisoner to his jailer. If he hung around after his shift, Tyler would sit at the far end of the bar, looking at his phone and talking to no one, making it clear the Shack would get out of him only the hours he was being paid for. He would accept the enemy's beer at the staff discount, plus his one free meal – as was his right – but no more than that. Everyone called Tyler *The Assassin* – everyone except Jeremy, who figured the guy had enough problems without having to carry around a nickname like that. When he came through the front doors in the morning, his hoodie up and his ears leaking earphone wires, Jeremy would already have a coffee ready and a copy of the *Sun* on the bar, open to the sports pages. Tyler would sit at the bar long enough to finish half of his coffee, then take the rest into the kitchen with him. Jeremy made a point of slipping in there throughout the day, always looking for an opportunity to draw the cook out a little.

"Working hard or hardly working?"

Tyler went about his work with about as much joy as a mortician. He stood over a pile of raw shrimp, pinching out the intestines with his fingers and turning his cutting board into a glistening black mess.

"Why don't they just get frozen ones with the shit taken out?" Jeremy asked him.

Tyler shrugged. "These are for the dinner special. They have to be fresh."

"Does it make a huge difference? Have you tried them?"

"I don't eat fish or meat."

"Oh right: no eggs, milk, cheese, steak, or pussy. Nothing that tastes good, right? Ha ha!"

"Milk's okay. I'm not vegan."

"So you can eat ice cream?"

"I don't really like it."

"God, someone put that guy out of his misery," Jeremy said when he was back in the safety of the bar. "He's like a dark cloud in there."

Charlene said Tyler was shy.

"*Shy.* Come on. How can you be shy and work in a kitchen?"

Tyler was far from the worst, however. There were lost causes and hopeless cases that had to be let go. A few times a year he'd have to sit someone down and deliver the bad news. There was the cook who kept missing shifts because of his band. Or the busboy who would disappear for half an hour at a time, even when everyone else was in the weeds, and would return to the floor with pie eyes and a shit-eating grin. Jeremy had to fire one server less than three weeks after hiring her because she was always late and always a little short in her cash-out. Also, no one liked her – not on the floor, not behind the bar, and not in the kitchen. The trifecta of hate. One bartender said the new server was a *total tampon.* Jeremy look baffled, so she explained: "They're both stuck-up cunts."

"Okay, pretty funny. But I'm not a big fan of that kind of talk."

He called the server in on her day off and they went out onto the deck. He had her sit at one of the tables while he stood with his foot up on the lower rung of the railing – she was a little taller than him, and he wanted to maintain the height advantage. He talked to her a little about attitude, about how there were always people who just didn't gel with the rest of the staff, and how sometimes, if things were not working, there was nothing you could do to fix it.

"Am I fired?" she asked.

The look he gave her confirmed it.

"Are you serious? What the fuck."

He started telling her again how the Shack only worked when everybody fit in and got along. She would find it was the same everywhere.

"So what do I do now?" she asked, cutting him off, as if only inquiring about the way to the nearest exit. She wasn't looking for advice, she just wanted the whole thing over with. In her mind, she had already started the process of sealing this job off from the rest of her life. It would be forgotten; she'd get better ones.

On the whole, however, he felt he'd done pretty well, despite what often got thrown at him. Staffing a place was like looking for diamonds in a haystack, he liked to say, but he could spot potential in people other owners might dismiss right off the bat. Patty, who worked the busier lunches alongside Charlene, was like that. Patty was a substitute teacher who had last waited tables back when she was in teacher's college in the mid-'70s. At first, he'd thought he was getting another sad old lady with no experience – nothing but a handwritten list of jobs with huge gaps of decades where the kids happened – but her resumé looked professional, and there wasn't a bit of hesitancy or gloom about her. She'd said she needed the money because her husband had retired, his pension left them short every month, and there weren't enough teaching jobs to fill the gap.

So why waiting tables?

"I just like meeting people," she said, with unexpected aggression, as if the idea were somehow controversial. "I never liked working in an office. My Shawn worked forever in a room with one little window – I don't know how he didn't go crazy. He worked with some nice people, at least. Sometimes when you're at one place for too long, people start to get their noses up, you know what I mean? People start to worry about the stupidest things."

"They do, you're right."

"That's the nice thing about being a substitute: you don't have to get involved in all the nonsense, all the gossip and who said what. I made it a personal rule, very early on, that I would never eat my lunch in the staff room – my favourite thing is to sit in the music room, if they have one, and listen to students practising. Some of the girls now are just lovely."

Jeremy felt oddly comfortable listening to her, as if he were being hypnotized. Most people couldn't stand the motor-mouthed type, the ones who got you in the grip of a conversation like the giant squids in those paintings of embattled sperm whales. Patty's chatter, however, had an almost narcotic quality to it. He wanted to put his head down on the table, close his eyes, and let her talk.

When he called her to say she had the job, she didn't sound at all surprised.

"I don't want to say this but I will: I knew I had the job as soon as I left your bar. I told my Shawn you would call, you can ask him."

"You didn't tell me you were psychic. That changes things."

"Oh, I don't go for all of that nonsense. That's just another way to lose your money, as far as I'm concerned. I always say there's only *one* part of the newspaper you can trust, and that's the obituary pages. Everything else you have to take with a thousand grains of salt. Especially the weather."

Jeremy told her he wasn't really able to train her beyond showing her how to work the computer and giving her a tour of the place.

"Well, I'm sure I'll pick it all up. I always do. I've learned to get right in there and do the best you can. They once had me teaching computers. I thought, *Oh, you've really stepped in it now*. But you just suck it up and get through it, one step at a time. That's all you can do. One step at a time."

Patty wasn't great at the start, but she got better and more confident and was able to handle a nearly full room all by herself. Eventually, orders stopped getting mixed up, drinks and baskets of bread that had been requested were delivered in good time, and Jeremy didn't have to stand near the bar just in case, ready to jump in and help when things got truly chaotic.

"I think I'm in the swing of it," she said proudly at the end of a day that netted her over $50 in tips, the most she'd made so far.

"Just like riding a bicycle."

"Oh it's a little tougher than *that*, I think. It's quite a workout."

Patty's husband, Shawn, always came at the end of the day to pick her up. He refused Jeremy's offers of coffee or beer, and would not let his wife accept a staff meal. She was already getting paid for her hours, he reasoned, plus tips on top of that. That should be enough. Most people don't get food just for doing their jobs. "Most people don't work in restaurants," Jeremy pointed out.

"Fair enough." But he still wouldn't let her eat at the Shack for free.

Shawn took Jeremy aside not long after his wife got the job. "I don't know, you know, how much she ever talks about it, but Pat was really happy to get this. She's grateful for it, you know. It's just waiting tables, but you know what? She really enjoys it. It really bothered her that they never offered her something permanent with the teaching – she kept waiting and waiting, but you know how those things work. It's who you know and all that."

"They were stupid not to grab her when they had the chance," Jeremy said.

"You know what? She's too good for them. Patty cared about what she did, and they screwed her around. Anyway, she's in a good spot now. The whole school system's full of goddamned horse manure, pardon my French."

"True enough. Well, I hope you don't mind that we steal her a couple of days a week."

Shawn winked. "Lets me catch up on my beauty sleep. And a couple extra bucks a month comes in handy."

"More than that, I hope."

"Not much more, but that's okay. We're surviving. And you know what? It's the thought that counts, as they say."

It was Patty who had first recommended Charlene. She'd been her teacher very briefly years earlier and knew her mother a little. The mother was not a *friend*, Patty made clear, just someone she'd spoken to sometimes. "I don't even know the husband – maybe there isn't one. That happens a lot, doesn't it? Charlene seems like a nice girl, though. She's a little quiet, and you can always tell she's listening, which is a rare thing. Most people her age now can't go two minutes without checking their phones."

At Charlene's interview, Jeremy asked her where she saw herself in five years. It was a question he'd picked up from a management course he'd taken before getting hired at Crane's, and which he asked of every person who came in for a job. He couldn't think of a single impressive answer he'd ever received, or even a particularly memorable one, but he kept asking it, feeling it must hold the key to something vital.

"Five years?" Charlene took a quick look around the room. Her mind was blank.

"Let's say 10 years."

"I've sometimes thought I might like to open my own little place. Not a bar, but maybe a little lunch place or a coffee shop. I don't even know if that's 10 years away. Anyway, that's one plan."

"I can probably help with that, when the time comes. Opening your own place can be a real boot to the balls if you don't have help."

"Thanks. That would be really helpful."

She liked the sound of the lie, though she was a little irritated at having to come up with it on the spot. Her mother had told her that the job was pretty much hers as long as the owner liked her. That was the impression she'd gotten from Patty, anyway.

Her previous job had been at a tiny lunch counter downtown where the owner was a shockingly muscular hippie whose entire body weight seemed to reside in his shoulders. He had thick dreads the colour of hot mustard and a goatee that gave him the profile of something animal. Plus he had hair curling up from his chest and shoulders.

He was like a centaur. He refused to carry a phone or use the internet, and talked about both as if they were evil spirits let loose upon the world.

Jeremy said he had trouble picturing Charlene in a place like that, and she admitted she had a hard time understanding how she'd lasted so long. The owner's wife was a small, sensitive woman who cut vegetables and made sandwiches in the kitchen and rarely came up front – serving customers made her feel faint. The two of them would sit with Charlene after they closed the place for the day and smoke gherkin-sized joints rolled from pot they bought off friends who grew it on a farm out near Peterborough. The centaur told her an old singer from the sixties named Ronnie Hawkins had a big place right nearby.

"That guy's *out there*. He knew Bob Dylan and John Lennon and all those guys."

His wife's eyes slid around like raw eggs in a bowl at the mere mention of such deities.

Charlene and the wife would listen to the husband talk about getting off the grid. The grid, and the absolute necessity of escaping it, dodging it, getting as far away as possible, was an obsession. Not just the electrical grid, he said: the emotional grid, the economic one, the psychological one. Even the sexual one.

Kyle wouldn't step foot inside the place. The whole time she was there, he kept trying to get her a job at the animal shelter where he worked. She told him he was being controlling. The centaur said Kyle was emotionally colour-blind. She needed someone who could see the entire spectrum – see and not fear it. She made the mistake of telling Kyle that, as a joke. He got angry and threatened to go in and confront her boss.

"*Please* don't say anything," she begged him. "I shouldn't have told you. That's just the way he is – he's always saying things like that. Just forget about it. Please."

She didn't tell him about the blowjobs that had happened more than once while Charlene was working out front. It made her sick to her stomach the first time she heard it: the centaur kept saying reassuring things to his wife, as if teaching a child to read. One time it happened while there were customers in the café, and she had had to turn up the Peter Tosh to cover the noise. She wasn't afraid of her bosses getting caught in the act, but of being found out herself: she didn't want anyone to know that this was the kind of thing she was willing to put up with. She didn't want people to see how low she'd go for rent money. She felt humiliated standing there, handing over biodegradable coffee cups and a paper bag that held two warm bagel lumps, with the reggae chopping away behind her. She worried the whole time the centaur would make a sound, some unmistakable groan.

What finally got her out was something the centaur's wife said. They'd wanted to bring her camping with them for a weekend – just her, not Kyle. Charlene was in the middle of politely declining when the wife declared that the centaur had opened her up sexually on a camping trip, not long after they'd first met.

"He wants to open you, too. It would be so amazing – we'd be like sisters."

Charlene couldn't make herself work behind the counter even one more day. Strangely enough, it was the wife who would not talk to her or look at her when she went in to get her final paycheque. The centaur was gregarious and easy with her, almost shrugging off the one that got away. The wife stayed hidden in the back.

For a couple of scary months after she quit, Charlene worried about money and wondered if she'd made a huge mistake quitting her job. Even Kyle started to hint that maybe she'd exaggerated the situation at the sandwich place a little and could've stuck it out, at least until she had something else lined up. Just when she was starting to panic, the job at the Ice Shack came up.

Charlene kept herself apart from a lot of the drama that went on at the Shack, the entanglements, feuds, and drunken couplings. She'd been married for the better part of a decade, and to her high school boyfriend no less, which made her feel as though she were decades older than everyone else on staff, part of some other generation that was more predictable and conventional. She had photos at home of herself in the exact kind of bright white, head-turning bridal dress that some of the younger girls imagined themselves wearing one day, or swore they never would. She'd been a bride, she'd stood there and said the words. She had an actual husband at home. She shared furniture and a bank account with someone, and had reasonable expectations of being a mother within a few years, maybe.

She'd been in the Shack a few times before she ever worked there, and had noticed how the staff seemed to be performing the whole time, playing the roles of servers in a bar-restaurant. They greeted each other with high-fives and fist-bumps, but did so as if they were making fun of the idea of greeting each other with high-fives and fist-bumps. Maybe they were – even after working there for a while she couldn't tell. She remembered seeing Jeremy moving through this happy, performing clan, talking to each of them like the playfully scornful head of a musical family, the bar's Baron von Trapp. The staff would sometimes swirl around him excitedly, as if begging for a song. She could imagine him striding onto the floor with a sly grin on his face, singing "Edelweiss" while the waitresses swayed.

Years later, after everything happened and the Shack was long gone, that was the image she liked to conjure up of her former boss: smiling, confident despite everything, and fully in charge of the situation.

When she told him about the lunch counter hippies and all the nastiness that went on, he didn't laugh like most people did, like her friends did. Instead, he got visibly tense.

Owners like that made it hard for the rest of them, he said. They all got painted with the same brush. "You shouldn't have had to put up with that kind of bullshit," he said angrily.

"That's why I quit."

"I mean you should've just walked as soon as it got weird."

"It was weird right from the start – he interviewed me with no shirt on. Just his apron and a pair of jeans."

Jeremy didn't know what to say. "Jesus, I've worked for guys who were pretty bad, but even the worst ones mostly kept it out of the place a little bit. There was one who was always getting waitresses to sit in the car with him in the parking lot. Just to chat, right? I thought for sure we were going to get sued."

Charlene wanted to know why hadn't he tried to stop things like that. Why hadn't he warned those girls? He said it wouldn't have been any use – he simply would've been fired, and the nastiness would've continued no matter what.

"You could've said something at the time, though."

He showed her the palms of his hands. "Look: I'm

totally on board with all the feminism business. Maybe not to the absolute craziest degree, but as far as being treated with respect and all that goes, I've always been right on the money. I actually prefer to hire women than men. Not in the kitchen – that's like throwing somebody to the wolves – but out here on the floor? Every time. Women don't have to worry about *me*."

When she'd first started the job, Jeremy gave her a tour of the bar that ended with him showing her the photos. He wanted to impress upon her how important it was to understand the culture of the Shack – as important as knowing where to find extra napkins or how to get the ice machine working again if it crapped out. Maybe more.

"You know *these* two, obviously," he said, pointing at the photo of himself with the mayor. Next to it was a shot of him wearing an oversized foam leprechaun's hat and being kissed on either cheek by two young women. He touched each of the people in the photos in turn: "*She* was a lab assistant at the hospital, maybe she still is, and *she* was studying to be a teacher. The dopey-looking guy with the muscles there was her boyfriend. Pretty sure he was a carpenter. Or no, wait: it was that he talked about Jesus a lot. And he was a bodybuilder. That's right: he was really into Jesus and Arnold Schwarzenegger, knew everything about both of them, all these little facts. Weird guy."

"You remember all this?"

Jeremy said he could tell her exactly what was happening in every one of the pictures, and exactly when they were taken. He pointed to a group of mallet-headed guys toasting the camera: a rugby team from Kingston, in town for a tournament and caught in a freak April snowstorm. One of Jeremy wearing a fake white beard and a bright red baseball cap: Christmas Eve, five years ago. Raised glasses at a New Year's Eve party, the one where the power died five minutes before midnight and they all sang that Nirvana song in the dark. There were a few pictures from the notorious Halloween party in which Jeremy, dressed as a cop, had had to step between two women dressed like pirates who were squaring off in the middle of the floor, brandishing their wooden swords. In the photo he was smiling and holding his handcuffs up to the camera.

Charlene smiled and pointed to a photo showing Jeremy and a few other men wearing dark suits and ties. "What's going on *here*?" They looked as though they might be part of some theatre production, either as ushers or as a chorus of 1920s gangsters. All they needed were fedoras and cardboard machine guns.

"That was after a funeral for a guy who came in here almost every night at the start," Jeremy said, suddenly sombre.

"Oh my God, I'm sorry."

"It happens."

"Was he sick?"

"In the head, maybe." He pointed one loaded finger at the underside of his chin and silently fired it. "I heard his wife found him – I hope it wasn't a mess, for her sake. He wasn't always the most considerate guy in the world, so you never know. People surprise you. So that's the tour. Any questions?"

At some point Charlene felt comfortable enough to admit that the whole thing she'd told him at her interview about opening a café was a lie. He replied that he'd known it at the time and didn't care, but looked slightly hurt. To make up for it, she quickly said that the idea of owning her own place sounded fun, that it must be exciting and scary to be your own boss.

"That's not how it works," he said, a little defensively. "Everyone who works here, and everyone who comes in – they're all my bosses. I work for all of you. The higher up you get, the more bosses you get. It never stops. Is that what you want?"

She said it wasn't.

"It's not something you do because it sounds fun or for the money, because there isn't any. A lot of people find that out too late."

That night, instead of insisting she join him for dinner after her shift, he embedded himself within a group of older men who were having some kind of reunion. He didn't even look at her as she left the bar.

———————

There were only a few things Charlene could remember ever truly wanting to be. When she was seven or eight, it was Wonder Woman. She would walk around the apartment wearing her blue-and-red swimsuit with a set of her mother's heavy bracelets around her wrists, a shoelace whip coiled on her hip, a paper tiara on her head. She kept the swimsuit under her clothes when she played in the park, or even at school, and it gave her a sense of secret power, the knowledge that she could whip everything off at the first sign of trouble and start windmilling her arms through a storm of bullets. After that, she wanted to be an African tribeswoman, leading all her children down to the river. She'd watched a documentary with her mother about a drought-ravaged village, and immediately felt an intense desire for that kind of silent, stoic nobility. She wanted to be tall and thin, the colour of no-milk coffee, with the soles of her feet as hard as a tire. She wanted six or seven children of wildly varying ages trailing behind. She wanted a baby in a sling around her, barely covering her chest – she was 11, and getting the first, faint swellings of breasts, like two anthills. That wish lasted an embarrassingly long time, almost an entire summer. She told no one, thank God.

In high school, she'd been fairly sure she wanted to be a doctor of some kind. That dream came with obstacles, one being that she hated science: it all felt too arbitrary and unmagical, and whenever she lost her place or got confused, the equations and formulas became like rolls of barbed wire that snagged her and stopped her from going forward. Numbers were inimical, so she loaded herself up with empathy in an effort to compensate, having decided that empathy was the greater part of medicine – the better part, the indispensable part, the unteachable part. She became the most empathetic person around. She sat out beyond the soccer field with girls she didn't even like who had just been dumped by their thuggish boyfriends and would rub their backs and listen, glowing with empathy, stinking of it. In Grade 9, her friend Stephanie's older brother was diagnosed with leukemia, and Charlene almost fainted from all the empathizing she was called on to do. She eventually had to draw back a little and stop hanging out in Stephanie's bedroom, where the two of them would lie on the bed for hours, sobbing and talking about how amazing and wonderful and special her brother was. When her mother asked her why she wasn't hanging out with her friend anymore, Charlene said she thought Stephanie was being overly melodramatic – from what she'd heard, the doctors had given her brother a 50-50 chance of recovery, which seemed like good odds, as simple as flipping a coin. Charlene was invited to the brother's funeral, but didn't go.

She went to school to become a nurse, and dropped out after less than a year. She came close to reapplying a few times, once getting so far as to request all the required documents and begin writing the slightly desperate-sounding letter explaining why she had left the program the first time, but the fact was the idea of a being a nurse held even less interest for her than being a doctor. She flirted with the idea of becoming a veterinarian, but she didn't think she could handle being Kyle's professional colleague as well as his wife. He wasn't crazy about the idea, either, though he was always pushing her to do *something*. He went on job and career sites and listed off the kinds of positions that seemed always to be in demand, and with large starting salaries attached. A lot of companies were advertising for research analysts, with only minimal experience required.

She said, "Those are telemarketing jobs."

"What? Seriously?" He read the rest of the ad, the parts about needing a confident phone manner and about the astronomical wages available through the miracle of commissions, and was silent.

"You think I'm wasting my life."

That wasn't fair, he said. He didn't think that, and he hadn't said that. Maybe she wasn't using her time the best way, but it wasn't like she was never going to do anything. She was too smart to let that happen.

"So if I'm not becoming a doctor, I must be a retard. Is that what you think?"

"All I said was that you're too smart to do nothing. Why would you ask me that?"

"But you think I *am* doing nothing. Right now I'm doing

nothing, is that it? Going to work, cleaning the apartment, eating dinner with you, having a life that isn't working all the time and studying every night – that's nothing. I get it. Being with you is nothing. Okay."

"I just, no, I just meant that you are not the kind of person who will end up doing nothing, not that what you are doing now is nothing."

"That isn't what you said."

"It's what I meant, though. You didn't hear me right."

"So I'm supposed to read your mind and not pay attention to the words coming out of your mouth. That makes total sense."

Charlene almost felt sorry for Kyle for not recognizing an unwinnable argument. Such a concept seemed wholly foreign to him. His arguments were regiments of smartly dressed soldiers marching in tight ranks up and down the main streets, unequipped to respond to counter-arguments that blew up cars, shot from windows, and sent women and children out with bombs under their shirts. His only response was to send in more regiments, keep parading, hold the line.

The one thing Charlene could not remember ever being fully certain she wanted to be was married to Kyle, to be his wife. It wasn't that she *didn't* want to marry him, just that she couldn't remember ever having a moment when she looked at him and wanted nothing more than to have their lives sewn together. She never felt it as a physical need. The whole time they were a couple, it seemed as though they were headed that way anyway, so she never felt any need to actively hope for it to happen. Like hoping for the seasons to change, or for ice to melt in the sun. They were simply being moved up to the next level, which was appropriate.

Her mother, who had never fully accepted Kyle (she thought he was too angry, and a bit of a snob; his family obviously had money) made no protest when told about the upcoming wedding. She did not even suggest they ought to wait a few more years, to when their lives were a little more settled and they had both their careers on track. Charlene got the sense her mother's concerns about Kyle were being overridden by her desire to finally get the apartment to herself – ever since Charlene was a little girl, they'd lived in the same small place. Before Charlene finally moved out, her mother started moving things into her room, stacking them in the corner in impatient piles.

The wedding was wonderful, even if it had been nearly wrecked by Kyle being sick with the flu and almost passing out during the reception because of all the medication he had taken. When she came down the aisle of the little schoolhouse to join him, it didn't feel as though they were being brought together in any formal or intimate way, it was more like the final dress rehearsal for a performance they'd been planning for years. They went on a trip to Manitoulin Island as a honeymoon, during which they fought only once. When the fight was over, he helped her build a crude inuksuk out of stones on a secluded beach, which he then knocked over while getting out his phone to take a picture. She didn't mind. They hadn't built it to last. She was just happy to be so far from her mother, from her friends, from the apartment. By the time they got home, her back was patchy with bruises from having sex in the tent. She never once complained about the roots and random stones that dug into her while they quietly grappled. It was all part of it, part of the experience.

All of that was years ago, nearly a decade. Charlene

sometimes had trouble remembering what had happened since then. She and Kyle had moved three times, into ever-larger apartments, and there'd been a lot of talk about possibly buying a house someday. Both of them had been hit with a vicious stomach flu two Christmases in a row, which Charlene took as a sign they should probably just ignore a holiday she'd never been all that crazy about in the first place. Kyle thought that making decisions based on either superstition or illness was a bad idea. It was just a coincidence. Small, bad things happened to them all the time, he argued. She broke her ankle falling off a playground slide one night when both of them had been out drinking sangria with another couple whom they didn't see much of anymore. After Charlene got herself off the ground, laughing and crying and holding her ankle, Kyle piggybacked her out of the dark playground, up the hill and onto the city bus that was just pulling up to a stop, and then through the automatic sliding doors of the hospital emergency room. He placed her across a row of seats as gently as he could and argued with the nurse to see her quickly.

"At least give her some Tylenol or something!"

They did. He let her sleep on his shoulder while they waited.

———————

It sometimes amazed Charlene's friends when she told them, truthfully, that she had never fucked around on Kyle. Nobody admired her for it – being with the same person since high school and not having at least a quick fling once in a while seemed perverse, almost masochistic. There was something smug and superior about it, too, like being a sexual vegan. Mostly they felt sorry for her.

Just Kyle?

Just him. "And I'm totally, totally happy about that!"

She'd come close a few times, though. A few months after they'd started going out, while they were still in school, Charlene went to a cottage party out near Bobcaygeon. Kyle refused to go – they'd had a fight about something; she could barely remember what. At the party, she split a bottle of vodka with another girl and followed everyone down to the lake to skinny-dip. It was past midnight. There was one boy there, a blond music student whom she'd noticed during the night and had made a few attempts to sit near. He nearly fell over taking his shorts off, and when he regained his balance, he caught Charlene staring at him. She tried to think of an excuse, but there was no hiding the fact that she wanted to know what his cock and his ass looked like. They swam close together and gave each other a few meaningful pats as they moved back toward shore. In waist-high water, they came together and kissed. His skin was cold, and so was hers. He moved his tongue around in her mouth: she tasted beer. He touched her nipples with the tips of his fingers and let the back of his hand brush against her pubic hair – very lightly, as if his hand were a clumsy fish swimming by in the night. Then they separated. Nothing came of it, but she knew, as she went back over the night in her mind later, that she'd been prepared to go along with whatever was going to happen, and she still remembered the mix of disappointment and relief she felt when he rejoined the group on the beach and got dressed.

Kyle knew something had happened at the party, but he never mentioned it. He was conspicuously nice to her for a while, buying her flowers and rarely saying anything if she had to cancel a plan at the last minute.

A few years later, a young cousin of Kyle's named Chad who lived in Ottawa came to stay with them for the summer while he worked at a day camp downtown. His mother's family was Spanish, and he had blue-black hair and olive skin, like he'd been rubbed with tea leaves every day since birth. He could read and speak Spanish, and on his first night in their apartment, he taught Kyle and Charlene some crude sayings: Charlene worked hard to get *me cago en la leche de tu puta madre* (I shit in your whore mother's milk) to come out right. That one bothered Kyle a little, and it bothered him that she liked it so much. Who was she ever going to say that to? It didn't matter, she told him, it was funny. He preferred *No me jodas!* (Don't fuck me around). It was simpler and more useful. Why didn't she use that one instead? Wasn't it better? She would not admit it was better. He vowed to use it at work, where a few people spoke Spanish.

Chad giggled and laughed at the slightest thing. He didn't like being alone, and would follow them both into the kitchen if they left the room, like a puppy. Kyle said it drove him crazy, but Charlene didn't mind – she thought it was cute. It was his first time living away from home, he told her. His girlfriend dumped him just before the beginning of summer.

"I think she wanted to be free to fuck around while I'm here. I know that sounds totally harsh, but you'd have to know her."

"Why is he telling *you* this kind of thing?" Kyle asked.

"I don't know. He just wants someone to talk to. He's always hanging out here at night."

She liked Chad – she was used to Kyle, who treated conversation like a precious resource to be used sparingly, or like something inherently suspicious, something corrupt.

"He should go out and make some friends."

"We're not his parents. He can do what he likes."

When Kyle did a run of double shifts at the shelter, Chad and Charlene would make heavy pots of spaghetti with garlic bread. Chad never offered to help clean up the dishes, she noticed, but kept her company in the kitchen while she did them, so she didn't mind. She would come out in the morning and find him asleep on the couch, on his back, with the cat on his bare chest.

"I'm surprised you can breathe with him on you."

"My cat at home used to do this. He's even fatter."

She noticed how dark the skin on his chest and arms was, and how smooth. After having a shower, he often walked through the apartment wearing only a towel. He ate lots of junk food, and would always eat tons of whatever they had for dinner, but there didn't seem to be any fat on him. He always walked to the day camp where he worked, though it was a few kilometres away. He walked there in the morning and jogged back at night. He used to work out a lot, he told Charlene. He had a whole weight set in his room at home, but hardly ever used it anymore. He didn't want to become one of those weird guys who gets all obsessed with that kind of thing, with getting big muscles. Chad's body had definition. He had a T-shirt he liked to wear that was tight and wonderful. Kyle's body was never something she could really focus any erotic thoughts on – they slid off too easily. She liked it when she and Kyle had sex, and she liked the feel of him, but just seeing him in the shower or covered in sweat from a run or a bike ride wasn't enough. Kyle could sometimes be so sweet and nervous with her that she would fuck him as a kind of reward, a treat.

"How long did you lift weights?"

"Honestly? Until my sister asked me if I was gay. I had all these muscle magazines I was always reading. It sort of ruined it for me. She really thought I was going that way. I started to worry about it, too – there's only so long you can spend looking at all these oiled-up gym rats before you start to, like, forget. So I just stopped."

On a night when Kyle was working an overnight shift at the shelter, and wouldn't be home until nearly eight in the morning, Charlene and Chad made their spaghetti, bought a case of beer, and watched movies on the couch. They huddled under some blankets, and before the first movie was even half over, their hands were under each other's shirts and they were kissing hard. Chad was hesitant, but Charlene pushed him into the couch, positioning herself so that, should he want to, he could easily get her bra unhooked and her shirt over her head. She felt like a deaf person whose hearing had been restored in the middle of an electrical storm. Her head was full of noise.

"We shouldn't do this," Chad said, pushing away from her and wincing.

"We shouldn't," she agreed, pulling him back.

She got his pants open and put her hand around his cock. She couldn't see it well because they'd dimmed the lights for the movie, but she imagined it had been rubbed with tea, as well. It hardened in her hand like a pet that was eager to show a new friend what tricks it can do. She bent toward it, but he began to resist. She allowed herself to be pushed away.

"I'm just, I'm still all fucked up about my girlfriend. And Kyle's like, my cousin. I don't know."

Charlene reached under the coffee table where they'd

stashed the beer and pulled out two bottles. She offered one to Chad, who took it from her without saying anything, a reflex gesture. She was a little thrilled with how blasé she was being, how in control, as if she did this all the time. It was almost as exciting as the thought of fucking him had been.

"I'm sorry," he said. "You must think I'm a total asshole for this."

She thought about it. "No."

Chad promised her he wouldn't tell Kyle or anyone else. He kept telling her it was his fault and that she must think he was a prick. She reassured him, telling him she thought his ex-girlfriend would probably come to her senses if he just left her alone for a while to think. He was a really nice guy. There was a small part of her mind that hoped these reassurances would lead to more kissing. She was determined, if it started again, to get her bra off before he could object and get his cock in her mouth. He offered to move out the next morning – there was a guy at the day camp who told him he could stay at his apartment if he paid some of the utility bills. He said again that he would not tell Kyle what happened.

After he left, his blankets and sheets were left on the couch. She found a T-shirt he'd left behind and almost inhaled it. She masturbated with it twice before throwing it away in a moment of panic and shame.

She told Kyle herself, weeks later, while they were on their way to get groceries. She immediately wished that she'd waited until they were already done their shopping, because now it would be hard to get everything they needed.

I don't get it, he kept saying.

What was there to get?

"I'm so sorry. It wasn't anything. It was stupid. It was really, really stupid. I wasn't even thinking. We were drunk and being stupid. Don't be angry at Chad – be angry at me. I'm sorry, I love you."

Kyle slept on the couch that night, and the next night, too, using the same sheets Chad had used. Charlene thought that was fair: they would end up smelling like her husband, like everything else did, and whatever craziness she had fallen into would evaporate. On the third night, he came into the room, sat on the bed, and made her promise it was just a stupid one-time thing, that she'd never done something like that before and never would again. She did, and meant it, and was happy to have him back beside her. As had happened after the cottage party, Kyle became uncommonly sweet and flexible for a while, and she decided that was what she'd wanted all along.

At some point, rumours started going around the Ice Shack about Charlene and Jeremy. That they had a thing going, that there was more to the dinners they sometimes had together, that she would stay overnight at his house when Kyle was out of town, and worst of all, that she got paid more than anyone else at the bar. Charlene found out from another waitress, who came right out and asked her if it was true.

"I'm married!"

"That's why I was a little shocked, to be honest – about you, not Jeremy."

Charlene carried her anger around with her for days. When she finally confronted him about it, he just laughed, which made her even angrier. There was no point even thinking about it, he said, trying to calm her down. The Shack ran on beer and gossip. Next it'd be him and Tyler who had something going on. Seriously, it wasn't worth it.

Did he know people were saying this shit?

He told her he'd had no idea. Which was a lie: he'd been hearing rumblings for a while. It had spread wide enough that one of the regulars had made what he must have thought was a clever sideways reference to it. A week or so later, another regular came up to him, swaying in an invisible breeze, and said it must be nice to have the pick of the staff.

Jeremy shut the idea down as best as he could: "The one thing I've learned long ago about this business – about *life*, never mind – is that you don't shit where you eat."

"That's gross, bro. I was talking about *fucking*."

Charlene could tell by the look on Jeremy's face that the rumour was not news to him.

"So basically everybody thinks we're having an affair?"

"I don't think *everybody* thinks that. And if some people do, so what? They'll figure it out."

"How long will that take? A year? It's insulting."

"Oh thanks a lot. I guess I'm not as big a catch as I thought I was. Thanks a lot."

"I'm serious!"

"I know, sorry. Look: this will die out. I'll take a couple of the biggest mouths aside and tell them to cool it. Then, in a few days or a few weeks, something will happen to somebody else that will get everybody all giddy and excited, and they'll all start talking about that instead. The harder you try to deny something like this, the more people believe it. That's how it works."

Charlene wasn't convinced. "What if Kyle hears something?"

"Who's going to tell him? One of the dishwashers? He barely ever comes in here – which I've noticed, by the way. But if you want, I'll call him myself and tell him there's nothing going on."

She thought about it. "That would make things worse."

"There you go," he said.

> **"GETTING OLDER IS NOT ABOUT CLOSING DOORS,**
> **IT'S ABOUT LEARNING TO OPEN WINDOWS."**
> *– Behaving like Grown-Ups, Believing like Children,* Theo Hendra

In the mornings, while Charlene set up chairs and wiped down tables, Jeremy would work away in a corner booth, totalling receipts and talking on the phone. He almost never worked downstairs in his office. If she brought in music from home, he always asked her what it was. He did this even when it was clear he hated it. One morning it was Yo-Yo Ma performing Bach's Cello Suites. Her favourite elementary school teacher used to put it on in class whenever they were working on group projects or doing silent reading. It always made her feel as though she were working toward something, preparing the ground for something momentous to happen to her. All she had to do was wait, be ready, and recognize the signs when they came.

Jeremy sat there for nearly 10 minutes while the lone cello sawed away, then finally asked her if the whole thing was like that.

"You don't like it?"

"It's sort of the same thing over and over again."

"Not at all! It's constantly changing."

She put the music back on, and the sawing began again in earnest. He tried to ignore it, then put up his hands in surrender. "Maybe stick to things with a little more get up and go. I thought I was floating on the ceiling for a while there."

In the afternoons, they took turns eavesdropping on the group of young men, mostly teenagers, who took over a corner booth to play Tactix, a strategic game in which each player was half-cyborg, half-medieval knight. They had asked Jeremy if they could hold their games there, having been kicked out of the library, their usual spot, for sneaking in food. After determining that the game involved no twisted Nazi shit, and that a disgruntled player was not likely to show up one day with a shotgun under his trench coat, Jeremy said yes. He needed the daytime business, even if it was only a dozen Cokes and a few baskets of fries. He and Charlene were both fascinated by the young man who adjudicated the tournaments: a little older than the rest of the group, his official title was Master Guardian. His name was Donnie. The younger men huddled near him, in awe of his skill with the game, his ability to anticipate everyone's next moves, and his card collection, all contained within a leather binder. Donnie was patient with them, like a fat mother pig being rolled and jostled by her rebellious piglets. After a game in which he was soundly defeated by a younger player, Donnie had to endure a few minutes' worth of teasing and boasts about who would be the next Master Guardian. Before leaving, he sat at the bar and finished his Diet Coke.

Jeremy said, "Sounds like they gave you a hard time today."

Donnie held his glass in front of him, swirling it slightly as if it were expensive Scotch. Charlene had to fight to stop herself from laughing. He reminded her so much of some of the guys she'd known in high school – awkward misfits who, having grown too large to be physically bullied, stopped being fearful and skittish and became angry about their exclusion from the brighter world of teenage popularity. That anger fuelled arrogance, which brought on the long, black coats, the wraparound shades, the heavy, buckled boots, and the black gloves. Some of them had been her friends in elementary school – she had to fight her way out of their orbit once they got to high school, where those associations would've been fatal.

"I don't get caught up in who's winning or losing," Donnie said. "You can't worry about one game, one day. They see the battles, I see the war."

Jeremy liked that – *they see the battles, I see the war* – and adopted it as his own. It was almost as good as anything he'd read in a Theo Hendra book. True victory was always just over the horizon; it was better to live to fight another day than lose everything trying to defend a lost cause. He told Charlene to make sure Donnie got a free Diet Coke the next time he was in, but to be discreet about it, or else she'd have that whole pack of monkeys on her, demanding free drinks.

If it were a warm and bright day, Jeremy would insist she come out onto the deck with him for a few minutes to soak up the sunshine. He sometimes brought peanuts for the squirrels, and the two of them would laugh at the contradiction between the animals' furtiveness and the massive facts of their tails. It was like trying to sneak into a house wearing clown shoes. He made her stand on the bench along the edge of the deck to look down into the ravine. She would almost get sick at the sight of the drop, but she did it. When she felt steady up there, she stretched out her arms in either direction and loudly declared herself king of the world, which Jeremy smiled at, puzzled.

"That from a movie?"

He pointed out where that poor kid had jumped from the bridge and been speared through the thigh all those years ago, a story she'd heard before, though in a much more gruesome form.

"Didn't it go through his neck?"

No, no, he said, and laughed, as if the very idea were absurd.

"Apparently, all the schools went crazy with safety lectures after it happened," he said. "My sister told me her class had a cop come in three times in one year to talk to them about not doing stupid dares. As if having a cop at school would stop anyone who wanted to be that goddamned stupid. Did they do all that at your school?"

"I . . . don't think so."

"You don't remember? It was a pretty big deal."

Charlene admitted, reluctantly, that the jumping incident had happened shortly before she was born, while her mother was pregnant with her. She knew this because her mother told her she'd spent about a week completely broken down over the idea that someone's child – who'd once been a baby in a belly, just like Charlene was at the time – had nearly thrown his life away for absolutely nothing, on a stupid dare, showing off, not even thinking.

"Didn't the guy almost drown? That's what she told me."

Jeremy ignored her question. "You weren't *born* yet?" He suddenly felt as though he were telling her about something from way back in history, like D-Day or the Beatles.

Her mother might've been talking about someone else, Charlene suggested. Another accident, another teen.

Jeremy shook his head. "You know how to spoil a day, you really do."

———————

Jeremy was not yet what he would call *old*, but he could already feel parts of himself losing the fight to stay young. He never missed a chance, when passing the broad mirror behind the bar, to check his reflection. What he saw there was a thickening man drawn tight by his own tools and clothes. His head of dense curly hair gleamed with the synthetic dew of hair product. It had been wood-stain brown his whole life, though a kind of frost was creeping into it. Wood stain after a few seasons of hard weather, maybe. The closely trimmed beard he'd worn for decades was gone, and he couldn't decide whether its absence made him look older or younger. It made him look a little less serious, which he decided was okay – he wanted always to be approachable – but it revealed the softening curve of his chin and jaw. His hair, his gut, and the flesh around his eyes were drifting away from the rest of him and falling asleep on themselves, like peripheral friends at the far end of a long table full of people, pushed out of the stream of conversation and too drunk and tired to fight their way back in. Every year something else gave up. His feet were growing tough and square. The pink rim of his ears kept producing long white hairs as hard as little feathers.

Ever since he'd quit smoking – at the urging of his mother, whose extended family seemed to contract different forms of cancer the way other people caught colds – food had rushed in to fill the void. He fought back, having only some kind of salad for lunch, and another one for dinner, then putting an exercise bike in his office. His stomach, if left alone, would happily spread out, the same way his hair was just waiting for the signal to clear a tiny helipad at the back of his head.

Next door, the old widower with the bagpipe music had finally given up trying to take care of himself and had moved out east to live with his daughter in the navy, who had two daughters of her own and an ex-husband with chronic fatigue syndrome. Across the street, Nicolas had gotten thicker, while his brood of white-haired children had gotten thinner – there was only one left at home now, and he no longer looked like a younger version of his father. Now when the boy greeted Jeremy in the morning, it was with a voice that was tenuously, willfully adult, and Jeremy would respond by deepening his own voice with mock formality.

"Your kids keep growing up," Jeremy said to Nicolas.

"It's the one thing they do without me telling them."

Jeremy looked to his parents for clues as to how his own old age would go, and was usually heartened. They looked and behaved like people at least a decade younger, though they were both already older than some of the drooling skeletons he saw parked outside in the sun at the seniors' residence. Gord and Anne were still self-sufficient, which was good. His mother and father kept the house clean, cleared the driveway, maintained the yard, and did almost all their own shopping. Once in a while he would get a report from his sister about there being all kinds of food rotting in the fridge or about the state of their bathroom, which Jeremy never ventured into when he visited. Marie had regular meetings with their parents' doctor, and knew all the troubling details about blood pressure, eyesight, arthritis, and bad joints. She would come to the Shack on her way home from those meetings and want to sit and fill him in. She sat in the middle of the booth, relishing all the unencumbered, childless space around her.

"He says Mom is losing sight in her left eye. It's not panic mode yet, but it will be if it keeps going."

"Will it?"

She didn't know. She was only ever given their current status. Their doctor, an Indian man whom Marie thought was gay because of his careful manners and soft voice, would not make predictions, even when pressed.

"And Gord still has his blood pressure thing and his clumsiness. Did you know he nearly broke his neck last week taking out the recycling?"

"Nobody told me that."

"Nobody told me, either! Apparently, he went right off the back stairs and whacked his head so bad he couldn't see for a while. He twisted his arm, too. Mom had a fit. They don't tell us this stuff, because they're afraid we'll put them in a home. You know what they're like."

"They're proud, and don't want people taking care of them. I get that."

"You get that – oh good. Except it'll be me who gets one of them when the other kicks the bucket."

"Why would you even say that?"

"Because it's true? Jer, this is something we will have to deal with. It's not all getting put on me. You're not going to pull a Gord on me and just pretend it doesn't matter."

Their father didn't like to talk about getting old. Getting old was getting old – what alternative was there? It was as pointless as trying to imagine the forms life might take at the far end of the universe. We'll know when we know. Gord had survived the first years of his retirement by throwing himself into the making of wine and beer using a kit. He still had cases of the stuff in the basement, some of it in green bottles and some of it in brown bottles, all of it foul and undrinkable. After the first few batches, he stopped pretending it tasted good and was a desirable drink, though he went on making it. Everyone was glad when that passed. After that, he attended weekly aqua-fit classes, and would bob and twist with a dozen other old folks while the young instructor danced on the deck with a scowl on her face. He told Jeremy the only thing he didn't like was how long he had to wait for all the fat old turkeys to climb their way up the shallow-end ladder and out of the pool at the end of the classes. He was sure some of them were secretly peeing during the classes, too. A suspiciously warm current would suddenly appear around him every once in a while.

"That's disgusting. How can you keep going?" Jeremy asked him.

His father gave him a scornful look. Once you started something, you had to stick to it, and he'd had worse things on him than a little pee.

His mother kept putting herself and her husband on life-extending diets. She always insisted, however, that staying alive for as long as physically and medically possible was never her goal: "My mother, your Gramma Jackie, used to say there was such a thing as an *over*-ripe old age," she told

Jeremy. "Her father held on until he was 95. She got so bitter about it, about everything she had to do for him."

Of course, she added, Gramma Jackie hung around herself until she was almost the same age.

"But *my* father died when he was 70," she said. "Younger than me!"

"He was the exception, though."

"That's exactly what he was. I have a feeling that, no matter what I do, I'll still be here when people start travelling back and forth to the moon every day like it's nothing."

One afternoon, his mother appeared in the Shack without having called ahead the way she usually did. Her favourite booth was occupied, so he found her a table in the corner, as far away as possible from Donnie and the Tactix players. They made her nervous. She was wearing a floppy hat and a big pair of sunglasses, though it was overcast outside.

"I'm sorry if I've got you in the middle of things."

"So you're a celebrity now? You still have your sunglasses on."

She reached up to touch them, but left them in place.

"Everything okay?"

Charlene brought over a bottle of sparkling water and two glasses.

"I like your hat, Anne."

When she'd gone to take care of another table, Anne said, "She's very nice, I've always liked her. Does she have any kids?"

"Not that I know of."

"She seems like she would be good with children. She shouldn't wait too long. Everybody waits so long now."

"I think she's doing fine."

He knew exactly what was happening in his mother's head: visions of her son lying on his deathbed, wracked with guilt over never fathering a child. He poured them both a glass of water and waited.

"I did something stupid," she said finally.

Jeremy felt ice form in his chest, imagining her sending the rest of their savings to a phantom Nigerian prince.

"What is it, what happened?"

"I had a little accident. It was stupid – I shouldn't have gotten up so fast."

She quickly removed the glasses, looking irritated, as if someone had put them on her face as a prank while she'd been sleeping. Surrounding her right eye and spreading up her temple was a dark bruise the colour of a grape. Her right eye was bloodshot, and there was a blood-red glow to her nose he hadn't noticed before. His first instinct was to tell her to put the glasses back on – quickly, before anyone saw. But having revealed her secret, she seemed wretchedly proud of it. The glasses stayed on the table. She'd fallen, she said, in the bathroom. She could laugh a little now at the whole situation. If he had to know, she had been sitting on the toilet and stood up too quickly, so that all the blood suddenly drained out of her head and she felt dizzy. Before she could sit down again, she found herself falling forward, and her head caught the edge of the sink. His father heard it happen, and almost broke down the door coming into the room. He'd wanted to take her to the hospital.

"Did you go?"

"Go and sit for hours, just to have them tell me to lie down and put ice on my face?"

Did Marie know about the accident?

"I tried to tell her, I called her, but she and Brian were in the middle of some fight about something. She's busy with those kids all the time, anyway – she has enough to worry about."

It was sore, and she still felt so embarrassed about the whole thing, but that's life, isn't it: things happen, and you have to get through them. She finished the rest of her water and put the glasses back on.

"If I don't get back, Gord will call the police to come looking for me. He must think I am completely useless. I guess I don't blame him after this."

Jeremy was sometimes alarmed to discover that his mother and father didn't look as old to him as they once did, their ages no longer like grotesque things kept in the upper loft of a barn with the ladder pulled up. He was climbing up there himself, however slowly, getting a better and better look with each step. Somewhere, in an interview Jeremy had watched, Theo Hendra said that the only thing he feared about getting old was being unable to help people as much as he wanted to. The interviewer objected, saying his work would go on helping millions of people even after Hendra himself was gone, and Hendra reluctantly agreed. Jeremy was less certain about his own impact: the good he was putting into the world – some of that would outlast him, maybe, but mostly it would all crumble the moment he stopped building it up and packing it down.

He gave the situation some thought: if things ever got so bad that he was becoming helpless, he would borrow a rifle from someone, drag himself into the woods, and swallow the barrel. Or else he'd drive to Niagara Falls, climb the little wrought-iron fence in the middle of the night, and drop down into the swirl and the foam. Assuming he could still drive and climb. They'd have to scoop out his body, fatter and wetter and whiter, a ways downstream. Maybe the only mess-free way was in the Jeep with the engine running and one end of a hose attached to the exhaust pipe, the other end poking in through a back-seat window. He debated with himself about the exact right music to have playing while he waited for the fumes to do their thing – "Bridge Over Troubled Water" was an obvious choice, but he'd never really liked the song. And he wasn't a big Pink Floyd fan, so *Dark Side of the Moon* was out. "Superstition" seemed inappropriate somehow, like tempting fate. He abandoned the idea without coming to a decision. If he did ever go through with it, he'd have to be spontaneous.

––––––––––

Jeremy shared a birthday with Glenn and Phil, two regulars at the Shack who often ended up sitting together at the bar, but who rarely betrayed any actual affection, as if their physical proximity were merely an ongoing coincidence. Jeremy hardly ever encountered them outside the bar. When he did, it was as if a crucial support beam for their relationship were missing. Glenn was a little older than Jeremy, Phil a few years younger. The three had an agreement to celebrate their shared birthdays quietly at the bar, with no singing, no gifts, no nonsense. It was less of a birthday party than a wake for the year that had just fallen away. The staff was under strict orders to nix any plans to surprise them with cupcakes and cards.

Jeremy asked the two men if they had any plans to end things early. "Let's say nothing's working anymore and you're totally at the mercy. Do you wait it out or take matters into your own hands?"

"You mean kill myself?" Phil asked. "Oh no, not a chance."

"You want to stick around as long as possible."

"I absolutely do. For the sake of my daughter."

"But does *she* want to see you stick around that long? It's not like the two of you will be going on road trips together. It might be a relief for her, too."

"It doesn't matter. Life is too precious a thing, too rare. You can't just throw it away like that."

Glenn declared that, if he were too old or sick to be of any use, he would take care of himself in a heartbeat.

"It's not like I have a plan – I'm not that morbid. But if I had to decide right now, I'd probably go down to the lake on a hot night, drink a bottle of vodka and swim out as far as I can, then just let myself drop."

"That's a good one."

"Oh don't say that," Phil said.

"I have no intention of being a vegetable waiting to die."

"Me, neither," Jeremy said. "The trick is knowing when to pull the cord though, right? What if they find a cure for cancer the day after you do it, or figure out how to make people young again?"

"Exactly," Phil said. "You have to live with hope."

Glenn shook his head. "Most great men in history accomplished everything they were ever going to do before the age of 30. There are exceptions: you have Winston Churchill and a few others. Nelson Mandela, I guess, though there's some black marks in that guy's past – no pun intended. But for the most part, the show's over before you turn 30. So unless you're one of those, Churchill or Mandela, you're pretty much done."

"I've still got a lot to do," Jeremy said.

"Alexander the Great died at 32. Think about it: 32. And that was *old*. My son will be 25 next year."

Phil gave him a friendly pat on the shoulder. "He's still got time."

"It never used to bother me," Jeremy said, "but sometimes I have to think about what my exact age is, for taxes or something, and I literally can't believe the number."

"I look at every year after 40 as a gift," Glenn said.

Phil liked that idea. "That's the best attitude to have, I think."

"I didn't say we were *doing* anything with the gift. We waste it. We do all this shit just to get another 10 or 20 years, then we flush it all down the toilet. Might as well go when you go. Or even better, go when you can. Before you're a total waste."

"I don't know if I can go along with any of this," Phil said. "My father-in-law is 83, and to see him, you'd think he was no more than 60. He built a storage shed behind his cottage a few years ago, almost on his own."

Glenn went on, a little annoyed at being interrupted: "Think about apples – with most of them, once they're ripe you get three, maybe four days before they start looking like shit. One little bump and they're fucked. Then you have green apples. Doesn't matter what you do – drop them on the floor, drive over them – they stay green, and they're like that for weeks. They never change, like wax fruit, because of radiation and dicking around with the genetics. We all want to be green apples. We waste so much effort trying to look ripe all the time. What's wrong with a few bruises, for Christ's sake? What's wrong with getting old?"

"Hear, fucking hear."

"A time to be born, a time to die – you don't fuck around with that formula."

"The Byrds, right?" Jeremy said. "My mother loves that song."

"It's *Ecclesiastes*, you pagan. From the Bible."

"Is it really?" Jeremy looked to Phil, who confirmed it.

"They left out the best part though," Glenn said, "about how men are no better than beasts and will die like beasts, and all is vanity. Put *that* in your pipe and smoke it."

Glenn owned a men's clothing store in the neighbourhood, a long, narrow place crowded with plain grey pants and white shirts on the first floor of a building he also owned. He had started the business with his ex-wife. When they split, she got the house, he got the business and the building, and moved into the apartment above the store. Their son, already an adult and living in Calgary by that time, showed his neutrality by never coming home. The only thing Glenn regretted leaving behind when he moved out was his hulking, silver barbecue. There was no way the thing would fit up the stairs to his apartment, so he abandoned it to his ex-wife and bought a little portable one that he stuck on the roof of the building. In the summer and fall, he would sit up there in a patio chair, cooking his dinner and drinking cans of German beer, throwing sausages to seagulls and pigeons.

Phil was also divorced, though much more freshly and messily so than Glenn, and it showed. Glenn treated his divorce like a public insult he refused to let bother him; Phil's seemed to have sucked out of him everything that had once been vital. He taught at a community college downtown and had been on his way to heading up the adult education department before his wife caught him fucking around with a woman who taught small business management and who saw sleeping with him as the least stressful way to burn off the excess lust she accumulated throughout the week. After getting kicked out of the house, he lost a lot of weight, shedding pounds like a cat sheds hair under stress. The weight walked away from him and so did a lot of his old friends. His shoulders sharpened and his chest sank. Occasionally, when the booze washed away the thin emotional struts that kept Phil upright, he would collapse at the bar like a downed weather balloon, leaking tears and apologies. Or else he would work himself up into a fit about his ex-wife until he was clenching and unclenching his fists and yelling about *bitches* and *cunts*, and Jeremy would have to get him outside and into a taxi. The next morning, he would return, looking for his car keys and smiling guiltily.

"I hit the giggle juice a little hard last night."

"Forgiven, forgotten."

After his wife kicked him out of the house, Phil moved in with his sister Paula and her friend Barbara. He and Barbara, having burned through most of the sustaining illusions they had about themselves, got along great, occasionally acting like a platonic couple: buying groceries, cooking meals, planning and executing repairs to the house. Barbara even helped Phil pick out a little folding bed for his daughter to use on her rare visits. It was Phil's sister who, still believing she deserved better out of life than to have her weak brother living in the basement, was resentful of the new arrangement.

"She makes me wear flip-flops in the house."

"What for?"

"She says my feet sweat a lot, and doesn't want me getting bacteria all over her floors. Even if I'm wearing socks."

"That is not true," Jeremy said. "Tell me that is not true."

"Yellow ones. She buys them by the dozen, I think, so I can't even pretend I've lost one."

Glenn said, "That is classic behaviour, just classic. It goes right back to the Old Testament – you should be *teaching* this stuff."

"That's got to be the exception, though. Flip-flops?"

Glenn shook his head and put his big hands out in front of him. "It comes down to this: in every culture and every race, women preserve the status quo. That's what they do, that's their role. Women protect the nest. Which is not even a bad thing – someone has to do it, right?"

"That's an interesting point, that's a very interesting point," Phil said.

"What men are supposed to do is go out there and explore. We map out the territory and fight off invaders. That's the deal. So you've got raising kids and keeping the house versus what, walking on the moon? Curing diseases? Fighting wars? It's *this*," he formed a small, invisible mound with his hands on the bar, "versus *this*." He spread his arms wide. "It's in Shakespeare, the Bible. Old Testament. It's probably in the Koran. In fact, I *know* it is: those guys don't fuck around when it comes to women. Not saying they're right."

"You're saying Phil's sister is like a terrorist?"

"Not at all. Exactly the opposite. She doesn't want anything broken."

Phil started giggling. "No, no, no. She's . . . she's more like one of those mothers in Rwanda who put their babies on their backs and went out to hack people up with machetes."

He made a slashing motion with the edge of his hand.

"I don't know about that," Glenn said, taking a wary

drink. "Anyway, all bets are off when you're talking about friggin *Africa*. Christ, we're way off the map now."

––––––––––––––

Less than a week before one of their shared birthdays, Phil dropped to the floor in front of a classroom full of bored business and cosmetics students being forced to read about a boxing match between Ernest Hemingway and Morley Callaghan. An invisible flying punch caught him between his ribs and the world turned white. He lay there for almost a minute before anyone thought to do something. Finally, an ambulance was called, and he was taken away to the hospital.

The news threw everyone at the Shack. Some of the waitresses cried. Even Tyler seemed upset. Charlene bought a large card for people to sign. She liked Phil: he reminded her of some of the absent-minded teachers she'd had in high school. There was one in particular: a science teacher who was always burning himself with something, and who had two sweat patches under his armpits that might as well have been sewn right into his shirt. For a while he had a thing for Charlene, mostly because she was his most attentive student, though she only showed interest in his lectures to be polite. He zeroed in on her, and then lost interest once her test results showed she had no actual aptitude for the subject.

When the card came back to her, she was shocked at some of the things in it: the messages were bad enough, but the crude cartoons were worse.

"What if his daughter sees this?"

"We can give him two. This one and a nice one," Jeremy said.

He said he would deliver the cards to Phil in person, and she volunteered to accompany him. Patty asked if she could come along, too – she had a friend on the same floor recuperating from a hernia operation, so she could kill two birds with one stone.

"Don't say that when we're there," Jeremy warned her.

On the elevator ride to Phil's floor, Patty talked about the time, years earlier, when her husband had been knocked down by a mild heart attack, and was taken to the very same hospital. They had tickets to go see the musical version of *The Lion King*, which she had been dying to see for years, and he went and had an attack a few days before. It was too late to even cancel.

In the hallway, a man in a wheelchair accepted the lunch being handed to him by his wife, piece by piece: juice box, egg salad sandwich, granola bar, banana. Across the way, an elderly woman held a stained Snoopy doll by the throat, as if it were responsible for whatever was ailing her.

"I swear some of these people were here when I came to visit my Shawn that time," Patty whispered.

Phil's room had two beds. One was empty and stripped of sheets and pillows.

"This is alright," Jeremy said, looking around. "You've got the place to yourself."

He had to stop himself from shouting. Something about hospitals made him act as though everyone in them were deaf. Phil was thin and pale, more so than usual, and his hair was standing up. He looked like a broom that had been enchanted and brought to life, only to fall ill before it could complete any of its appointed tasks.

"It was supposed to be shared," Phil said, looking happily at the cards that Jeremy had brought him. "The other guy gave up the ghost just before I got here."

Charlene's eyes went wide, and she put her hand over her mouth. The empty bed was propped up in the sitting position, as if the other patient had been violently ejected the moment he died. Jeremy moved closer to the open door.

"Still, that's a kind of luck," he said.

"When can you go home?" Charlene asked.

"There're not saying anything yet."

"It was exactly the same when Shawn was in here," Patty said. "They ask you all kinds of questions and do a million tests, but can't answer a simple question. Nothing has changed."

Jeremy noticed a new-looking air purifier humming away on the floor next to the bed.

"That's handy. Who got you that?"

Phil smiled brightly. "That was Glenn! He was in here yesterday. He said he'd had one when he was in for an operation some time – he thinks it saved his life."

"That's what you do, good for him," Patty said, though she had never liked Glenn.

Charlene gave Phil the nicer card and made Jeremy hand him the one that had been vandalized. Phil grinned like a little boy at the cartoon boobs. There was already a homemade card from his daughter on the nightstand, next to a pile of empty containers of applesauce – the only thing he could eat at the moment, he said. Everything else hurt his throat. He didn't even like applesauce.

"When you get back to the Shack, there's a 10-inch steak waiting for you, buddy. On the house."

Phil laughed, then coughed and turned red enough that Jeremy and Charlene began to worry they might need to summon the nurse. Patty didn't seem to notice.

"What I really want is a beer," Phil said when he'd recovered.

"Now, should you be drinking?" Patty asked.

He said it was fine; it wasn't a bad attack, just a Death Knock.

The other three looked confused.

"You've never heard that? Really? My mother used to say it when I was a little kid. After my grandfather died of pneumonia, my sister got it, too, less than a year later, and I was so scared she was going to die just like him. My mother told me Death sometimes knocks on your door just to see if you are home. If you're old enough, you might forget and answer the door by accident. Or even on purpose, if you're so old that all of your friends have already gone."

"That's so sad," Charlene said.

"That's the craziest thing I've ever heard, buddy," Jeremy said.

"Is it? I still sort of believe it, to be honest."

"Now you'll have me scared to answer my door!" Patty said.

After a half an hour or so, Phil began to float away, his eyes closed, and his chin touched his chest. On the ride back down in the elevator, Patty listed off all the teachers she knew who'd had heart attacks. There were a lot. Even the ones who'd been mean to her did not deserve it, she insisted.

Jeremy was unable to shake the thought that what had happened to Phil meant Death was no longer a far-off threat or an abstract concept. Death was a pack of wolves that had started going after people in his own group, which meant anyone could be picked off at any time. It would start with the weakest and most vulnerable, like Phil, and make its way up the chain until it got to him.

"You know in movies when one of those little laser dots appears on a guy's forehead just before he gets shot?" he asked Charlene. "That's me sometimes."

"You're waiting for a Death Knock?"

He truly wondered if he was.

"Most of the time – you know me – I'm the happiest guy around. But then something like this happens and I can't get it out of my head."

She asked him how long it'd been since he'd taken time off – not a day or two here and there, but a week or more away from the bar.

Right away, he said: "Three years. Remember I had that stomach flu? I couldn't get off my couch for almost four days, and could barely walk for a few days after that. Had to run the place over the phone."

"That doesn't count. I mean, when's the last time you did something fun, just for you?"

"That's easy: last night, and every night this week," he said, smiling. "This is my permanent vacation."

But she was right. He sometimes found himself fantasizing about having a small cabin somewhere – something close enough to get to within an hour or two, but far enough away to be out of the gravitational orbit of the bar and the city. He imagined standing on the shore of a body of water as clean and clear as a new contact lens. He wanted to stand there and feel as though the scene laid out before around him – rich kids buzzing from shore to shore on Jet Skis, a chainsaw revving somewhere way back in the woods, water folding brightly over the rocks, birds talking shit in the trees – had been created exclusively for him. He imagined stepping into a pond and pulling a plump fish from the water with his bare hands, roasting it in a fire pit, and eating it while standing on the rocks, the warm evening wind cleansing and soothing him, bringing the sound of kids tumbling in the lake for a swim and the smell of reeds and campfire smoke. He wanted to sip at bourbon that tasted like it had been distilled from all the colours in the woods around him, and to spend evenings watching the sun char the sky and fall behind the trees at the other end of a kidney-shaped lake.

His sister had a cottage, an ostentatiously wooden place on a strip of land near the bottom end of Algonquin Park. Marie and Brian bought it after their first child was born, Brian's family cottage in Quebec being too far a drive for a little baby and a recovering mother. Jeremy got invited out every summer, and would spend his time sitting by the fire pit in a wooden chair that might as well have been scalloped out of a tree especially for him. He would sit there, too sick with resentment and envy to move, waving off the children's pleas to be thrown into the water by their uncle. Each night, Marie and Brian would collaborate on a meal that looked as though it had been created for a photo spread in a glossy magazine. They'd have to wait while Brian took pictures of each heaping plate and bowl with his phone. When the kids were asleep, the three adults would sit around the fire.

"I need a place like this," Jeremy said, staring out into the darkness.

"Everyone does. If people could see this kind of thing a couple of weekends a year, you wouldn't have anyone going nuts shooting people or blowing up airplanes. It just wouldn't happen."

Brian raised his glass to toast the sentiment. The lake shimmered its agreement.

"You should loan your place out as a retreat for troubled youths."

"If I thought it was needed, I would. But it's not. Right now, the government is sitting on so much land they're not even doing anything with. It's crazy. There's probably enough for everyone in the country to have a little spot like this. Or share one, at least."

Brian raised his glass again.

On his way home from Marie and Brian's cottage one time, Jeremy pulled over to look at a cabin with a *For Sale* sign out front. It was barely dawn, and there were no cars in the driveway, so he walked up to peek into the windows. There was a raft moored in the lake, about 50 feet from shore. He pictured himself sitting on it in a lawn chair, dozing and waving at passing canoes. On the lake side of the cottage he looked into a small window he guessed to be for the kitchen, and immediately drew back, his heart frantic: inside, standing next to a steaming kettle, were two elderly women, both completely naked and embracing each other in a lingering hug. He stood for a moment, waiting for the inevitable shouting to come from inside, but everything was silent. They hadn't seen him. A sand-coloured chipmunk approached the toe of his shoe, sniffed it, then stood on its hind legs to consider his worthiness as a source of food. After a minute, he carefully stepped away from the building and walked in a wide half-circle back to where he had parked the Jeep, his entire chest burning with a desire for the exact kind of raw intimacy he had just witnessed.

———————

"I will say this for getting married," Jeremy said to Glenn and Phil, "you at least know you won't die alone. That's gotta take the sting out of it a little, I think."

Neither of the two divorced men jumped in to agree.

"Maybe if your carbon monoxide detector's not working, and your furnace starts leaking in the night," Glenn said.

"That's just awful," Jeremy said. Phil agreed.

"I'm talking about dying together – that's the only way it works. Otherwise, only one of you gets the benefit of the arrangement, because one of you goes first."

Jeremy admitted he hadn't thought of that.

"Some ancient societies solved that problem by burying the wife with the husband, whether she was dead already or not," Glenn said. "There are probably a few nasty fuckers out there who still do it."

Phil said that he had made one of those agreements where two people promise to marry each other if they were still alone at 80. Back when he was in teaching school, one of his closest friends was a woman who had moved back in with her ailing parents, and thus had trouble maintaining a decent social life. "She was also more than a little overweight, but really smart and fun," he said. When Phil knew her, she hadn't been in a serious relationship – *any* relationship, in a long time. One time when they were both out celebrating the end of a particularly thorny assignment, they started talking about the future, getting old, all the rest of it. That's when they made the pact – it was her idea, though he signed on right away. When they reached 80, if neither of them were married, they would marry each other and wait out their last years together.

"You plan to honour that?" Glenn asked.

"That's the thing: she got in touch with me a couple of years ago when her parents finally died. Not even sure how she found me. She's married and has two little kids."

Phil looked down into his drink, suddenly glum. "I honestly didn't think I was going to be the one who got left out," he said. "She's a lot thinner now, too."

"Oh buddy, a lot can happen between now and 80."

"You're right: I might end up married again myself by then."

"I was thinking more like her husband could bite the dust." Glenn nudged him on the shoulder and chuckled. "More likely scenario there, right?"

Jeremy asked Charlene, at a quiet point in the day, if younger people still made those kinds of pacts, or if they were something that had become extinct. She surprised him by saying she knew at least four people who'd sworn themselves to one, and had heard about a few more. One of her best friends had pledged herself to the woman she'd been roommates with in university, though neither of them were particularly gay. At that age, they figured, it wouldn't matter much what they were.

"I hope it happens," Jeremy said.

That would mean neither of them find somebody in the meantime, she reminded him.

"What about you?" he asked. "Is there someone out there who's got you as their old-age insurance policy?"

She said there was not, unless you counted Kyle, of course.

"I'm picturing Kyle as a senior citizen," he said.

She laughed. "And?"

"There's a guy who won't be sitting around watching butterflies, put it that way."

Charlene agreed, and said it was one of the things she admired about him. "He has always been like that – totally unable to relax. He makes me feel so lazy sometimes. I once said he should paint the living room on one of his days off – we were fighting about something, and I said it just to bug him. By the time I got home, it was all done. He was pulling off the last of the tape when I walked in the door. I would never have done something like that."

"Good for him. Why wait? But did he do it because he's such an on-the-go kinda guy, or just to get back at you?"

"Probably both, but the room still got painted. It looks pretty good, too. He's a good painter."

Why was he so obsessed lately with getting old and dying, she wanted to know.

He had to admit that he didn't know for sure. All he knew was that he kept catching himself feeling as though he had run out of time to do certain things. It was something he had never thought about before – he never cared about time at all. Most of the time, he still didn't. But there were those moments when he would feel as though big life possibilities were drifting past him, and vice-versa.

"But look at all you've done, look at what you're doing – you've got the Ice Shack."

It was true, he said. Most of the big life possibilities he truly cared about could be found within those four walls. And anyway, age was a matter of outlook.

"It's all up here," he said, and tapped his temple with the tip of his finger.

––––––––––––

At the very least, Jeremy felt, there was nothing seriously wrong with him. No big threats on the horizon. He had reserves of energy, and could ride hard on the stationary bike in his office for a half-hour without feeling as though he might topple over. Sleep wasn't always the easiest thing to negotiate, but he was still able to function just fine on five or six hours of the stuff per night, as long as he gave himself one night a week in which he went home early and fell asleep right away.

The worst that had been happening lately were the panic attacks, which had started around the time the Shack went into a long dry spell that was particularly long and particularly dry. Most of the attacks were fairly mild – just a sudden thudding of the heart and an unaccountable surge of breathless terror that went away after a minute or two. Sometimes they came in the middle of the night, when he was already asleep. Dreaming of lava pits, he would jolt awake, face down in his pillow, already covered in sweat and unable to breathe, tinsel swimming across his field of vision. Not even a long, territorial session on the toilet and an extra-hot shower could dispel the lingering sense of unease. One afternoon at the Shack, Tyler, of all people, found Jeremy sitting on a beer keg in the downstairs fridge, trying to calm his heart. Jeremy had come down to check the draft lines, and had been overtaken by fear.

"You okay?" the cook asked him. There was some graffiti on the wall, just past Tyler's head: *Ozzy Rules*, in red marker. Someone had added the word *football* below it in black marker. Jeremy had seen those words thousands of times, but it wasn't until that exact moment that he got the joke.

"We have some real smartasses here, dude."

Tyler nodded, and filled his apron with lemons from one of the cases stacked in the corner.

Charlene came to Jeremy the next day, looking worried. "Tyler says he saw you having some kind of attack."

"It's amazing how chatty that guy can be when he feels like it. Really amazing."

"What's going on?"

It was nothing, he told her. He just hadn't been sleeping well lately, and was a little worn out. Which was true: every day, it seemed, more trouble came down on his head.

Someone had stuffed an entire roll of toilet paper into each of the men's room toilets in the middle of a busy Friday night, flooding the basement and forcing Jeremy to spend a messy hour down there with a mop and bucket. A week later, a hose split in the kitchen's walk-in fridge during the night, spraying everything with water and ruining hundreds of dollars' worth of food. Everywhere in the Shack, little things kept failing or breaking. For a while, Benny became a near-permanent fixture in the bar. In the morning when Jeremy arrived, he would already be there in the parking lot, sitting in his truck, drinking coffee mixed with whatever else out of a plastic travel cup.

"Another day, another dollar," Jeremy said.

"Better be more'n that."

He did what he could to swim through those rough waters, to stay as cheerful and confident as possible, to maintain his Personal Power, but he felt as though all of his instincts were abandoning him. He was stumbling. One night he asked a regular how his wife was doing – he didn't see her around much anymore, was she avoiding the place? – only to be reminded, with some irritation, that the poor woman had been diagnosed with breast cancer a few months earlier. Another time, he laughed out loud at a woman who kept putting her head at a strange angle whenever he spoke to her. "You're like a bird!" he shouted, before being told, angrily, that she was deaf in one ear.

He took a succession of women to dinner, but it never went anywhere. It was like trying to start a campfire in a rainstorm. When he finally convinced one woman, a teacher who dealt with special-needs kids, to come home with him, he ended up locked in his bathroom, trying desperately to catch his breath, caught in the sharp talons of a panic attack, flushing the toilet and running the water to cover up the sounds of his struggle. She waited almost 20 minutes, then said through the door that she was calling a cab. He cursed his body for its treachery.

His new doctor, whom he'd started seeing after the one he'd been going to half his life finally retired and died, was young. He always mentally registered her youth when he entered her office, the way he might note her height or her hair colour. Officially, she was Dr. Harwood, but Jeremy sometimes called her Christine, which he was fairly sure she had told him to do on his first visit. On her desk there were framed pictures of a little boy and a little girl at various ages. She sometimes referred to someone named Michael who liked to do something with the kids – Jeremy couldn't remember what. Go fishing? Take them out to dinner? She didn't wear a ring. He figured she took it off while she was working. Either that or she and Michael had kids but weren't married. That arrangement, his mother said, was like turning on the furnace and leaving all the windows open. He didn't see it as a big deal, however. They had the relationship they wanted. So long as they were happy, what did it matter? She was undeniably cute, however, and he stayed alert to possible openings.

Dr. Harwood was attentive, solicitous, and always greeted even the smallest problem with an overabundance of concern. She never dismissed anything Jeremy said, never told him not to worry. She moved in on him right away like he'd scraped his knee on his first day of school. He wanted to be thinner for her. He didn't like having to reveal the bulk of his belly every time he took his shirt off in her examination room. She had a big poster on the back of her office door, showing the tall, thin one from Monty

Python in a black suit and a bowler hat carrying a black umbrella and suitcase and walking on the sidewalk as if to an important job. He was photographed in mid-stride, with his knee at the same level as his shoulders – he seemed about to step directly up into space and out of the picture. At the bottom of the poster, written in marker, were the words *Make Excuses to Walk*: her motto, and something she tried to drill into all her patients.

Jeremy got points for having quit smoking, at least. Of all the terrible things a person could do to himself, smoking and drinking were the real bad guys, she told him.

"Well, I'm halfway there, then."

"Halfway."

After his first appointment, she sent him to a clinic downtown to get some blood work done. A woman in a white jacket who looked as though she'd been born in an age before happiness gave him a jar with a cap and told him to *go make a pee*. When he got back, carefully holding his little jar, she made him sit in a straight-backed chair, leaned over him so far that he thought for a moment she was going to mount him, then tied off his arm and jabbed it. He watched blood as dark and red as nail polish fill three or four thin glass tubes. There were plants all over the woman's office, all harsh cacti and twisted green things with serrated edges. This woman had seen what people were made of, so no flowers for her. Nothing that required care.

"You have a low platelet count," Dr. Harwood told him when the results came back.

"That sounds ominous."

"There are red blood cells and white blood cells and platelets. They're like the army and the navy and the air force – they all work together, but they each have their own

– 133 –

job. You always hear about white cells and red cells, but hardly ever about platelets. Yours are a little low."

Jeremy wondered how things would've gone had the tests brought some darker news. It had been years since he'd heard about anyone, anywhere, dying of AIDS, but he assumed it was still out there, like some dark rider killing hitchhikers in the dead spaces between towns. What if he'd caught it from the blood of a customer with a nosebleed? Or from cutting his arm on a broken pint glass? Or from unblocking the toilets with his bare hands? He was dimly aware that the process of becoming infected was a little more complicated than that, but didn't want to look it up in case he was wrong. He didn't want to put a white flame under his paranoia. As it was, the missing platelets eventually returned in full force.

"You don't hear much about AIDS anymore," he said to Tyler one morning while the cook was sitting at the bar, looking at basketball scores.

Tyler's arm froze as he was lifting his coffee to his mouth. "Should I?"

"Not at all. And that's a good thing. People always say things are shitty these days, but they're wrong: this is an amazing time to be alive. Maybe not the best, but getting there. Never forget that."

Once a year, Dr. Harwood gave Jeremy a full physical, which required that he strip right down to his underwear and sit on cold, crinkling paper with his sock feet dangling. On those days, he would mentally transport himself into a state of being in which erections, the very possibility of them, did not exist. She always asked his permission before telling him to lower his underwear so she could press two no-nonsense fingers against the underside of his crotch. The blood usually began to arrive in his wild-eyed cock just as he, almost sighing with gratitude at the narrow escape, was pulling his underwear back up.

A new wrinkle had recently been added to his annual checkups: after a lifetime of being rewarded for its diligent service by being left utterly alone, Jeremy's prostate had become an area of interest, like a tract of unspoiled land suddenly getting noticed by developers. Dr. Harwood had warned him that this new interest was coming, giving him lots of time to prepare for the fact that he would one day have to accept her curious, lubricated finger into his unwilling rectum. But it still came as a shock when she told him there was a new item on the checklist as of that day, and that it was important that he be relaxed. He tried to remember something he'd read in a Theo Hendra book about managing fear by envisioning the worst, most catastrophic outcome possible. Instead of some small measure of social embarrassment, imagine cascading disasters on the scale of a total organ failure, the collapse of the building, a new ice age arriving overnight. The idea was to overdose on fear, to get your mind to the point where it could no longer believe in the scenario, allowing you to laugh it off. It had never worked for him – his mind was always able to stay fully engaged with the original, wholly rational fear. The true fear stayed visible like a bright beacon in a storm.

He asked if the procedure could be deferred to another date, and she seemed amenable, but said he probably wouldn't feel any better about it next time. It had to happen eventually, and it was better for everyone if he just took a deep breath and got it over with.

"It's not like I'm all into doing it, you know."

"I hope not. Can you give me, like, five minutes?"

It all went just fine in the end, and was over much more quickly than he'd expected – in some of his nightmare scenarios, she'd found it necessary to root around in there, going up to the elbow like a country veterinarian trying to inseminate a cow. The reality was quick, painless, and efficient. Going through it brought the two of them closer together, he felt. The examinations eliminated the need for dishonesty; they were like a couple who'd managed to stay friends after the end of a wildly sexual but unsustainable relationship.

"If you didn't know me, and I just walked into your office, how old would you think I was?"

"Such a loaded question!"

"But how old?"

She sat back in her office chair and gave him an amused look. "I don't think people always *look* an age."

"If you had to guess."

"I know how old you are – it says so right at the top of your file!"

"Just guess."

"If I really had to guess, I'd say . . . 40? Or just a little over?"

"That's what I would guess, too!" he said, relieved. "The thing is, I can still remember a time when I would've been so pissed off if anyone had ever said I looked anywhere *near* 40. Now it's a compliment."

"I can remember being a little girl and asking my mother how old she was, and she told me 30, and I thought that was *ancient*. Now I'm almost 35, my god."

As always, he did some quick, frightening calculations in his head.

When he finally told Dr. Harwood about the panic attacks, she put aside her files and asked him to describe them in detail. She gave him another examination, sent him to the cactus lady for more blood tests, and spent five minutes making him breathe in and out while she probed his bare chest and back.

"It's not physical," she told him. "And there are no respiratory problems that I can find. Which is a relief, though I'm going to keep an eye on that, just in case – these kinds of things can be serious if you don't pay attention to them. For the moment, let's focus on calming back down when they happen, okay? That should be the most important thing: just getting everything back to normal. Breathing. Let's work on that."

He loved how she made his problems her problems, too. Whatever was wrong with him, they would find a way to fix it. They were a team, they'd get through this.

He told her about Phil's heart attack and his falling down in the middle of a class. He didn't want to suddenly drop while talking to some group at the bar or hauling some kegs around. She said that was always a remote risk, given his age, but not likely. And his panic attacks were nothing like what had happened to his friend, who sounded like someone who had been abusing his body for too long.

"He's a big boy, he makes his own decisions."

"That's right. We all do, especially the really bad ones. How much time do you spend at your bar?"

"All of it."

"Maybe you need to slow down a little."

"You first," he said, and basked in the laugh that followed.

At their next shared birthday, Glenn and Phil were sub-dued. Phil's daughter had not called him to wish him happy birthday as she usually did. All night, he kept pulling out his phone to check. His doctor had given him strict instructions to stay away from alcohol, so he was sticking to beer. Glenn was not drinking much, either: he had gone home late a week earlier and nearly fallen backwards down his stairs. His wrist was in a cast, which he had to stop himself from banging on the bar as he complained, with less fire than usual, about the carelessness verging on maliciousness of the people who'd designed and built his building. He used his good arm to demonstrate the impossible steepness of his stairs.

Glenn's flame sputtered out a few times, leaving him quiet and grumpy before his pint glass, which he barely touched. At around 9, he got off his stool and called it a night. Phil lasted another hour before announcing sadly that he had an early department meeting the next day that he was not looking forward to but could not miss – he'd skipped the previous two, and had found himself in the Dean's office, being spoken to like a misbehaving student.

"Well, *happy birthday* anyway, buddy."

"We made it through another one," Phil said as he put on his coat.

"Jesus, don't say that. We're not a hundred years old."

Phil stopped for a moment to think, then smiled. "Add us together and we almost are!"

Not quite ready to give up on the night, Jeremy wandered through the Shack, looking for distractions. He talked with two older women who were playing hooky on their book club, which had once been a perfectly good excuse to drink wine and gossip in someone's living room, but had lately been taken over by an abstemious and self-important former elementary school librarian who insisted they wait until after the conversation was over to open a single bottle, and who prepared actual discussion notes in advance, which she emailed around to all the other members. Sitting at the other end of the bar was a silver-haired man with a phone clipped into a leather case on his belt. He had a South American accent and two small scars on his neck. When asked where he got the scars, he told Jeremy that, as a teenager, he'd fought in the streets against the police in his home country, standing with gangs of other kids, throwing stones and flaming bottles until the government was toppled. Now he was a web developer, and preferred to talk about the blazingly obvious superiority of open-source programming codes to the kind developed and sold by rapacious tech corporations, his new and more formidable enemy. Each time Jeremy tried to lead the conversation back to exploding bottles and clubs crunching skulls, the man shook his head with a slight, impatient smile – all that was ancient history – and would begin again to explain how grotesque profits were being made by selling weak and buggy operating systems.

After checking that the kitchen had been shut down properly, Jeremy called Charlene, getting her voice mail. He called again. This time, she picked up, and less than a half an hour later, she appeared in the bar, a little breathless. "I got you this," she said, smiling and handing him a plastic ring topped with a giant candy jewel. "Nothing's open. It was this or some licorice cigars. Would you have wanted those instead?"

"Maybe, but you know what? This is great. Order yourself some wine. On the house."

She was wearing a dark green dress that looked like velvet. It clung tight to her all over. He wished he were wearing something a little smarter than khaki pants with bleach stains around the ankles and a golf shirt he'd been given by a wine rep – little bunches of grapes were stitched around the breast pocket. She touched the grapes and said they were cute. She didn't appear to be wearing a bra. The silver-haired web developer caught his eye and raised his glass. Jeremy nodded, but did not smile.

"Where did everybody go? Glenn and Phil?"

"See, this is the problem: those two keep getting older, while I keep getting younger."

"You definitely look like you are."

"You don't have to be sarcastic. I just bought you wine."

"I was being serious! You look better than ever, I think. I would never guess you're that old."

"My doctor said the same thing. And she's seen me at my worst."

"What do you mean? What's your worst?"

"You don't even want to know."

They toasted his birthday, and then hers, which had happened a few months earlier. Then they toasted Glenn's and Phil's birthdays. Jeremy asked her what she had done for her own birthday, and she told him she and Kyle had simply stayed home and watched a seemingly endless movie about an ordinary kid growing up in small-town America. Or rather, *she* watched a movie about an ordinary kid growing up in small-town America, while he read about Mikhail Gorbachev on the couch next to her.

"That's pretty sad," Jeremy said, then apologized.

"No, it *was* pretty sad," she said. "I go back and forth between thinking you should still get birthdays as an adult and thinking maybe you should just forget about them."

He raised his glass and waited for her to do the same.

"You know what my mother does on her birthday? She visits her parents' graves. And some of her aunts and uncles. By herself."

"Oh, fun," Charlene said, and then covered her mouth in shock. "I'm so sorry – that was mean."

"No, you're right: it's friggin grim. My dad won't go with her for that exact reason."

Having established a baseline for depressing birthdays, they began to goad each other into having a good time. Jeremy made the bartender line up shots in front of them – two each, plus one for the bartender – which they threw down without a hitch.

"*Glasnost*," he said, by way of a toast.

"What does that mean? Oh, right – don't remind me."

She told him about how she'd gone out with a bunch of friends a few weeks earlier to celebrate someone else's birthday, and while they were out, the birthday girl announced she was engaged.

"And you didn't come to the Shack? It's not like we need the business or anything."

"I didn't pick the place, and it wasn't fun."

The weird thing, she said, was that for years they'd all suspected this particular friend of being a lesbian, and either not ready to admit it, or not aware of it herself. And the guy was a real guy-guy, too, with a beer league hockey team, action movies on Blu-Ray, and everything. While everyone made a fuss, Charlene had turned to whoever was sitting next to her and asked, a lot louder than she'd intended: "You think he knows she's a dyke?" That stopped the celebration cold. It was as though she'd hiked up her dress and peed on the floor. She had to leave quickly, but was so drunk she almost ended up going out the back, through the kitchen. She didn't even remember getting home – some of her clothes were on the landing outside their door the next morning. None of her friends had spoken to her since, and they weren't answering her texts.

Jeremy could barely speak, he was laughing so hard. "What the *hell*, girl . . ."

She sat up straight in her stool. "Part of me doesn't care, to be honest. Kyle was mad at me for getting so drunk and for embarrassing myself, but whatever. Fuck *off*." She swayed back in her chair to emphasize her dismissal, and almost fell off.

"Kyle doesn't ever have a few too many?"

"The last time I saw him really drunk – really, *really* drunk – was maybe two or three years ago." The two of them were at the wedding reception of one of his high school friends, someone he rarely saw anymore. He hadn't wanted to go, but she'd convinced him that it would've been rude not to. The reception was at a fancy golf course, and Kyle had spent the entire time refilling his wine glass and muttering. During the speeches, which went on for over an hour, he made a point of loudly noting every cliché, at one point shouting out the punchline of a joke the father of the bride was struggling to tell. Charlene said she responded by getting horrifically drunk herself and turning the dance floor into a sweaty, spasmodic display of rhythmic aggression and clumsy simulated stripping. Had there been a vertical pole in the centre of the floor, she would've flung herself onto it and likely fractured a rib.

Somehow, after the wedding, it was only her awful,

drunken dancing that got remembered and commemorated on Facebook. No one ever mentioned his shouts and grumbling. She had to convince herself not to care.

"Good for you – you can't worry about that shit," Jeremy said. "The minute you do, it's over. Hard enough to keep focused on what you want to happen with your life. Worry about what someone else might think you should be doing? Fuck that. Seriously: *fuck* that."

"Fuck that," she replied, and drank down another glass.

"I think it's amazing that anybody finds anybody. But then there's those weird things, like that married couple who found each other in a picture of themselves as kids at Disneyland. She's standing there with Mickey Mouse ears or whatever, and there he is in a stroller going by in the background. And they don't actually meet for another 30 years. That blows my mind. It's a million to one."

"That's why Kyle thinks it's not a big deal. He said it's a million or a billion-to-one odds, and so the one time it actually happens, that's the one time in a billion. It happened as many times as it was ever going to happen."

"So it doesn't matter because it only happened once?"

"Basically, that's it. That's what he told me."

"I completely disagree – I think that's why it's so crazy. That's when you start thinking maybe there is some kind of fate or pattern to things. That's when you start wondering if that was always going to happen, those two together."

"I disagree," she said, putting her glass down hard for emphasis. Then she corrected herself: "I mean I *agree*, with you. I can't even talk tonight. The only depressing thing about it is that if you think they were supposed to meet later and fall in love and all the rest of it, what about the billions of other people who were not together at Disneyland or wherever when they were five years old? What about the rest of us?"

"We have to work it out on our own. Simple as that. If your boat doesn't have an engine, you get out the paddles. If there aren't any paddles, you fucking swim for it."

At closing time, he offered to drive her home. She stumbled getting into the Jeep, so he came around to help her and buckle her seatbelt. It was tough, because she was laughing the whole time he was trying to make the buckle connect, saying he was tickling her. Taylor Swift came on mid-song when he started the car, and they both sang along as loud as they could. After that came Stevie Wonder's "Superstition," which she admitted used to scare her as a little kid whenever it came on the radio – it always sounded as though something bad was about to happen. "But listen to that guy *play*," Jeremy said, turning the dashboard into an electric piano.

"It's still scary!"

A few minutes into the drive, Jeremy had to admit he could barely focus on the road, and pulled into the parking lot of a grocery store.

"Is it okay if I put you in a taxi from here? I think I'm past my limit. In fact I know I am."

"That's fine," Charlene said, though she was busy scanning through radio stations for another fun song. She landed in the middle of someone singing "Hallelujah" by Leonard Cohen. It was her mother's favourite version, though she couldn't for the life of her name the singer. He sounded German. They sat behind the grocery store with the engine running, back with the abandoned shopping carts, until the song was over. Instead of announcing the name of the performer, the station went straight to a commercial for discount furniture.

"Happy birthday," she said.

"Hope this year's a little easier. No, fuck that: I'm lucky."

She looked at him, smiling. "I love that! I *love* hearing someone say they're lucky."

"*You* are lucky, too, even though you never act like it. You're young and smart and beautiful – that's three things most people don't even have *one* of."

"I feel old and stupid."

"You're stupid if you really feel that way, because neither of those are true, and you know it."

Someone came out of the back of the building to smoke a cigarette. He stood framed by the glare of the lights inside and stared across to where the Jeep was sitting, though it wasn't clear the car was even visible from that far away. As if they really meant to conceal themselves, neither of them spoke while the man was there. When he went back inside and slammed the door behind him, Jeremy said, "Anger issues."

Charlene thought again about the wedding she'd gone to with Kyle where he'd heckled the speeches and she had danced like an idiot. When they got home that night, she had locked herself in the bathroom, worried that she might throw up – other than the million glasses of white wine she'd downed, she had also done vodka shots with the maid of honour, whom she'd never met before. Kyle banged on the door and demanded to be let in: he assumed she was angry with him, which she was, though that wasn't her primary reason for shutting herself in there. He banged again.

"This is childish," he shouted.

She said she agreed, but made no move to open the door. The room was still spinning.

The next bang was so loud it made her squeak involuntarily, and it took her a moment to realize he had kicked the door this time. Actually kicked it. The absurdity of it made her laugh, and she told him he was acting crazy.

"Downstairs they probably think you're trying to *rape* me. This is so ridiculous."

She didn't hear him retreat to the bedroom, where she found him after she finally felt well enough to open the door and come looking for him. He was standing beside their bed, his dress shirt messily untucked, his jacket and tie off. His face was dark and he was shivering with rage.

"Don't you *ever* say that again."

"Say what?"

"You called me a *rapist*."

She guffawed without meaning to, and immediately regretted it: he picked up his phone from the side table and flung it hard to the floor. She apologized, and he eventually accepted, but they had not been to a wedding together since, though they'd both gone to a few on their own.

Charlene pressed a button to silence the stereo in Jeremy's car.

"It's kind of nice here," she said, which made him laugh.

"Those dumpsters are lovely, it's true."

"I was supposed to be doing a ton of laundry tonight, so this is an improvement."

"I spent the night trying to cheer up Glenn and Phil."

She unbuckled herself, put her seat back, and closed her eyes, as if they were on a long drive. He wondered if she were planning to go to sleep right there in the car, but after a moment she spoke up. "Did you think Phil was going to die that time?" she asked.

"There's a cheerful question."

"Did you?"

"I did, actually. It was a surprise, but not really a shock, put it that way."

The weird thing was, he said, after being so certain that Phil was going to die, it was almost harder to accept that he wasn't – in his mind, he'd already started the process of dealing with the loss.

Charlene opened her eyes and turned to him with a look of surprise. "Me, too! And I felt awful about it."

"You shouldn't. Anybody can go at any time, as fucked up as that is."

"And it could still happen," she said, closing her eyes and settling in the seat again.

"Don't say that. Christ, I don't need him dropping dead in the bar."

He said one of his biggest worries was what a bummer it would have been in the Shack if Phil had not made it. "I don't mean in terms of people not buying drinks or coming in, just that it would be a little less fun from now on. I didn't want people feeling bad about it all the time. That sounds really shallow, but I mean it. People have enough to feel bad about."

"You're always worried about everybody being happy."

"Not everybody, just people in the bar. And not even *happy*." He tried to think of a better word, but couldn't. "Theo Hendra has this thing about how, in a disaster or an emergency, you see two different kinds of people. One fucks off and does whatever they can to survive, *fuck* everyone else. The other one tries to save as many people as possible, even though they'd probably have a better chance of making it if they just tried to save themselves. You get zombies walking around everywhere, and some people will barricade themselves in a house until it's all over, others will go out to fight them."

Charlene burst out laughing. "Oh my God, that's ridiculous . . ."

"It is a little," Jeremy admitted. "I sort of think it's true, though. You can see it anywhere you look."

"And you're the type who'd rescue everybody?"

"I'd try, at least."

She sat up, leaned over, and pretended to pin a medal on his chest and salute him. He laughed and let himself be teased, and was unprepared for the sudden feeling of her mouth against his. Her hands left his face, slid down his side and along his thigh, and stopped at his knee. The other got his ear in a delicate grip. He shifted over so he was closer, and put a hand on the back of her neck, the other on her hip, then quickly removed them both.

"I'm sorry," he said.

"I don't think I am."

By the time a late-night delivery truck honked at them to move the car a few minutes later, one of his hands was creeping under her dress and up her thigh. Jeremy waved at the driver and moved the Jeep to a far corner of the parking lot. When the taxi arrived, they both got in without any discussion and headed to Jeremy's house.

"ONLY BABIES ARE TRULY HELPLESS; THE REST OF US HAVE OPTIONS."
– *Recharge Forward*, Theo Hendra

In the middle of everything, the Shack's bookkeeper came to tell Jeremy that, for the first time ever, the bar might not be able to cover payroll. The accounts had dropped below the safety line, and she'd already used almost all of their credit to top things up over the past few months. He would not believe it at first; he was certain they were doing better. He'd been seeing weekend lineups again at the front door, just like when they'd first opened. And some of the lunches had been busy enough to require both Charlene and Patty on the floor. She showed him the spreadsheets she'd been working on, which he spent a long time reading over.

"How did we not see this coming?"

He was careful to say *we*, not *you*. Though he meant *you*.

She pointed out there'd been a lot of unexpected expenditures lately, like the new chairs he'd bought for the bar without telling her. He hadn't even tried to sell the old ones, but had given them away instead. Benny stacked nearly a dozen in the back of this truck, and Phil now had two with him in the basement of his sister's house. The rest Jeremy dropped off at the Salvation Army.

He had also – and this was likely a larger cause of the problem – quietly handed out raises to a few, select employees. Tyler got one, though he hadn't asked for it. A couple of the better bartenders got a bump up. He'd thought about giving one to Charlene, too, but decided against it – he worried a gesture like that might be taken the wrong way.

"I knew it was going to be tight," he told the bookkeeper, "but it was the right thing to do."

"Okay, but things like that need to be accounted for and planned for. You should've let me know."

"Would you have told me to go ahead?"

"Probably not."

"There you go – I saved us a pointless conversation. Not having to listen to anyone else is one of the privileges of being the boss."

"You have to have something to be the boss of, though."

He felt the first prickles of a panic attack move across him in a slow wave.

"I really don't need to hear that kind of thing right now."

"Could you maybe tell people not to cash their cheques right away?" she asked.

He straightened up and put his hands flat on the table between them. "Whenever I hire someone," he said, "I make them a promise. And that promise is this: I tell them that as long as they act like adults, show up on time, do their jobs, and don't act like assholes and keep the fucking around to a bare minimum, I will not make their lives more miserable than I have to. And I will *never, ever* fuck them around on their paycheques. Once you start that, there's no going back."

Jeremy had already burned through his own line of credit, and had remortgaged the house the year before. He called around to his suppliers: could they hang off on invoicing him, just for a couple of weeks? He told the kitchen to order only the absolute essentials, to use up the contents of the freezer before bringing in anything new. And if they had to shrink the menu for a bit, they would. He'd field the complaints. Whatever could be done to stretch things, they should do it. He asked Tyler if he could handle the kitchen alone during the day, dishes and all.

"You can keep your raise either way – one has nothing to do with the other. Well, not nothing, obviously: I wouldn't have given you that boost if I didn't think you were capable of being a rock star when the time comes."

Tyler said he could do it.

Jeremy told the bartenders to keep people on the house brands as much as possible, since the markup was so much better for those, and to cool it with the comp'd drinks.

"I don't really care if it's someone's birthday – let their friends buy the drinks. And if they have no friends, too bad. And speaking of friends, I want all of you bringing people in here. At least five each. Minimum. And don't be going somewhere else to meet up with people. No more feeding the competition."

He thought seriously about letting Patty go, and spent an entire day working out how he'd do it – he knew that if he didn't frame it just right, the disappointed look on her face would crush his will and he wouldn't be able to go through with it. Or worse, he'd have to lay off Charlene instead, which would've been punishingly awkward. They hadn't spoken much since the night of his birthday. Mostly she avoided him while she was working and went home immediately after her shifts. After a few failed attempts to talk things over with her, he started staying away from the bar for big chunks of the day, wandering the aisles at hardware stores and at Costco. One time when he was at Costco, he turned a corner and nearly walked into Kyle from behind. He had no idea the guy would ever be caught dead in that place, yet there he was, standing still in the centre of an aisle, staring down large buckets of black olives. Jeremy backed away as quietly as he could.

When the payroll came due, it was like navigating an 18-wheeler with flat tires between two sets of rickety scaffolding overloaded with schoolchildren. They got through it with no room to spare – an inch either way would've brought the whole works crashing down. On his way to the bar in the morning, Jeremy had to roll down the windows of the Jeep to let out the panicked air. The traffic lights fell asleep on red, and the radio hosts paused nervously between jokes about the Oscars and the weather. He fully expected to arrive to find the Shack had slid down the hill into the river in the night. He stood out on the deck, breathing deeply the way Dr. Harwood had shown him.

Jeremy knew there was no point talking to the bank about further loans, or in trying to change the terms of the ones he already had. His meetings with his loan managers were painful. They made him wait while they chatted with each other in glass-walled offices. He could see them in there, and they knew he could see them, but would only call him in once they had flirted themselves out. The woman he dealt with had to keep refreshing herself on the details of his business, and always seemed perplexed by the notion that he might require money to help stay afloat, money from the very bank for which she worked. She wore silk, button-up shirts that opened at the top like a scoop every time she leaned forward to find something in the drawer of her desk, giving him a lingering view of the tops of her breasts. He openly drank the view in, staring hard, committing it to memory. Normally he would have been more discreet and pretended not to notice, but he felt that he was owed *something*.

And so, after another close call with the payroll, he resigned himself to asking his sister and brother-in-law to invest in the bar. Marie and Brian had refused to put any money in the bar at the beginning – or, at least, *Marie* had refused, telling him that having a kid was a bigger investment than he could imagine. Brian may never have been given the option. Out of pride, Jeremy had never asked again. What made him change his mind was the new pile of money that had slid into their lives. Brian's elderly mother had finally died after nearly a decade of being confined to a rest-home bed in Montreal. When the inheritance came through, Marie invited Jeremy to dinner at their house to celebrate. He got the sense, from the way she worded the invitation in her email, that they'd already had their *real* friends out for an inheritance party, and that he was being asked over partly out of duty. Maybe he'd be eating and drinking the leftovers from the first one.

He said yes.

They lived out in the country, between two working farms. Theirs was a *faux farm*. That was what Marie called it – she always acted dismissively toward the things she was most proud of. Nowadays, aside from some vegetables she had planted in the backyard garden and some pear trees way out back that shed rotten fruit for the squirrels and raccoons, there was almost nothing actually growing on the property. Mostly dandelions and some stray cats. There were at least five cats sitting on the long driveway up to the house when Jeremy arrived. He had to drive slowly enough so that these arrogant squatters had time to stand, stretch, give their fur a significant lick, and wander out of the path of the Jeep's wheels. He parked near the barn, which Brian had converted into his studio. Through the window, Jeremy could see the oversized poster his brother-in-law had once made as a kind of art project: a shot of a thickly mustachioed Joseph Stalin looking gruff and self-satisfied, with the old, rainbow-coloured Apple computer logo in the corner next to the words *Think Different*. He'd planned to do a whole series of them using people like Karla Homolka, a Newfoundland priest who'd been caught molesting children, and an illiterate Texas teenager who was on death row for beheading his girlfriend in the bathroom of a Walmart. Marie let him make only the Stalin one, and insisted that it stay in the barn.

She met Jeremy at the door.

"I'm surprised you don't have a butler doing this now," he said.

She stepped back and lifted her foot. She had on a pair of red high heels that gleamed.

"These are literally the only thing I've bought that hasn't

been groceries or clothes for the kids. I haven't even had my hair done in months."

Jeremy held up the case of beer he'd brought – samples from a microbrewery in Kingston. A treat for Brian. Each bottle had an ace of spades symbol on the label.

"Those look dangerous. Don't get Brian drunk. He's got a meeting in the morning."

"Oh, he'll be fine. He's a big boy."

Marie took the beer from him, as well as the flowers he'd picked up at the last moment. They walked down her long front hallway. There was dark wood everywhere – they had preserved as much of the original farmhouse as they could. His sister liked to say that she wanted some of the spirit of the house's original occupants to be absorbed by her children. She hated the idea of them growing up in a world where so much was disposable, and hoped the house would give them some sense of a connection to an older, sturdier time.

"Creaky floors build character," Jeremy said.

"I know you're making fun of me, but sort of, yes."

Some of the framed photos on the walls in the hallway were old portraits of hard-looking farmers and random pioneers that Marie had found at flea markets and antique stores. These, too, were there to communicate a spirit of endurance and inheritance. To Jeremy, it always seemed as though they were being forced to stare out from their own grim and deprived times at the relative playground that was his sister's life. By forcing the ghosts in the portraits to watch, Marie was rubbing their noses in it.

She stopped and leaned against the hallway wall with her eyes closed.

"You okay?"

"Brian has been so vulnerable lately. Because of his mother and everything."

She leaned in closer. The hardest part, she whispered, was having to listen to him go on about how wonderful the old woman was. What a *joke*. She never came to visit them: they had to go all the way to Montreal if they wanted the kids to see their rich grandmother. And when they were there, she wouldn't talk to anyone but Brian. Never said a word to her daughter-in-law, not even hello – it was as though she thought Marie was the nanny. And nothing for her grandkids.

"Anyways, we're all going to miss her, *blah blah blah*. Oh, by the way, don't get mad if there's no red meat tonight. I have to hear about it from Dad every time he comes over. I don't need to hear it from you."

That meant Brian was cooking, so Jeremy could look forward to some kind of salty Asian salad full of bitter weed-like greens that would cut the insides of his cheeks.

"I'm okay with anything."

In the kitchen, Brian leaned against the counter with the sleeves of his shirt rolled up, looking as though he'd been waiting to be discovered in that pose. Next to him on the counter was a tray piled high with expertly scorched chicken breasts. Most of the space in the room was taken up by a broad wooden table, made from the floor of an old shed they had found way at the back of the property when they first bought the house. On it were plates of fresh-baked bread, a big bowl of Caesar salad, gleaming strawberries and blueberries, and little plates of olives and cheese. No sign of the bitter salad.

Jeremy offered his hand. "Sorry to hear about your mother."

Brian looked thoughtful, and paused before extending

his own hand.

"It was hard to accept for a while, but more and more I'm thinking I'm just glad I got as close to her as I did while she was here. That's what life is about, right?"

He smiled broadly, his face cracking on either side into long, deep dimples like ruts left in the ground by a storm. Brian was tall, and even Jeremy could admit he was handsome, if a little ape-like in his features. He was much better looking now that he'd cut short the long curly hair he had when he and Marie first started dating. Jeremy used to call him the Rock Star, which he, aggravatingly, never took as an insult. At their wedding, Brian had longer hair than Marie, who at the time – unbeknownst to everyone except the bride and groom – was two months pregnant with their first baby, the one who died in the womb.

Two of the children were already asleep upstairs. Marie had spent the day with them at the zoo, she said, then took them to her gym to use the pool. Logan, the oldest, was sitting at the far end of the kitchen table, picking away at a small bowl of fruit cocktail. There were scraps of paper all around him, as well as markers and pencil crayons. He didn't acknowledge that Jeremy had entered the room until told to by his mother.

"Hi, Uncle Jeremy."

"Hey!" Jeremy shouted. "Hulk Hogan! Fruit cocktail? Cool!"

"Eat up, sweetie," Marie said.

Beyond the sliding doors at the back of the kitchen was the barbecue that only Brian was allowed to use; it looked as though it could fit a whole cow inside of it. Brian took the beer away from Jeremy and held one bottle up to the light to admire the label.

"I haven't tried this one before. I thought I'd tried them all."

"You have a meeting tomorrow morning, remember," Marie said.

"He's a big boy," Jeremy said. Brian gave him the thumbs-up.

The food was mostly ready, but Marie insisted they sit around the table and chat. "This isn't a diner; we can wait a couple of minutes before stuffing our faces." From out of nowhere appeared a bottle of expensive bourbon that Brian had brought back from their last trip through the American South. He'd smuggled three bottles of the stuff back. While they drank, Jeremy told them a few stories about the bar – he knew they liked hearing about the messier things that happened there, as it always helped confirm the wisdom of their decision to avoid all such messes. Someone had set some napkins on fire in the middle of a dinner rush while trying to demonstrate a trick with a lighter, he told them. Someone else lost her eyebrows trying to put it out. A dishwasher went to a birthday party before his shift, came in drunk, and fell asleep on some bags of flour, which is where Jeremy found him. Phil managed to beach his car on a concrete barrier in the parking lot on his way out, and had to call a tow truck to get it free. The city was demanding Jeremy pay to replace the barrier.

"If it had been anyone else, I'd be royally pissed off right now, but not that guy. Not sure why. Maybe because if I started getting mad at him, I'd never stop."

"Which one's he?"

He gave them Phil's highlights – his fling with the other teacher, the divorce, the occasional collapse into tears and yelling, and the heart attack that had landed him in the hospital.

"That's a sad case," Brian said.

"There's nothing sad about it," Marie said. "You said he cheated on his wife, didn't you? Well, now he has to live with it."

"You should be a social worker," Jeremy said.

"Oh, I'm sorry – I should feel sorry for him? He had his fun. His wife has to be on her own now and raise their daughter while he's out getting piss-drunk at your bar."

Brian cleared his throat and nodded at Logan, who was busy drawing what looked like a whole colony of ant people living on a giant tank bristling with weaponry.

"I'm sorry," she said in a quieter voice. "I'm sure it sucks to be him, but I don't feel a lot of sympathy for guys like that."

"Honestly, when I look at someone like Phil," Jeremy said, "I don't see how messed up he is, or what mistakes he's made – or *keeps* making, more like. I look at him and I'm just impressed he's still walking, you know what I mean? And he's harmless – there's a lot worse out there, people who give off a real negative energy."

To change the subject, he told them about the repairs he'd been doing to the Shack. Some were routine, he said, the kind of thing you had to do every year, but he'd also been looking to improve things, to freshen up the place. It was mostly small things so far – new paper dispensers in the bathrooms, new baskets for the condiments – stuff most people didn't even notice. He had grander plans, though. The Shack was overdue for a renewal.

"The hard part is finding the money. Even if I do most of the work myself and get Benny to help out, the materials alone are killer."

"Oh fuck, not that guy."

The sound of a swear word made Logan look up from his drawing.

"He's not still hanging around your place, is he? That creep?"

"Oh, come on – Benny's all right. He's been around forever, and if the job's easy enough, he does it cheap."

"You get what you pay for," Brian said.

"You get more than that – you get that creepy guy coming into your house when you're in the shower!"

Jeremy laughed, but Marie's face was stern. "I'm not kidding!"

"Who's looking at you in the shower?" Logan asked.

"Nobody, honey. Mommy was making a bad joke."

Having put the idea of money out there, Jeremy was happy to cede the floor and drink more of his brother-in-law's good bourbon. Brian talked about going to Montreal for his mother's funeral. He had gone alone, saying it would have been confusing and upsetting for the children to see their father in such a state. Jeremy suspected that Brian simply wanted a weekend on his own, with no wife and no kids.

"My brother and I sat in the lobby of the church and we bawled our eyes out. We've always been pretty tough with each other since we were kids, but we just broke down completely."

Brian lowered his head, and Marie put her hand on his arm. The room was quiet for a while, except for the sound of Logan jabbing his markers into the paper. Jeremy helped himself to more of the fancy bourbon, which had been left on the table.

"Montreal can really mess with your mind," Brian said.

"It's so beautiful, you get sucked up into it. And all you hear all day is French – oh my God, I felt like I was constantly being seduced. I was amazed to find I could still carry on complete conversations. You never totally lose it."

Logan looked up from his drawing. "*Parlez-vous français*, Uncle Jeremy?"

"*Un peu*. Just *un peu*. You're probably a lot better at it than I am, hey?"

Logan said he was and went back to his drawing. He had his father's habit of accepting every compliment as his due, deflecting none of it out of some inauthentic sense of modesty. At some point, many generations back, Brian's family ditched a sense of humility from its genetic code.

Marie must've given a silent signal that they had fulfilled their pre-dinner conversational quotas, because Brian got up and started bringing the chickens to the table. He did so solemnly, as if he were recreating his mother's funeral. Marie and Logan both stopped what they were doing and bowed their heads as the tray of heavy, artfully scorched birds were placed in the centre of the table, right next to a bulbous knot in the wood that must've tripped up those long-dead hunters when they came back to their cabin late at night. The rest of the food came to the table in the same solemn way. Jeremy poured himself more bourbon and filled his plate.

"This chicken is really good, Brian. What kind of sauce did you use on these? I could sell this at the Shack by the shitload."

"Jeremy."

"Oops." He turned to Logan: "Sorry for swearing, Hulkster."

"I could tell you what's in the sauce, Jer, but then I'd have to kill you."

Marie laughed, almost choking on her wine. She was on her fifth or sixth glass.

"You would kill Uncle Jeremy?"

"No, no, of course not – it's just a joke."

"An *old* joke," Jeremy added.

"Speaking of old, whatever happened with all of your mother's things from the home?" Marie asked Brian. "What happened to the Eavesdropper?"

Jeremy laughed. "What's the Eavesdropper?"

Marie pointed at her right ear. "She could barely hear us speak when we were there."

"She could hear just fine," Brian said.

"Well that's worse – that means she was ignoring us. Anyways, it's not true: she was as deaf as a doorstop."

"When you said *Eavesdropper*, I imagined, like, another old lady hiding in the closet, listening all the time," Jeremy said.

"I would not be surprised," Marie said, then turned to her husband. "So what has happened to it? And all the rest of her things?"

"It's all taken care of. I donated the books and the magazines to the other residents. The photos are in a box in my studio – I might do something with them sometime. I have some ideas. The Eavesdropper I gave to the staff as a gift for whoever needed it the most."

"That was an expensive little gadget, and she wouldn't ever put it in," Marie said. "I had to keep telling her what people were saying. We'd sit there and watch TV, and I'd have to repeat everything."

Brian smiled. "She was stubborn, all right. I can already see that stubbornness in Emily."

"Emily was driving me crazy today, by the way. I think

you need to talk to her."

"She's alright."

"Here's to Estelle," Marie said suddenly, lifting her glass. "And thanks for all the money!"

"Take it easy," Brian said.

Marie pouted. "I was just *joking*."

"That was funny, Mom."

"Thank *you*, at least."

"So what's the plan?" Jeremy asked. "Do you have one?"

"Well, we've still got more chicken, we've got all this salad still, and I think there's a pie warming up. I'm definitely going to have some more of this beer you brought."

"You have a meeting, remember."

"I mean plans for the money from Estelle."

"The money?" Brian seemed surprised that Jeremy had heard about it, despite it being the reason for the celebration. "It's still a little early to be making any decisions, I guess."

"Well, *I've* made some decisions," Marie said, straightening in her chair. She wanted to completely renovate the house, she said. They'd been feeling cramped lately, now that there were five of them. She talked about expanding the kids' playroom, knocking out the wall between the dining room and the living room, and putting an addition on the kitchen so that it would finally be big enough to fit an island in the middle, something she'd always wanted.

"Your house is going to look like it's busting out all over. You might as well get a bigger place."

"Oh, I couldn't leave here. I love my little faux farm."

She moved over to sit on Brian's lap and started nuzzling him. Logan moved to the kitchen floor, where there were newspaper-sized sheets of sketch paper on which he drew scenes of tiny armies slaughtering each other on hills and in vast caves loaded with missile launchers. The dishes vanished from the table, and in their place was a bowl of raspberries that looked as though they had been picked in the middle of a light rain less than an hour earlier, from a hidden patch that maybe only Brian and some bears knew about. Jeremy picked one out and brought it to his mouth, where he held it for a moment, as if struck by a sudden thought.

"All the stuff you have planned makes me even more sure that I need to spruce the Shack up a little. It's humming along really nicely, but I've got a big list of things I want to do to really fire it up."

"No rest for the wicked," Brian said, watching his son draw as if the boy were a kitten in the midst of cleaning itself.

"Exactly. It's like anything else, though: once you've finally got all the day-to-day stuff covered, there's no time for anything more long-term. Even if you're firing on all cylinders, you're still only going to be able to do so much. But I do have some ideas, and ideas are the greatest natural power source that has ever been discovered."

"Don't start quoting that Hendra guy," Marie said.

"Wasn't planning to."

"Mom, do I have to go to bed now?" Logan's eyes were red and half-closed. He looked as though he'd had more to drink than the rest of them.

"You probably should, buddy."

"Good night, Hulk Hogan!"

"Don't call him that, Jeremy. He doesn't know who that is, and I don't really want him to."

"Who's Hunk Hogan?"

"He was a boring guy who looked stupid and talked like

a big idiot and didn't do anything important," Marie said. "That's all you need to know. Now let's go, mister."

She took the boy upstairs. As soon as they'd left the room, Brian took out his phone and began tapping at it. He had some kind of finger painting program on it, and he wanted to show Jeremy the digital pictures he'd been making with the kids. Each one looked like a puddle of melted ice cream, but Jeremy made the appropriate noises of appreciation. For a while they sat there in silence while Brian grinned at the tiny screen.

"So, you're a rich man now, eh? Rich*er*."

He expected Brian to laugh, but instead, his brother-in-law put down his drink and gave the darkened kitchen window a thoughtful look. "I've never been sure what *rich* means. I've never in my life stopped and said, *I'm rich*. I don't really think about it."

That's because you're rich.

"And it's not like Marie and I don't worry. It's not like we don't sit down here and try to figure out how we're going to cover everything. I still have to work hard to make sure we're okay."

"That's the way to do it. People who just live off someone else's money – it does something to their heads. I see people like that sometimes in the bar. You can tell right away. They're not from the same planet."

"If I had the choice between the money and having my mother still alive, I'm not going to pick the money. As it is, I wouldn't have cared if I'd gotten none of it."

Jeremy knew that wasn't true: the inheritance was originally supposed to have been shared out equally between all three brothers, but the youngest was living in a kind of commune in Northern Quebec and had renounced all connections to his family years ago. He sent a letter refusing the money. They talked about putting it all in a trust in case he changed his mind, but Brian's lawyer told him the letter could be considered formal enough for legal purposes, and that he and the other brother might as well split up the youngest brother's share. So they did, though not without a few weeks' worth of legal wrangling and lawyers' letters. The other brother wasn't onside at first with the idea – he wanted their younger brother's share to be given to charity, maybe something to do with heart disease, which was what had killed their father. Marie had given Jeremy frequent updates as to the progress of the battle. She talked about the money as if it were a child they were adopting from some third world country, a fragile thing that did not deserve to be put at the mercy of lawyers and paperwork and courts.

"I know so many people who would get money like this and blow it all in about six months," Jeremy said.

"I'd have Estelle's ghost after me if I lost it like that."

"Exactly – she knew what she was doing. She was no dummy."

"She was a tough woman," Brian said.

"She was tough, and she knew money was useless unless you were doing something useful with it."

Brian raised his glass for a toast: "To the root of all evil."

"And to seeing the war, while everyone else sees the battle," Jeremy said, raising his own glass.

Brian paused with his glass at his mouth. "That's a weird one," he said.

He began to stroke his phone again, checking texts and emails. Jeremy slipped his own phone out of his pocket and took a peek. The Shack had called twice, but there was no voice mail message, which meant that whatever perceived emergency had been avoided or cleaned up.

"How's that beer, Brian – not bad, eh?"

"Have to say it: this is good stuff."

"Have another one." Jeremy stretched himself as casually as he could. "You know, one thing you could do is take a closer look at the bar."

"Which bar? Yours? Why? What's going on there?"

"No, I mean as an investment."

Brian laughed. "Sure. I should buy a bar. Marie would love that."

"I don't mean *buy* it, but maybe stash some money there, away from the tax vultures. It wouldn't even be that much."

"Ah. I'm pretty sure Marie has plans for the money. I know she wants to put a lot of it away for the kids."

"That's exactly why I'm suggesting this. The Shack is as solid as a bank, with a better return. When they're ready to start heading off to college –"

"University."

"Right, exactly. And when they're ready to go, here comes Uncle Jeremy with a bag of cash in each hand."

Brian laughed again and said that he liked *that* idea, at least, but honestly doubted they'd be able to make the rest of it happen.

"I know about as much about running a bar as I do about the dark side of the moon. Probably less, actually. That's your world, and I envy you for it."

"You envy me?"

"I never had one of those jobs," Brian said. "A service job. I never waited tables or tended bar or any of that. It always looked like a blast. I think it would've been fun to do for a summer or two."

"Try doing it the rest of the year. For 30-plus years. It's been a total blast."

"Yeah well, I don't know that I'd be totally happy doing *that*. But you'd probably be bored stiff doing what *I* do, too – sitting and staring at computer screens, trying to make the colours look exactly right. Adjusting type sizes and leading."

"I have no idea what leading is."

"Exactly."

Jeremy smiled, happy to let Brian sprinkle his superiority around with practiced casualness. His brother-in-law had been born rich, and would die rich, no matter what he did. Money went where it knew it would not be alone, not where it was needed, because it didn't *want* to be needed. It wanted a life of comfort, and could sniff out the people who could give it that. It would rub up against their legs and purr. It had sniffed out Marie and Brian, and had settled in. It settled into the very skin of their children, giving them the warm, dumb glow of people who already knew, instinctively, that they didn't have to worry about much, who already knew there were no cars or trucks bearing down on them, who knew they would be warned about every hole in the road ahead – warned, and then lifted gently over. If he went upstairs and fell asleep in one of their little beds, he wondered, would the money settle on him, too? No, money could smell desperation. You couldn't just *ask* for it, you couldn't grab at it.

Jeremy heard the floor upstairs creak: Marie was moving around, checking on kids. He'd hoped she might fall asleep in Logan's bed. She sometimes did that when they had company over and she drank too much wine.

"The thing is, the Shack is humming along pretty nicely right now," Jeremy said. "It just needs an extra shot in the arm, a bit of turbo fuel to really get to the next level. You know what it feels like when you have so many ideas you want to make happen."

"When I have too many ideas about how to do something, that's usually a sign I need to go for a walk or a drive. Or take the kids swimming."

"Oh, absolutely. Totally, totally. But listen: the fact that you've got three kids means you can't just sit around and hope for the best. You have to find somewhere to put it that will pay off for you."

Marie came back in the room, moving more slowly than before. "Are we still talking about money?" she asked. "I don't want to talk about money. The kids are asleep, so I want to talk about grown-up things, I want to talk about sex – I get about an hour a day when I can pretend I'm an actual adult. Who are you fucking this week, big brother?"

"*Whoa,*" Brian said, laughing.

"Oh, I never kiss and tell."

"Such a liar. Every time I see you, you've got some new thing going on, some new waitress or somebody. Who is it now?"

"Swear to God, I'm on my own right now. Too much on my plate."

"Yeah right. I know what you've been putting on your plate."

"Okay now," Brian said.

"Who's that one I met when I was in there for lunch that time with my friend Mel? She's got big eyes, a little chunky. Not the old one, not Patty."

"Oh, I remember *Patty,*" Brian said. He and his wife shared a private joke.

Jeremy pretended to think. "That was probably Charlene."

"Really nice cleavage. Even Mel was jealous, and *her* tits are huge."

"Oh, come on."

"I'm not saying it's bad! It's just a fact!"

"Charlene's great, but not really my type. For one thing, she's really young."

"Does that ever stop you?"

"The other thing is she's been married since forever. Her husband is a real piece of work, actually."

Marie sucked at her teeth. "Oh, don't tell me he's a bully. I friggin hate that. I *hate* guys like that. He doesn't hit her, does he?"

"No, no, nothing like that. At least I hope not. No, I really doubt it. His problem is more that he's got his asshole sewn shut."

"Okay, I hate that, too." She recovered the half-full glass of wine she'd left on the table. "So boring. You'd almost rather be with someone who gives you a smack every now and then. At least you get to have crazy make-up sex. And they feel so guilty they go down on you for like an hour."

"Jesus, Marie."

"I'm joking! I love boring guys!" She poked her finger playfully into the centre of her husband's chest. "If you tried to hit me, I'd run you over with the car. I really would. Twice. I'd back over your corpse and be out of here so fast . . ."

Brian looked offended. "I have been in *one* fight my entire life, when I was 11. I tried to hit a guy because he was picking on my little brother. I got a single punch in, and he demolished me. One punch, my entire life."

"That's why you go for their balls," she said, kicking her leg out and nearly sending an empty chair clattering across the room. "You kick them where the sun don't shine so they don't get up again. That's what I always did."

"When were *you* in a fight?"

Marie straightened up in her chair and flexed her thin, yoga-hardened muscles at him. "I've had a few unfriendly encounters. I can take care of myself. You remember Cory," she said in Jeremy's direction. "That guy I dated in high school? You met him at Christmas once."

"Vaguely." The name sounded familiar, but all Jeremy could conjure up was a neon green ski jacket with half a dozen crumpled lift passes attached to the zipper. "Did he ski?"

"That's him! That's the little gaylord!"

Brian made a noise of exasperation. "Marie, come on. Seriously?"

"Oh, he *was*. He came out of the closet in university. I looked him up on Facebook – he looks like a male stripper now. He'd do well, actually – he was hung like a butcher."

"Fuck's sake." Brian got up to put away some of the food and picked up Logan's paper and pencil crayons from the floor.

"So you kicked him in the balls for liking guys?" Jeremy asked.

Marie screwed up her face. "Come on, give me *some* credit. I had all kinds of gay friends in school. People you didn't even know were gay, I bet."

"Good for you."

"It *was* good for me. Very good for me. I learned a few things about –" She jammed an invisible cock in her mouth and made her cheek bulge out with her tongue.

Her husband crossed his arms with righteous anger. "My *lawyer* is gay. He's one of the sharpest guys I know." Jeremy and Marie ignored him.

"So why'd you kick him?"

"Because we were sitting in his dad's car fighting about something, and he just reaches over – " Marie, laughing so hard that tears appeared in her eyes, slammed her hand down on the table like she was winning an arm-wrestling match. "Smacks my head right on the dashboard! Seriously! I got out of the car and he tried to follow me to apologize. I turned around and got my knee right in there, right in his crotch, as hard as I could. I thought for a second I'd busted them. I wish I had. He threw up."

Jeremy and Brian stared silently at Marie while she struggled to stop laughing.

"Good for you," Jeremy said, quietly and sincerely.

Marie dabbed at her eyes with a paper towel, then blew her nose. "Well, it was fun sometimes, probably because he wasn't always trying to get into my pants. And, you know . . ." She spread her hands apart. "I think he just lost his mind for a second."

"I think the whole idea is messed up beyond belief," Brian said. "The idea of hitting your wife or girlfriend. I have trouble sometimes even thinking about it. That time you told me about, when your father threatened your mother in the car – I still think about that sometimes. It's hard to believe."

Marie bristled slightly and took a long drink of wine. "He never would've done anything."

Jeremy had no idea what Brian was talking about. "What is this? Gord threatened Anne?"

Brian turned to his wife, who suddenly looked guilty. "We were coming home from some backyard party," she said to Jeremy, in a slow, even voice, as if giving evidence. "They were both a little drunk, so I was driving – I had just got my licence. Gord was pissed off about something. You know him: he's talking shit. He wouldn't have done anything."

"I don't know – people can surprise you," Brian said. "Even Gordon."

"What did he say? I've literally never heard this."

Marie sat up in her chair. "People *are* surprising," she said to Brian. "Remember when we were visiting *your* mom the time Logan threw up in the car, and you took him to the hotel to put him in the shower? I was sitting there waiting for you to get back, and your mother starts saying all this shit about how fathers were different when she was a kid, and how *her* dad used to beat the crap out of her brothers, all your uncles. He used to slap them on the ears and hold them against the wall."

"I'd heard that," Brian said quietly. "My Uncle Roger used to joke about it. It wasn't as bad as that. Everybody hit their kids back then."

"Oh, Uncle *Roger*. Uncle Roger was a peach. He was the one who used to throw you and your brothers into the middle of the lake and drive off with the boat, wasn't he?"

"He thought it was funny. There were always people around watching us. Roger would've come back if we were in any real trouble. We were good swimmers."

"Lucky for him."

"It was just a bad joke."

"Sometimes good jokes go bad," Jeremy said.

"That's what smacking kids around does," Marie said. "It turns them into cruel assholes who almost drown kids as a joke."

"Uncle Roger wasn't a cruel asshole. My dad *definitely* wasn't. He didn't hit people. He never even threatened anyone, as far as I know."

"Oh, really?" A look of evil triumph appeared in Marie's eyes. She cocked her head at him and opened her eyes wide, waiting.

"What's that look?" Brian asked.

"I don't even want to say it."

Jeremy could tell she did. "Maybe we should change the subject."

"I don't even know what you're talking about."

"Her *jaw*, Brian. He dislocated her jaw. It wasn't even a smack – it was a *punch*. Estelle told me it didn't even hurt at first, she was so shocked. You were a baby and thought it was the funniest thing ever. That's the thing she remembered: you sitting there cackling while your father stomped out of the house and left her holding her poor face."

"That's nice. That's really fucking nice." Brian got up from the table and walked out of the room, taking his phone with him. He carried himself straight, but Jeremy saw that his eyes were already flooded. Marie's eyes were glistening again, too, and her shoulders were stooped with guilt. She made no move to follow her husband. They heard a door slam upstairs.

Marie tried to smile. "Guess I'm not getting laid tonight, eh?"

Driving back down the long laneway, Jeremy was less careful about avoiding the cats. He felt that a sacrifice was necessary.

———————

At the Shack, on his eighth bourbon, Jeremy announced to Glenn and Phil that he'd figured out how to eradicate the shittiness of the world. It was simple: everyone had to forgive everyone else. Just like that – a one-time, all-encompassing round of forgiveness to wipe the slate clean.

"What if they dig out another Nazi war criminal?" Glenn asked. "What happens then in this new world of forgiveness?"

Jeremy waved his hands to dismiss all these objections – they were getting lost in the details.

"It's a one-time offer. If, after everything is forgiven, they still go out and be all Hitler, then fine: we throw away the key."

He reached for one of the keys on his belt and nearly tipped over. Glenn caught him, and with the help of the bartender, got him downstairs and onto the couch in his office. He awoke there the next morning, covered in a coat from the lost and found. His grand idea had reversed itself in the night: now, instead of forgiveness, he wanted judgment, blood, the sky in flames, a great sword the size of highway cutting in half the guilty and innocent alike. The feeling lasted until he was able to wobble his way upstairs, make coffee, and fill a pint glass with grapefruit juice. When Tyler arrived, he requested a fried egg on toast and a large slice of fridge-chilled watermelon, and asked that the cook not play any music for a couple of hours.

Brian called a few days later. Jeremy couldn't remember his brother-in-law ever calling him about anything, and so braced himself for news that Marie and the kids were in the hospital. Or that a divorce was imminent. Or else his mother was the one who'd been in an accident, and his sister was too broken up to call. But Brian's news was good, at least potentially: he had been thinking about the idea of investing in the bar, and had even talked about it with his lawyer, who'd not only said it sounded like a good idea, but that he himself might be interested in putting some money in the bar, too.

"That *is* good news. For you, especially, I think."

"Can we talk some more about it?"

Brian and his lawyer, a thin man named Stuart, came to the Shack one afternoon to work out the details. The three of them sat in a corner booth, and Patty brought them a tray of snacks and a bottle each of sparkling water, exactly as Jeremy had arranged beforehand. He'd had the bookkeeper prepare a folder full of financial documents, all carefully edited to show the business as unquestionably strong, but in need of an outside boost. While Brian sipped at the sparkling water and checked his emails, Jeremy showed Stuart around the place. He showed the lawyer the photos behind the bar and pointed out the one with him and the mayor. He showed him the kitchen and introduced him to Tyler, who barely said hello. He showed him the office and apologized for the mess.

"Brian tells me you're gay."

"That's right."

Jeremy said he was happy for him.

"It's not like being pregnant, but okay. Thanks."

"This is a totally open-minded place. We're a family, and everybody's a part of the family, no matter what: gay, straight, black, white, blue, purple, yellow."

"Purple. Okay."

The meeting went better than Jeremy had hoped and, at the end of it, an amount of money was proposed – most of it from Brian, with a small, supplementary chunk from Stuart. It was more than Jeremy had been expecting, though it came with the condition that the three of them meet regularly to talk about how things were going with the bar. Every two weeks to start, then, if need be, once a month.

"That's more than I see my parents."

Stuart smiled and said, "We're not your parents. We don't need to know every time you're planning to fire a dishwasher. Just keep us in the loop for the big stuff."

"Marie's okay with you coming to the bar every couple of weeks, dude?" Jeremy asked Brian, whose expression didn't change. "How'd you convince her to let go of the money?"

"This has nothing to do with her."

"The inheritance money is administered through my office," Stuart explained. "So there's no real legal issue as far as Marie is concerned. I think we were hoping . . ." He gave Brian a quick, sideways glance. "I think it'd be easier all around if this investment was kept somewhat confidential, at least from the standpoint of the staff and people outside the Shack. It's not really anything anybody else needs to know about, honestly. There's no legal issue, like I said, but it just makes things simpler."

"So don't tell Marie, in other words," Jeremy said.

Brian winced, which increased the glow of happiness growing in Jeremy's stomach.

"For example, sure," Stuart said. "Let's keep it among us for now."

"Happy to keep it on the down low."

Stuart smiled again. "Not exactly the expression I'd use, but okay."

Part of the agreement was that the other two men's names would be put into all the Shack's files as part owners, with equal say on the bar's future. They'd also have equal shares in the business, shares that they could not sell to anyone other than the other two. Jeremy chose to see all that as mostly theoretical, even ceremonial, like singing "God Save the Queen" in school when he was a kid, and so readily agreed.

There was just one detail left that Stuart wanted to work out.

"There's some money owing to your parents, right?"

Jeremy looked at Brian, who was staring down at his phone. The glow in his belly receded slightly.

"Some, yeah. Not a whole lot, but they helped out early on. It's not a problem."

"But – and I'm just asking so it's clear in *my* head – this loan does not show up on any of your financial statements. Did I miss it there?"

"It was just a loan. A gift. They're my parents, and it was years ago. It's not like I'm paying interest on it."

"I totally understand. And that was really great of them. I've only met your dad once, and he seems like a great guy. I'm sure your mother is, too. I will say this, though: it's not great to have a debt like that outstanding, even a casual one. So here's what I'm thinking: why don't we pay them back their money, above and beyond what we're talking about here? Put everything in the clear."

Jeremy felt as though the warmth, ease, and optimism of the meeting were already slipping away. "If I had the money to pay them back, I would've done it already."

"Oh for sure, I'm sure you would. That's not the question. It's more about timing. So how do we solve that problem? Here's what I was thinking: maybe *I* pay them back. I'm putting less money into the bar than Brian, so that would even things out, right? I'll write them the cheque, and we can figure out what that means later in terms of all of this."

He waved his hand at the papers in front of them. "I can always write up a supplemental document to show Revenue Canada once we're all fine and good."

"*You* would pay them back? Personally?"

"To get us in the clear, debt-wise, yes. That way, we wouldn't have to worry about screwing around with family."

"They're not getting screwed."

"Sorry, let me be clear: that's not what I meant. I'm just saying it would be easy to do, and would make everybody happy. How many things in life can you say that about?"

"Not a lot," Brian said, looking up from his phone.

"None," Stuart said. "Okay."

"They're really not waiting for it. They haven't even asked."

Stuart looked at Brian, who told Jeremy, reluctantly, that his parents had been bringing up the subject with Marie. His mother, mostly. She had asked her daughter more than once how if she, Marie, could ask about the money for them. She didn't want to do it herself.

"She's worried about your dad, about Gord."

"What the fuck did Gord do?" The other two looked at Jeremy with alarm. He tried to laugh off his sudden anger. "Not more home brewing, I hope."

Stuart turned to Brian. "Didn't you say she wants to renovate their bathroom?"

"She told Marie she wants hand rails and one of those sit-in showers in the bathroom. I guess because Gord fell over that time in the backyard."

"She just wants to make sure your father will be okay," Stuart said. "That both of them will be okay, really."

"Of course they'll be okay. That's ridiculous – they have a chunk of their money in the Shack, but I can give it back to them whenever they need it. With interest."

Stuart held up a piece of paper. "Can I say something? Not to be an asshole or anything, but looking at the bank statements you gave us, you can't. Not right now, anyway. And it sounds like your mother is anxious to see at least *some* of it soon. Honestly, this would be good for everybody – we need you to be totally clear and focused on growing the business and not worrying about tiny things like that. Okay? Let's just get it done."

Jeremy said he would think about it, and they ended the meeting without toasting their new partnership. After they left, he told Patty he was unavailable for a while and went out to stand on the deck.

He called Stuart the next day, while sitting in the Jeep across the street from the bar.

"Let me be the one to give my parents their money."

There was a pause. He thought he heard the lawyer sigh.

"I don't know if you can really afford it right now, Jer. That's sort of why we've been having these discussions in the first place."

"I mean let me physically give them the money. You give it to me, and I'll give it to them. I don't want them to know where it came from, I just want to be able to hand them the cheque."

"Oh. Of course, sure. No problem. That works."

"But don't say anything about it to anyone."

"Understood. We keep it on the, ah, on the down low. This is the smartest way to handle it, Jeremy, so I'm glad we're getting it all taken care of. Okay?"

——————————

When the arrangement with Brian and Stuart was completed and the money had moved into the Shack's account,

Jeremy went to a bank machine and withdrew a few hundred dollars in twenties. He folded the money and put it all in his shirt pocket. At the bar, he walked around purposefully, handing each staffer a crisp new bill. "Little bonus," he said. "Keep it up." The Shack could not be defeated that easily. He'd gotten through worse. He handed out bills in the kitchen, where the cooks had already closed things down for the night and were sitting and passing joints around beyond the delivery door. "Just a little bonus," Jeremy told them. "Don't look so shocked. It's not much." He pinned a bill behind the next day's prep list for Tyler, then gave one to the poor kid who'd been left to mop the floor and finish the dishes. He had a split-second's regret that he hadn't also stocked up on smaller bills for the more junior staff.

"Make it shine. I want to see that floor sparkle."

He offered a round of shots to everyone sitting at the bar, and to the servers out on the floor. People smiled, thinking it was someone's birthday or an anniversary. Benny stood at the bar, drinking a beer, his lower half speckled with white paint and plaster dust.

"Can I get you another one of those, on the house?" Jeremy asked him.

"I wouldn't say no."

"I don't know about that – you've said no to me a few times." He blew a kiss and popped the cap off the bottle.

Feeling as though the powers that had been stripped from him were finally, magically being restored, and sensing that he was once again able to resolve the stickiest of conflicts, Jeremy swiped a bottle of wine from the bar, left with a few of the bills still in his pocket, and drove to Charlene's apartment. He parked across the street. There were lights on inside. She came down to the door in yoga pants and a T-shirt printed with a haughty-looking cat and the word *OBEY* below it in big letters. She put her arms around herself as soon as she saw him in a gesture that was partly a reaction to the cold air, and partly a reaction to him.

"Good evening," he said, and doffed an invisible hat.

"What time is it?"

"No idea." He held out the bottle of wine. "This is for you. For you and Kyle."

"Kyle's not home," she said. "He's out late with some people from work."

She made no move to let him in, nor to accept the bottle from him. She stared at the ground between them.

"Hey look, I know things have gotten a little weird, and I'm sorry about that," Jeremy said. "I completely understand if you hate me right now."

She relaxed a little against the doorframe. "I don't hate you."

Jeremy could tell she was weighing the idea of letting him into the building, and gaming out the possible outcomes if she did. He wanted to tell her he was only stopping by, that he hadn't intended to come in, that trying to bring about a repeat of his birthday was the last thing on his mind . . . but he couldn't make himself do it. It was as if he were in the grip of some primordial instinct, instilled in his default male genetic coding back when his ancestors were scrambling around trying to build tribes big enough to survive the winter, that would not allow him to preempt the possibility of sex, no matter what. He thought of the moment in his bedroom when Charlene had removed her bra, making him realize how much he'd been coveting her breasts without being consciously aware of doing so. And then, all of a sudden, there they were. Despite everything that had happened up until then, *that* was the exact moment when he was sure they were going to go through with what they were going through with. He had been waiting for her to call a halt to everything, to say that they were being crazy and stupid. Even a word of doubt and he would've instantly agreed with all of it, would've apologized sincerely and done whatever he could to repair things. But she didn't, and he didn't, and she was naked in his bed within a few minutes of the taxi dropping them off at the house. He was impressed with himself – and he was certain it made an impression on her, too – the way he'd handled himself. He had learned a few things in his time; he had a few tricks up his sleeve.

He was far less proud of how things turned out the next day, and still cringed involuntarily at the memory of slipping out of the bleary bed first thing in the morning and into the bathroom. He had woken up in mid-panic attack, with his body screaming judgments at him. He stood in the shower, trying to breathe his way to calmness, and when he came out, she was gone. The texts he sent her later that day – worded as ambiguously as possible, in case Kyle looked at her phone – were not returned, and the next time she came to work, her face was set in an expression that made clear she was not prepared to acknowledge what had happened, or even speak to him at all, for that matter.

"I'm glad you don't hate me," he said. He was still holding the bottle out to her. "Here, this is for you."

She took it without thanking him, and announced she was tired – she'd spent the day with her friend Samantha, who had a two-year-old. "You've met Samantha; she's been in the bar. Anyway, her little girl had me running around the whole time, so I'm exhausted."

Jeremy nodded: *message received*. It wasn't in his coding to force the issue; they would all survive the winter just fine. He took a step back from her door and began fiddling openly with his keys.

"I'll let you go."

"I'm actually glad you dropped by."

"You are?"

"Yeah. It's sort of hard to talk about anything at the Shack with everyone there."

Jeremy wasn't sure that was true, but nodded anyway.

"I'm still sorry about all this," he said.

"Do you know what Samantha said when I told her? Oh, I told Samantha, by the way. Hope that's okay. I didn't tell her who it was."

"Do I want to know?"

"Maybe. She said that as long as the sex was good, I shouldn't feel too bad about it."

He stood frozen in place, feeling as though the two of them were standing at either end of a beam balanced high in the air, waiting to see who would step off first, sending the other tumbling.

"So I've decided not to feel too badly about it."

"Okay."

"But it's never going to happen again."

"Of course."

"Thanks for the wine."

In the Jeep, he removed a small bundle from the glove compartment: a pair of Charlene's underwear, which he'd found twisted up in the sheets when he'd stripped his bed to put everything in the laundry that morning. They were in the Jeep waiting for the moment when he could return them, or maybe sneak them into her bag. They were orange, amazingly – he hadn't noticed the colour in the dark that night. Even more amazingly, they said *Orange You Glad I Wore These?* across the front. When he'd first found them, he stood for a while, staring at them, searching for the answer. Now, with Charlene's words still in his ears and his skin flushed, he knew: he'd been very, very glad. He got out of the car and stuffed the panties into the nearest garbage can, pushing them down deep so they couldn't be seen. As he re-buckled his seatbelt, he began humming the song that had been playing in the bar earlier in the night, the one about getting knocked down, getting up again, and never being kept down. *Perfect*, he'd thought at the time, and *perfect*, he thought now. There was a pretty part where a woman sang, then a list of drinks that everybody in the place seemed to know by heart. The whole bar shouted along. As he turned the car toward home, he decided that, from now on, that song would be played every Friday and Saturday night, right at midnight, so that the entire room could sing about how the week had knocked them down, and there they were: up again.

"IT IS AT EXACTLY THOSE MOMENTS, WHEN YOU ARE LOCKED IN *NO*, THAT YOU NEED TO LOOK AROUND FOR A NEW KEY: THE KEY TO *YES*."
– *Escape into Great*, Theo Hendra

With the Shack's finances back on solid ground, and most of the staff complaints falling away, the desire for a place to escape to became a constant in the back of Jeremy's mind. He began to spend his afternoons sitting in a corner booth with the Shack's long-suffering laptop, scrolling through online listings for cottages within easy driving distance. If he found one that looked promising, he would arrange to see if the reality matched the photos. It usually did not: every place he saw had a sagging roof or floors that looked ready to give way, or was little more than a sleeper cabin parked within spitting distance of a busy rural highway with only a few thin sickly pine trees in between.

One realtor showed him a cottage that was being sold off for next to nothing as part of a forced bank sale. It wasn't even a cottage, but a small house that'd been owned by a young couple who'd lost their jobs and stopped making payments. They'd spent their last days in the house kicking holes in the walls, smashing the bathroom sinks and the toilets, and taking apart the kitchen. It looked like a pack of enraged gorillas had been set loose inside. "It's not a pretty sight right now," the realtor admitted. He tried to move Jeremy quickly past a closet door that seemed to have been attacked with a steak knife. "The good thing is the price is so low, you've got lots of room to renovate. And it's the off-season, so right now you could bring in a contractor for next to nothing. I could recommend a few names. Local guys."

"How much would it cost me to bring in an exorcist?"

The realtor, looking confused, offered to show him where the river touched the back of the property.

It was Dr. Harwood who finally found the ideal place: a cottage owned by two elderly patients of hers who'd first bought it when they were newlyweds, and were now looking to sell. It was a sad story. Their daughter had died in a car accident while driving through a snowstorm outside of Kingston. She was 35 years old and had her two-year-old son in the back, so they lost their only child and their only grandchild in one blow. Her husband, who'd been driving the car, was in a coma for nearly six months before he, too, died. From what they'd told Dr. Harwood, the grieving couple had stopped going to the cottage after that. And now they wanted to be rid of it.

"And I'm supposed to take it from them? I'd feel like a vulture."

"I can't even imagine what they are going through," Dr. Harwood said. She spoke very slowly and carefully, and in the same tone she used when telling a patient about a troubling growth, an x-ray with an ominous shadow. "I do know that if I was in that position, I wouldn't want to go somewhere that reminded me of my grief. And I'd want it to make someone else happy if it could."

She added that having access to a place like that might also help with his panic attacks, which were still a problem. The medication she'd finally elected to put him on only created a barrier between him and the worst of their surges. It was as if he could feel them pummelling him while he was safe inside the kind of giant suit men wore when they served as targets at women's self-defence classes. He noticed, too, that he was more willing to leave the bar earlier in the night while things were still humming. He sometimes slept for eight or nine hours at a time, which he could not remember doing since he was a teenager. It was a blank and dreamless sleep, as if he were literally powering down and being recharged.

"And you've stopped drinking, right?" she asked him.

"Absolutely," he lied.

He invited the elderly couple to the Shack. When they walked in, he wondered if he ought to give them a hug, given all they'd been through. They introduced themselves: she was Rose, he was Dennis. Rose wore glasses with lenses as thick as her thumb and did most of the talking. Dennis seemed preoccupied by the napkin dispenser on the table. He drew out a large clump of napkins, then found it impossible to restore them in proper order: they spilled out like a parachute opened too late. Jeremy told him not to worry about it. Charlene brought out a platter of vegetables and springs rolls from the kitchen, which the couple ignored. Jeremy kept hoping they would take something, as he hadn't eaten anything all day, and his stomach was starting to protest.

Rose said that for a few summers in a row, they'd only gone to their cottage twice: once to open it and once to close it, which they did over the Labour Day weekend.

"I don't see the point of driving all that way and spending the weekend cleaning it out if we're not even going to use it. And neither of us really enjoy ourselves up there anymore. It's too quiet."

Most of their friends were too old to think about such a purchase, or had places of their own. Rose didn't like the thought of their place being taken over by the wrong kind of people, the kind who'd keep everyone else on the lake up at night and drunkenly crash boats into the dock.

"When Dr. Harwood told us you owned a bar, I have to admit . . ."

Jeremy laughed in the most non-threatening way he could manage. He wasn't looking for a place to party, he told them, and he understood completely why they wanted someone who would treat the place with respect. With some reluctance, he brought out the story of the cousin who had broken her neck jumping off the dock, the cousin who wasn't actually his own, but whom he once again employed for what he felt was a worthy cause. This time, he added a post-funeral epilogue in which the cousin's family, after a year's absence, made an emotional return to the cottage with the fatal dock for a final goodbye before selling it altogether. He'd been told that something like that had actually happened at the time.

"I don't think anyone stopped crying the whole time we

were there. We emptied the place, and had a big campfire where we all just talked about her and told stories. Before we left, my aunt and uncle spent about half an hour looking out at the water. They knew they couldn't stay there anymore, but they wanted to say goodbye."

Jeremy could feel his eyes moistening involuntarily: the story was taking him. Rose and Dennis were listening intently, their expressions full of mixed joy and pain, as if he were speaking to them with the voice of their own dead daughter.

He said that, whatever decision they made, he would understand.

He got the call a few days later, the two of them on the line. Rose told him the place was his if he wanted it. Dennis was less eager to sell than his wife, and tried to add some conditions to the purchase, such as that Jeremy had to keep both the interior and the exterior exactly as they were, and that he and his wife could stay there for a weekend at least once a summer. He also wanted Jeremy to sign an agreement not to erect any other building on the property or remove any of the trees. The place had to be left exactly as it was when their daughter was small, and theirs. And alive. Jeremy was just starting to wonder if it might be easier to simply walk away, when Rose spoke up to tell him her husband was being unreasonable.

"We'll never see that place again, whether we sell it or not," she said. "You can do what you want with it. I don't even like to think about it. In my mind, it's gone."

And by the way, she added, as much for her husband's sake as for Jeremy's: he could keep anything he found there. They weren't driving all that way to pick up old plates and bowls and some rotten curtains. Throw it all away, burn it. She didn't care if there was a shoebox in the wall with a million dollars in it – she didn't want to see it or know about it.

"Tell you what: we'll split the million-dollar shoebox 50-50."

Dennis didn't come when it was time to receive Jeremy's cheque and hand over the keys. Rose drove herself to the Shack and hinted that her husband was sulking. She turned down the offer of a glass of sparkling wine to celebrate, saying it would put her to sleep and upset her stomach. She folded the cheque and slipped it into a hidden pocket in her handbag. He had a brief thought that she might not even cash it, seeing it as insufficient compensation for the loss of her daughter. Instead of getting up after closing the deal, Rose seemed to slump a little in her seat. She sighed and looked out the front window, as if she were on a bus about to take her to a new life. Jeremy decided to wait until she was gone to add the keys to his belt.

"It's supposed to be hot this summer, so you'll be lucky. When Dennis and I were up the last time, it was just all rain. We spent three nights out there, the longest we've gone since everything happened, and it rained the whole time. I took that as a hint."

"Well, you're welcome to come out anytime."

She sat up quickly and got ready to leave. "Thank you, but you really don't have to worry about that. We had our time."

Jeremy looked to see if she would sit in her car in the parking lot for a while, but she was gone almost before he got to the window. Patty came up behind him to ask how it went. She'd heard the whole story about the crash, and the daughter, and the husband's strange conditions, and had been lingering nearby.

"So he didn't come after all!"

"I'm glad he didn't. He never would've let go of the keys."

"Men can be such babies."

"So I've been told."

Jeremy found almost nothing in the cottage when he finally took ownership, and was glad for that. His worst fear had been that he would come across a long-lost doll or an album of happy family photos. There were a few scribbles on the walls inside, and one spot where some kind of poetry had been scratched into the wood with a pen in tiny block letters just below a window. Maybe lyrics to a song. The building itself was pale green, like the interior of an old hospital, and the paint was flaking away at each corner. It had one big bedroom, plus a smaller one that wasn't much bigger than a closet with a tiny window, which he figured the daughter had used. The first time he'd seen the place, with the old couple lingering in their car, unwilling even to come show him around, he'd been a little disappointed, having imagined wide-open rooms and walls that were all glass and opened onto the lake. It was barely possible to even see the lake from the cottage, though the edge of the water was only a few steps away from the front door. Small trees had grown up to block the view. There was a dock on wheels that had to be dragged back up on the rocks in the fall to keep from being squeezed and snapped by the ice. Dennis left at least three messages on his phone about this.

Jeremy brought Benny out to take a look. As they circled the lot a few times, Benny shook his head. He said it was built solidly enough, but any real changes made would be expensive, given how old the place was. They'd need to do lot of reinforcing inside and outside. And he was worried about the wiring, which had been done a few decades ago and was probably one short-circuit away from lighting the whole place up.

"Maybe just burn it. I know a guy, if you want, who could come take care of it."

"That'd look suspicious, wouldn't it? To the insurance people?"

"They'd rather pay you the friggin money than have to send someone out to check, trust me. By this time next year, you could have a whole new place sitting right here."

Jeremy didn't give the idea much thought. Given the kind of person Benny would get to do the job, the fire fighters who arrived on the scene would likely trip over a charred corpse holding an empty gas can and a partially burned note with Jeremy's phone number on it. Instead, the two of them cleaned up the place and cut down as much of the foliage growing along the edge of the water as they could to clear a view of the lake. As they sat and ate meatballs and mushrooms that had been cooked in tinfoil right on the fire, Benny told Jeremy about how, when he was a lot younger, he and his brother used to drive out to cottage country with masks, flippers, and snorkels, then spend the day swimming up under people's docks, stealing the beer and wine that had been stashed in the water to keep cool. People wouldn't even realize for hours that the booze was gone.

Jeremy said it was a good trick.

"Wasn't a trick," Benny said. He meant it.

Jeremy waited until after they were mostly done for the day before bringing out what he'd loaded into the Jeep that morning: the two dragons from the Chinese restaurant that had become the Ice Shack, which had been sitting in his basement for years. He had them wrapped in old blankets, and checked them for chips and cracks after lifting them out of the car. Benny helped him carry them down and set them on either side of the front door, where they could bare their thick teeth at the woodpeckers and the mice.

"I'll have egg rolls and rice and those good chicken balls," Benny said.

Jeremy didn't care; he thought they looked as though they were finally at home.

He'd been told the country air would knock him out, but instead it gave him a kind of charged insomnia. He was sometimes still awake when the birds started up in the morning, and wondered if this might also be a side effect of the medication Dr. Harwood had him on. He finally drove into town one afternoon to buy a small TV and set the thing up on top of an old beer cooler in the corner of the cottage. With it, he watched the news and infomercials and reruns of *Star Trek* on the one local channel he received. The reception was tenuous at best, and on nights when rain and wind conspired to dissolve the intergalactic future into frantic grey static, he would find himself standing under the wind-twisted tin eave over his door, flanked by his dragons and listening hard for human sounds amid all the noise out there.

"It's pretty much silent when I wake up," he told Charlene as he sat at the bar. "Then some idiot goes racing across the lake on a Jet Ski and ruins it. First thing in the morning on a Jet Ski: why?"

"It sounds like fun, actually."

"Not my speed. If you need something like that to have fun, you're not doing it right."

Charlene said it sounded better than the place she'd

been dragged to as a kid, owned by one of her aunts – one whom her mother could not stand, and the feeling was vividly mutual. There was no water anywhere near it, just rocky hills covered in prickly bushes and farmers' fields that stunk of cow shit. The other place she remembered had belonged to a man whose name she could not recall – her mother must've been dating him. His cottage was beautiful, but she had spent the whole time reading in the back of her mother's car to escape the bugs and the man's two sons, who didn't like her at all, yet seemed intent on getting her naked.

"My place is a stress-free zone," he said quickly. "I almost want to put a sign over the door that says that."

He told her about the tree that loomed over the cottage, which he guessed was at least a hundred years old. He couldn't put his arms all the way around it. He talked about the chipmunk that lived under his step – he fed it peanuts and pumpkin seeds and had already named it Phil, because it looked a bit like Phil. And he told her about the weird stone he'd found under the dock: it was shaped like a valentine heart, and he was convinced it was an old arrowhead. He thought he could maybe donate it to the little local history museum, get it on display with a little card with his name on it just below. His other idea was to take it to the nearest First Nations reserve. He imagined handing it over to the chief, or the elders, or the band council – whoever was in charge – and humbly declining their expressions of thanks and gratitude. It never belonged to me, he would tell them. They would all nod deeply, in total understanding. He ended up not going, just in case they decided to claim the land around his cottage as some kind of sacred hunting ground. The whole thing might end up in court or in the hands of the government, then there'd be no end to the mess. So he put it on top of the TV.

"It's an amazing piece of work. Really historical."

———————————

The first person he brought out there with him, other than Benny, was Carla, whom he'd been seeing off and on for a couple of months. It was serious enough that he had not yet brought her to the Shack since their initial meeting, worried what Glenn or other people might say to her. She worked in the office of a member of provincial parliament whose riding was out in the boonies, and with whom, Jeremy was certain, she was deeply in love. He was a tall man with wings of grey hair on either side of his head and who seemed to be laughing in every photo Jeremy had ever seen of him. Standing onstage: laughing. Holding one end of an oversized cheque: laughing. With the sleeves of his shirt rolled up and one foot on the step of a tractor: laughing.

"He *hates* it at his riding," Carla told him, confidentially. "He grew up there, and couldn't get away fast enough. Now he's stuck with it."

"Does a good job hiding it," Jeremy said.

"Not with me."

Carla was constantly running around to get things for her boss, and always preoccupied with what kind of mood he was in that week, and whether his schedule was overcrowded. She had hesitated before accepting the cottage invitation, saying that he sometimes needed her for something over the weekend. Then she insisted on driving there in her own car – in case there was an emergency, she said. Jeremy arrived more than two hours ahead of her, and had already emptied three beers and gone for a quick swim by the time her car pulled up.

"Is there anywhere I can quickly check my email? I'm not getting a signal on my phone." He made her sit down in one of the Muskoka chairs by the firepit and brought her a glass of the sparkling wine he had chilling in the refrigerator.

"Check out these crazy trees." He put his arms around a fat trunk right next to the cottage. "How old do you think this sucker is? I'm guessing a hundred years at least."

She drank half the glass in one gulp.

"It's really nice. What's the nearest town to here?"

"*One night*," he told Glenn and Phil when he got back. "We drive all the way out there, I have all this food and wine, and she stays one night. She didn't even stay for breakfast – took off the second she woke up."

Phil looked sympathetic, at least until he could no longer resist Glenn's laughter.

Carla's boss had called, of course, while they were walking along the road above the cottage.

"Don't answer it," Jeremy had said. He was in the middle of pointing out where he'd seen a real, live fox run past the last time he'd been up there. "You're allowed to go on vacation."

"It might be an emergency."

When she got off the phone, she said she needed to go back first thing in the morning. Jeremy protested, trying his best to sound reasonable, but felt like flinging her phone into the lake. The cottage was full of quickly fading possibilities – they could get drunk and go for a midnight swim. They could have sex on the dock. Chances at happiness didn't come along all the time; throwing away the opportunity to have some fun seemed almost criminal.

She didn't eat much of the dinner he made for her. They had sex, though not on the dock, and she was distracted throughout, as if withholding the most intimate part of herself for someone else. When he finally came, which he hadn't even been sure he'd be able to do, she didn't seem to notice, and looked momentarily puzzled when he rolled over next to her, as if he had just appeared there.

"Did you . . . ?" he asked her.

She didn't answer, and he didn't ask again.

After she left, Jeremy decided to stay another day. He swam, napped in the Muskoka chairs, then cooked the lamb he'd bought especially for that evening. As it sizzled, he debated driving into town and asking the young woman who worked at the little butcher shop to come join him for the evening. He could serve her the very lamb she'd cut and weighed for him, then show her around the property and then walk her down to the dock, where they'd sit and talk about her life in the butcher shop, and his life in Toronto and at the Shack. He would make her look at the night sky – truly *look* at it.

Instead, he went for a swim, and as he tread water a few dozen feet out from the dock, a young couple appeared around the bend on a pair of floating water bicycles that moved over the surface of the lake slowly and silently. Jeremy submerged himself up to his eyes, like a crocodile, and watched them go by. The couple was not talking. They moved forward with slight, identical smiles on their faces, peddling their way to a bright new future on the other side. Jeremy felt as though he'd been visited by a pair of shy deer.

Whenever Jeremy spoke about the cottage in the bar, Patty would make a point of telling him how she and her husband used to rent a wonderful little place owned by one of her husband's co-workers. It was a small one-bedroom cabin in a little cove that was buggy and humid and didn't get a lot of sun, but they loved it. Shortly before Shawn retired, the co-worker died of cancer, and the wife, spurred on by her adult children, chose to sell the property for an astronomical amount of money. Patty knew she had no claim on the place, but she would have liked the chance to go there one last time, even just for the day, to say goodbye to a spot that had meant so much to them both.

"We tried staying in other ones, but those rental places – some of them, you might as well be sleeping in a tent by the highway. There's no privacy, and you get all kinds showing up. The last time we tried it, we had to pack our things and leave in the middle of the night because of the parties going on. Shawn nearly called the police. It broke my heart."

She sometimes remembered new things about the place they used to go to: how her husband had fallen asleep reading the paper in a chair by the edge of the water, and woke up with a turtle the size of a Frisbee right at his feet. Or how they'd opened the door one morning to find an old fox sitting and staring, just a few steps away. They threw it a burger patty that had fallen in the sand the night before, not knowing what else to give it, and it took the offering and tiptoed away on its soft paws. Or how they had sat at the fire eating fresh raspberries from a farmer's roadside stall, throwing the mushy ones into the woods; the following year, there were baby raspberry bushes growing along the edge of the trees. Shawn, who cared nothing about gardening, had been especially impressed by that one, by how their mere presence had so effortlessly altered the landscape.

Eventually, Jeremy told Patty that his cottage was hers whenever she wanted it; she just had to give him a little notice and maybe fill the propane tank when they were done. She nearly cried right there in the middle of the bar. Shawn came over to thank him the next time he picked her up after work.

"This really means a lot. Pat's been wanting to get out of town for a while. She's probably told you about the place we used to go to."

"She did."

Shawn told him all about it again, anyway.

"Your spot sounds just as good," he said. "So thanks."

"It's nothing. Make sure you get in there swimming."

The older man put his hands in his pockets as if rooting himself in place.

"I'll tell you something, Jeremy: I haven't been in past my knees since I was a kid. You know what? My favourite thing is just sitting in my backyard with a newspaper and a beer. That's all the vacation I need. But Pat loves going, so that's that."

"I bet she can be pretty hard to say no to sometimes."

Shawn considered the idea for so long that Jeremy wondered if he ought to make clear he'd only been joking.

"We both like to get our way."

"Well, I hope the weather stays good for you," he said. "Try not to think about all of us stuck here working."

"You know what, Jeremy? And I know you're not supposed to say this, but I don't miss working. I really don't. I put in a lot of hours, and a lot of days, and a lot of years. I worked a lot of hours that I will never get back. So you know what? I don't mind this."

Patty and Shawn always left the cottage in an immaculate state – even the dragons got wiped down. And there was always a note from Patty on the fridge door telling him how much the weekend meant to them, and letting him know there was a gift for him in the bottom of the closet. Under a folded beach towel he'd find a bottle of some expensive wine, which he'd open right away and have with his dinner. Afterward, he would drift off in one of the chairs while the firepit glowed and clicked just beyond his feet, and the first thing he'd see when he opened his eyes a few hours later was a bat crossing the sky above him, as fast and slippery as if it were greased, or the moon, looking as though it had been watching over him while he slept. He tried to think when he had ever in his life felt so relaxed, and could not. He had done the work, he had built his success with sharp eyes, a willing mind, and an open heart, and at long last he was being rewarded. The deer had dropped dead at his feet, the fish had leapt into his boat. He was sleeping in the golden bowl of his trophy.

As expected, the bookkeeper made a fuss when Jeremy let slip that he'd bought the cottage – or rather, that the Shack had bought it, since that was the only way he could afford it. "It only looks bad now because the place is still new," he said. "Have you ever seen a snake swallowing a rabbit? The snake lies there with this big rabbit-shaped lump in its body. After a while, the lump goes away and the poor thing gets digested. We just have to wait it out."

She said she was worried the snake might choke on the

rabbit before he had a chance to digest it, which Jeremy thought was a very strange thing to say.

"You haven't seen it yet," he said. "To be honest, I consider it a mental health expense."

There was one small thing: he asked her to conceal all the cottage expenses in the reports she made up each month for Stuart and Brian. Even if she had to fudge things a little, he didn't want to have them all over him because of it.

"What if they want to see the books?" she asked.

They could cross that bridge when they came to it. For the moment, everything was going fine, that's all they needed to know. He wanted to have things really humming before he told them – which he would do eventually, of course. Though he was unlikely to mention that the money he'd used was supposed to have gone to his parents.

Did it matter? Did it matter that he had diverted the money? Sitting in his kitchen at home, or driving in the Jeep on the way to the Shack, he spun the question in his head, waiting for the answer to drop down like a bingo ball. Yes, the money had been earmarked for his mother and father, but it was money they had never asked for directly – at least had never asked *him* directly. And the way he had used it – to buy this lakeside cottage, this escape hatch, this glittering prize – would ultimately benefit them, too, once he told them, as he definitely would, as soon as he felt the information would be received in the open-hearted and generous manner in which it was given. That time would come, but for the moment, there were too many conflicting emotions and too much unnecessary tension twisted up in the issue. He needed all those green stems of conflict to yellow, wither, and snap, leaving things clean and clear again. That day would come. He wanted to help his parents down the hill to the place, wanted to surprise them with the lake, shock them with the dragons, and then leave them alone to drink in the sunshine and air and all the rest of it. They would thank him, he was sure of it. Everyone would.

For the moment at least, things were going well. Stuart and Brian were pleased with some of the improvements he'd made to the Shack. Just in the past few months, he'd had the interior and exterior of the place repainted, taken out a few ads, and helped sponsor a neighbourhood charity run, all of which brought new people in. It also helped get the Shack included in a *Toronto Life* list of bars that were "off the beaten track," and though he didn't agree the patio was "vertigo-inducing," or that the typical stereo selections were "a classic rock time capsule," the write-up was mostly positive, and so he had it photocopied, laminated, and posted in the window.

"I think we're looking good," Stuart told him. "We're definitely headed in the right direction."

"We're more than headed in the right direction – we're starting to really cook here."

Brian said he'd heard from friends about the *Toronto Life* thing. They were interested in coming to check the place out. "And these are real *food* people," he made clear.

Jeremy could not hide his smile. "I may need to revise the wine list."

"Not a bad idea, actually," Stuart said. "Get some higher-end bottles on there, bump everything else up a few dollars."

"Worth a try, sure."

"Could probably do something like that right across the board. Adjust the price points, maybe switch out some of the more budget items for things that are a little more special. It all helps with branding."

"As long as we're smart about it and it's not too much of a pain for the staff, I'm all for trying whatever."

"That's a question, though," Stuart said. "The whole staffing issue. Let's say the kitchen – do you think they can handle a menu with a little more polish to it?"

"It's a big room, we've got all the equipment."

Brian gave Stuart a quick, meaningful look, and Jeremy had the feeling he was witnessing a routine that had been worked out in advance.

"I meant more with the actual kitchen staff itself," Stuart said. "They're a solid bunch of guys for what we're doing right now, but can they take it up a notch? Are they the right people going forward? I honestly don't know. Your lunch guy, what's his name? The Killer?"

"Tyler," Jeremy said. "Tyler is a bit of a pet project of mine. He's a character, sure, but he's not a creep, which is worth more than you think. I'm working on him – he's a work-in-progress, let's call it."

"Is that the best use of your time, though? Trying to get a lunch cook into shape? This isn't an internship."

"Oh, I think Tyler will surprise you. Even some of the floor staff who were down on him at first have come around. He and Charlene work well together."

Stuart and Brian looked at each other again.

"Well, the floor staff is a whole other question we should talk about some other time," Stuart said.

"I've got time right now."

Stuart looked uncomfortable, then became as direct as a lawyer laying out the grim facts to a client at the centre of a slim-hope case. The day shifts, he said, were an anchor, dragging everything else down. From his research, a lot of places lost money on lunches, or barely broke even, but kept doing them as a kind of loss leader, just to get people in the place and maybe convert them to nighttime customers. He wasn't sure that was the best strategy to pursue.

"I never expected the days to make a ton of cash," Jeremy said. "But they're not a total disaster, not anymore."

"I don't know if not being a total disaster is really the standard we should be using to evaluate this kind of thing. We have to be realistic, and we can't be sentimental."

"What am I being sentimental about?"

"I'm just saying there might be emotions at play here that are confusing the issue a little."

"If you're saying I care too much about my business, then guilty as charged."

"That's good to hear – you have a perspective we don't, and your passion for this place is what we're counting on, frankly. But that's not really what I meant."

Brian, unexpectedly, spoke up to say they'd heard about a possible romantic connection between Jeremy and Charlene. It had come up more than once.

"This is absolutely none of our business," Stuart said, jumping in. "We're all adults, this has nothing to do with us – *except* insofar as it maybe makes it just a little harder for you to have a clear perspective about certain aspects of the business. No one is judging here, it's just that we want to be sure you have the focus you need and the clarity you need. We would never make these decisions for you."

"No, you wouldn't. And I can tell you that I am more focused now than I have ever been. What the fuck – if there is anything that is going to be a distraction to me, it's having meetings like this that don't accomplish anything and just throw a lot of useless smoke in the air." Stuart seemed about to object, but Jeremy continued. "Just a second, here," he said. "Just so we're clear here – and I have no secrets to hide, you can ask anyone: I'm not fucking my staff. I have a rule, and that rule is you don't shit . . . well, it's never the smart thing to do, put it that way. I've seen it mess things up right fucking good and completely throw a place off balance. I'm a little shocked that I have to even talk about this kind of bullshit, to be honest. Honestly: what the fuck."

Brian and Stuart looked suitably chastened, so Jeremy smiled and softened his tone.

"Look: this is a bar, a bar full of overgrown children. I love them all, and I trust them all – mostly – but that's the reality of it. All bars are the same – some are worse. The Shack is actually pretty good as far as these things go. But in the end, the people here are good at their jobs because they're still kinda like kids. That works when the place is busting at the seams and everyone's in the weeds. That's when you see some real action happening and that's when it gets fun, but the downside is that you get a lot of stupid shit, too. And all the gossip and chatter, that's the stupidest shit of all. There is always all kinds of stories going around, about everybody. You're not used to hearing it, maybe, so here's my advice: ignore it. You'll just get sucked in so bad you'll have no idea what's really going on after a while."

"This is why you're the boss," Stuart said. "I think we had some legitimate concerns there, but I'm not even going to try to justify them, so let me just apologize. We screwed up and stepped in it."

"This is what happens. You have no idea the kinds of things I hear in a week. If I believed even half of it, I'd have to close the place down. And anyways," he continued, in a lower voice, "I think if I was going to bang a waitress, I would probably pick one without a ring on her finger."

The other two men chuckled, and finished their drinks. Brian went outside to answer a call while Stuart put his coat on.

"Hey, Jeremy – I was trying to get in touch last week, but your phone wasn't picking up. I called here and talked to someone who said you were out of town. You on vacation?"

Jeremy laughed and said he had no time for vacations. He must've had his phone off, or else the battery died. It happened. In reality, he'd spent most of the day in the middle of the lake with one of his cottage neighbours, who'd wanted to show him some of the best fishing spots. He had stashed his phone in a drawer in the cottage kitchen, and when he got back, burned and happy and more than a little drunk, he had left it there, untouched. There was nothing it could tell him that he needed to know right away.

———————

Jeremy began to let staffers and a few trusted regulars use the cottage. As he told the bookkeeper, he did it out of a sense that the place truly belonged to the Shack – and not just technically. He also did it, paradoxically, as a way to keep a lid on the fact of its existence. "If you go, it has to be our little secret, okay?" he'd tell people. "If I get all kinds of people asking to go, then that's it, party's over. I want this to be a kind of hideaway. So mum's the word."

One waitress took her boyfriend out for a few days. When Jeremy went up afterward, he found the door unlocked and dirty plates still in the sink. Worse, there was a used condom on the floor of the bedroom – he had to go outside to find a stick he could use to pick it up. Another waitress went with a couple of friends, and Jeremy got a call a week later from the cottage owners' association, saying there'd been complaints about the noise. A family with a place nearby had watched, shocked, while the young women took turns running off the end of the dock and leaping into the water, completely naked and swearing so loud you could hear it clear across the lake. When he went around to apologize, two young boys sat at the picnic table, grinning at him hopefully, waiting to hear if the miracle would be repeated.

He offered the place to Tyler, who reacted as though he were being told to climb into a metal cooking pot perched atop a pile of firewood and surrounded by torches.

"You should get out there. Have some fun."

"Do I have to?"

"Obviously not," Jeremy said, his smile slipping away.

Benny parked a small camping trailer on the lot, and for nearly a week, cottagers nearby were treated to the sight of him standing on the dock first thing in the morning, wearing nothing but distressed-looking underwear and a pair of work boots, toasting the dawn with a can of beer. Phil went for a weekend and ended up locking himself out in the middle of a rainstorm. He had to break in through the window, bending the screen and leaving scuff marks all over the frame and mud everywhere. When he got back, he showed everyone his poison ivy rashes and the scratches on his arms and legs.

"I'm starting to think I can't trust you to take a piss on your own," Jeremy told him.

"This is what happens when you lend your getaway spot to the people you're trying to get away from," Glenn said.

He offered it to Glenn, more out of a sense of duty than out of any desire to have the man out there, and was relieved when the offer was declined. Glenn had his own place, more than five hours northeast of Toronto, just on the fringes of Algonquin Park. It was nothing more than an enormous lot in the middle of the woods, on which he had installed a semi-permanent trailer. The nearest neighbours were a half-hour's drive away. He got water out of a nearby stream, and ran the place on propane and solar power. All he did all day was clear brush, read thick books about the Mongol invasions or the roots of the First World War, and occasionally stare back at the curious fox that crept out of the woods to check him out.

"That's where I'll be when everything goes to shit," he said.

"Sounds kinda vulnerable, doesn't it? Out there in the middle of nowhere?"

Glenn hinted that there were guns hidden beneath the floor. And, he said, he could take care of himself pretty well out there with just a baseball bat. He'd once spent a night with his feet up against the inside of the door, pushing back against a black bear that grew more and more irritated at not being given a share of the pan-fried fish he could smell from miles away. Glenn said he'd left some of the gouges on the side of the trailer where they were, just for show. That was a lesson learned. He now kept a few cans of bear spray in the drawer and one in the car.

"Nothing gets at me," Glenn said. "I could live there, no problem."

"I'd give it a month before you were trying to fuck the bear," Jeremy said.

———————

He waited for Charlene to ask to use the cottage. When she didn't, he finally insisted she go. It was like free therapy, he

– 210 –

said, not that she needed it. It would clear her head – she should get out there on her own and just absorb the light coming off the water, let it renew her. Or go with Kyle, too, obviously. Sure, that'd be totally fine.

Things were still slightly awkward between them, and she went home as soon as her shifts ended, but they found they could talk again during the day without acting as though one might suddenly jump up and burn the other with a lit match. They began listening in on the Tactix games again, marvelling at the way Donnie led his flock of hyperactive young men. Once in a while, if a regular were in for a late lunch or an early beer, and there was nothing else going on, Jeremy would get her to sit with them for a few minutes. The two of them managed to convince Phil not to go through his daughter's school bag – he was worried she might be smoking pot. If she was, Charlene told him, there was nothing he could do about it except let it run its course, and if she wasn't, all he'd be doing was letting her know he didn't trust her.

"Once you pull that kind of move," she said, "there's no taking it back. You're better off with a daughter who maybe gets high every once in a while, but knows that you love and trust her."

Jeremy was impressed, and told her so. She replied that she was probably just quoting an old episode of *Degrassi*, and that her mother used to go through her stuff all the time, looking for weed and worse.

"Girls are going to do whatever they're going to do. You can't stop them."

"I'll try to remember that."

When she'd first brought up the cottage idea with Kyle, he had laughed: *no way*. She eventually wore him down, pointing out that they hadn't gone anywhere together for over a year. Once he agreed to go, his reluctance disappeared, and he threw himself into the preparations, pulling his mother's Honda Civic out from behind the house, gassing it up, and filling it with windshield wiper fluid. He went out and bought a few hundred dollars' worth of camping equipment, even though Charlene insisted it wasn't necessary, they'd have all they need at the cottage. "And what if we don't?" he asked her. "What if we get there and it's full of rot or raccoons or has a huge leak in the roof? What if we get there and there's a half-dozen people from the bar already inside?" They left in the morning to beat the traffic and bought groceries on the way, then stopped at a liquor store beside the highway, where Charlene, after convincing the one employee there to let her use the staff washroom to pee, grabbed two bottles of sparkling wine at random. She wasn't crazy about the stuff, but it made the trip seem more festive, more celebratory. It would be worth the headache the next day and the slippery, racing feeling she got while drinking it.

When they finally found the cottage, after numerous wrong turns and bad guesses – Kyle had refused to even look at the directions Jeremy had supplied, and had mapped out his own route – Charlene was surprised at how small it was. She was shocked, too, by the dragons, as was Kyle. The two sets of partners – human and plaster – stared across the threshold at each other. The beasts were covered in the bits and bites left over from squirrels making meals of pinecones while standing on top. She imagined coming back up from the water after a late-night swim and almost peeing herself at the sight of those two glowering monsters.

Kyle took a picture of them with his phone. "I figured

there'd be at least *some* racist shit out here – every cottage has some – but these take the cake."

"I don't get how they're racist."

"Chinese restaurant. *Chinese.*"

"It's racist just because they're from a Chinese restaurant?"

"He might as well have a cigar-store Indian out here."

"Don't tell him that."

Kyle smirked. "Why, because he might go out and get one?"

They spent the day going in and out of the water and dozing in the Muskoka chairs. They hung their towels over the heads of the dragons to dry and so that they would not have to see their angry faces. Charlene washed and ate an entire basket of strawberries, and felt calmness creep up through her as though she were being slowly and pleasantly poisoned. She left her phone, which had buzzed a couple of times during the drive, up in the car. Kyle walked around the edge of the property, right through thick brush, and she worried that he'd gone into a sulk. Instead, he came back with armfuls of sticks for the fire and a look of triumph on his face.

"See? We didn't need to buy firewood. I told you."

He sat and read a book about the fall of the Soviet Empire, while she tried over and over to get through the same page of the novel she'd brought, one she'd been reading on and off for months, never seeming to get any closer to the far shore of the back cover. It was the size of a small briefcase, and so heavy it made her wrists ache when she held it. It was about three families in India. No: Pakistan – she kept getting it confused. Each time she picked up the book, it was as if all the fake-sounding names inside had been shuffled around, so that now the person she'd thought was the father who baked samosas according to a generations-old recipe was suddenly the angry son who had fallen in amongst Islamic radicals, and the woman who tended to her ailing grandfather in a dark room at the back of a house was now the widow who took over her dead husband's delivery route on her little motor scooter after he had his face blown off by a terrorist bomb unwittingly set by the angry son. She wished she'd brought something in which the body of a man was found under a bridge with a bullet hole in his back and a note in his pocket.

Charlene had hoped they might have sex as soon as they arrived. During the drive, she thought of ways to help make that happen. She wished she had thought to buy a new swimsuit – the one she had was brown and shapeless and coarse from too many washes and too many heavily chlorinated city pools. She could've got herself something revealing and sexy, and then modelled it for him in front of the cottage. She pictured him getting so excited that they'd do it right there on one of the chairs – no time to get all of their clothes off. Then they would go out for a swim together, and later do it again – more slowly and patiently this time – in the bed, for which they had brought clean sheets.

Clean sheets: Kyle had insisted they bring their own, plus pillow cases, freshly laundered and smelling like flowers and bleach. He refused to sleep on sheets that anyone else had used, or that had been sitting for weeks with spiders, mice, and squirrels running over them. Lying in the bed on their first night after having sat on opposite sides of the fire like two strangers in hoodies, she had to admit he was right: fresh sheets were wonderful. The smell of the fire and the lake was on both of them. She was just starting to drift off when Kyle put a hand on her bare shoulder. The suddenness of it made her jump a little. Even now, after so many years, he didn't know how to start, and always tried to signal his intentions as clearly as possible so that she would get the hint and take over the responsibilities of starting the operation. His bare arm snaked around her and pulled her to him, and his right leg landed on her thighs. She could feel his cock touch her side very lightly, like a celebrity on a talk show waiting backstage to be introduced, knowing everyone there was aware of him and excited to be in his presence. The thought made her giggle involuntarily. Before Kyle could freeze up at the sound of her laughter, she said, "I really like it here." Then she rolled over to face him, happily.

The first time she and Kyle ever had sex, they did it on the living room couch in her mother's apartment, careful not to mess up the homework they had spread across the coffee table, and which Kyle was helping her with. Sex with Kyle was completely different from sex with anyone else with whom she'd done it. Kyle didn't grab at her like a furious gorilla, he didn't push against her as though he were trying to smother her, and he didn't take off afterward or suddenly get all weird and sullen. Matthew used to grab her hand and put it on his cock, holding it there and jerking himself off with it. It made her feel like Helen Keller, with her clumsy hands on the water pumps. Kyle never forced her to do anything – though there were lots of times, she had to admit, right in the middle of everything, when she sort of wished he would. She didn't want to be hurt or tied up, and she would not have been able to keep a straight face at the sight of Kyle playing dungeon master, but she wanted to feel as though he were being driven a little bit crazy by her and had been pushed outside his usual limits. Instead, he kept to his limits, and always tried to ensure the pleasure was evenly divided, that they both ended with an orgasmic checkmark in their columns. Sometimes, when she simply could not get over the hump, he would brood about it, and she would have to assure him it made her just as happy to know he was happy. Which was true: she liked that she could do this for him, that she could help bring about such a release of tension. She rarely saw him so relaxed. It helped to know that she would likely get there the next time, that being left in pleasure's lobby was only an occasional thing.

As she stared up at the unfamiliar cottage ceiling, listening to her husband's slow drift into sleep, she began to wonder if that had been the one, and if in a few weeks she would discover she were pregnant. She was surprised at how calm she was about the idea. Normally, whenever she realized they had forgotten the condom, everything turned to panic and worry. But this time, the panic was far off, drowned in the lake. She had seen the look on Kyle's face, and could feel the message being communicated by the muscles of his ass, and had said nothing to prevent what she knew was about to happen. It wasn't even that she had done something unnatural – what was more natural than two humans fucking and one coming in the other one? How else was it supposed to work? She was surprised, too, that he had gone through with it, and hadn't realized at the last moment and quickly redirected the coming spurt of life. Maybe he'd been thinking along the same lines as her. Maybe he felt ready. He came fully inside her, which no one had ever done before. There was a slight bloated feeling, but also a pleasant warmth and sense of satisfaction that was more concrete than usual.

Charlene awoke to the sound of something moving around on the roof just above her head. She'd been dreaming of walking along a beach made entirely of dry clam shells. In the dream, she had struggled to explain to Kyle that the reason she was falling behind was because she was barefoot, while he had on thick rubber boots. The sun looked as though it had only just risen, and it was already warm and humid in the room. The bottoms of her feet held a phantom soreness from all the imagined slices and cuts. She felt herself sink into the mattress at the thought of being responsible for nothing that day but to enjoy herself. They wouldn't even have to go into town. There was more than enough food and beer for the rest of their stay, and though she always enjoyed poking around in the stores wherever they went, staying put meant not having to deal with Kyle's anxiety over behaving like a lazy tourist in a place where, for the people who actually lived there, it was just a regular workday.

She wasn't worried about anything. She wasn't worried about finding out if she was pregnant, about telling Kyle, about having to decide whether or not to keep the baby – though she probably would, no matter what. She was pro-choice in theory, and didn't judge anyone, but felt she had too little authority over her own life to cancel out someone else's. She wasn't worried about getting sick in the mornings, getting fat, being in pain, not being able to drink, or even being in labour and delivering a baby. She couldn't yet think what it would mean to have an actual child around, in the room with her, in her arms, at her feet. The only thing she feared was telling her mother, who'd been begging her for so long to make this exact thing happen, to be careless for one moment and allow new life to come into the world. To make something and to start to live for someone else instead of going along as she was, making every decision based on her own happiness and her own fears. She didn't want to have to tell her mother that she was right – that letting Kyle's sperm go flying up inside her had somehow finally fulfilled her as a person and a woman. She didn't feel that way just yet, anyway, though she figured she might start to over the coming months. She was willing to at least entertain the idea, if it came to it.

She could not help but contrast her current feelings of contentment with the way she'd felt waking up beside Jeremy, in the intrusive glare of his bedroom. The shock of remembering where she was had quickly replaced the disorientation. She'd been naked, with a sheet wrapped so tightly around her ankle as to make her worry for a brief second that getting tied to the bed had been part of the previous night's proceedings. It hadn't been, though there was more than enough else to work through. It had clearly been an opportunity for her to try on a new sexual persona, one with sharp teeth and nails and more willing to make demands. He, on the other hand, had moved slowly, constantly pausing as if waiting for her to leap away from him and flee in horror. His reticence had annoyed her, and thinking of the way she had whipped him on – only metaphorically but for the want of an actual whip – made her weigh the consequences of murder-suicide. She pictured herself sneaking down to the kitchen to retrieve a knife big enough to put a fatal hole in his neck with one thrust. Then she would swallow every pill in the house and set it on fire. Instead, she snuck out the moment he went into the bathroom and turned on the shower, even leaving behind her leggings and underwear, which were nowhere to be seen. She couldn't remember if she had worn a bra to the bar the night before, and gave up the search rather than have to work through why she had not.

For the entire walk through his oddly treeless neighbourhood, searching for a taxi, she kept expecting the white Jeep to pull up beside her. Had it done so, she would have climbed in and resigned herself to this new life as someone who fucked around with her boss. The Jeep never appeared, which told her that Jeremy, getting out of the shower and finding her gone, had decided that this was the best possible result. And so, on the cab ride home, she focused on the twin tasks of creating a plausible alibi – she texted her friend Samantha, telling her there'd been a need for an extra pair of hands with the baby the night before – and rebuilding the concrete fact of her marriage in her mind.

With the sun already gleaming behind the cottage curtains, Charlene lay in the bed and scratched at her bare thigh – something had bit her there. Likely a spider, of which she'd seen many inside the cottage since they arrived, all of them sitting frozen in the corners, looking as though they hadn't expected human visitors and had been caught at something. The happiness she was feeling was proof, she decided, that things had worked out for the best that morning after Jeremy's birthday, that her finding an empty taxi before his Jeep found her was the way her fate was meant to play out.

She tried to picture herself as a young mother: brighter, more engaged, more focused, less lazy. She would be tired all the time, but she would also glow with newfound purpose. Nine months of reading deeply about nutrition and diet would transform her meagre cooking skills into something more than up to the task of feeding her husband and child in a way that was dense with health benefits and full of variety. She imagined doing remarkable things with squash, sprouts, and whole grain flour. During her pregnancy, she would bring about peace between Kyle and the couple downstairs, and when they finally moved out for something bigger, it would be amid a sustained flurry of hugs and tears. Even Kyle would cry a little. On their first night in their new house, one of their last pre-baby nights together, they would sleep on the floor, the new mattresses not having been delivered yet, their old bed on its way to the dump or to Value Village. Kyle's parents would help them pay for it all. He would spread out their new comforters and pin the corners down with her books about breastfeeding. They'd both be awoken in the middle of the night by the unfamiliar sound of the furnace coming to life to warm them where they lay, and they'd smile at each other in the dark and have delicate, careful sex, then fall back asleep in each other's arms.

Kyle was not next to her in the bed, and she couldn't hear him moving around the cottage. That didn't surprise her: she was used to waking up on her own anytime they were on vacation. Whenever they went camping, he always got up early to go for a swim. If she got up, too, she would wander down to the beach, holding her instant coffee for warmth, and sit on the damp sand while he swam. He didn't seem to mind, though she always got the feeling he was just as happy, maybe happier, when she let him go on his own. The dawn swim was Kyle Time. She went out into the small kitchen area and made a cup of coffee with the last of the crystals in one jar, then opened a new one so it would be ready when Kyle got back. She worried a little about the mark just above the wall socket next to the fridge, a black smudge like a birthmark. Had there been an electrical fire at some point? Should she have the kettle plugged in at all? How else was she going to make coffee out here? Her momentary wave of concern dissipated in a rush of desire for more coffee. There were empty beer bottles on the counter, many of them fringed on the bottom with dirt from around the campfire. Kyle had collected them himself the night before, saying that even a swallow of beer at the bottom of a single bottle could attract bears. She didn't believe it, but was happy to let him clean things up.

She wondered how he might take the news about her being pregnant. It wasn't as though he could say he'd been tricked: the cock was his, the sperm was his, he'd bought the condoms himself and had already used most of the box, so it wasn't as though he didn't understand how the whole business worked. She hadn't put a hex on him, he hadn't been roofied. He couldn't accuse her of committing a sin that he hadn't also committed, at least by omission.

She'd once heard a regular at the Shack say that coming inside someone was a sin of *emission*. Would Kyle find that funny? She doubted it.

Maybe he already knew. If the woman could know right away, was it impossible that the man could, too? Maybe he was off collecting his thoughts, trying to assess how fatherhood would change his world. She wondered if he was better able to imagine the actual child as it would be. Probably he had just as much difficulty picturing anything more than a faceless, sleeping lump wrapped tight in blankets they had to carry everywhere. Even so abstract, the thought of being responsible for a baby calmed her. It slowed her movements and gave her a welcome feeling of mystery and superiority.

With her coffee, she went outside. She didn't feel like going back into the bedroom to retrieve her hoodie, so she reached behind the door for a heavy raincoat that must've been left out there for people to use. It was the colour of egg yolk, and the sleeves went past her hands. She liked the crinkling sound it made as she stepped among the roots and stones. Later they might pull out and play some of the board games that were stacked up on the floor behind the TV. Yahtzee would be fun. And maybe Trivial Pursuit. Monopoly was a no-go, as she hated the effect it had on Kyle: the one time they'd played it together, with friends over for dinner who'd brought the game with them, everything went wrong. They were playing it as a joke, as a tribute to the fact that they were too old for board games and smart enough to find better ways to amuse themselves. The joke died quickly. Kyle started losing almost right away, repeatedly stumbling onto other people's squares and having to pay up. The chance cards never went his way, and he wouldn't buy any of the cheaper places he landed on. He was told to loosen up a little and a buy a few things, and so, with a quiet, determined look on his face that only Charlene recognized, he started buying up everything he could, clearing out all his money doing so. The other couple started snagging themselves on his properties, which were positioned at fiendishly unmissable intervals. Within three rounds, Kyle had turned a whole side of the board into an impassable wall of hotels. One by one, the other three died on its sharpened edges. He played until there was only one other person left in the game, Charlene's friend Samantha, who sat there silent as she was bled to death by his railroads and other holdings. They played it again, and he did it again, and when the others complained that he was ruining the fun, he said there was no other point to the game: "It's called *Monopoly*, not *Everybody Have Fun*."

Maybe Hungry Hungry Hippos instead, she thought.

She walked down to the water's edge, expecting Kyle to emerge from the water at any moment, dripping, shivering, and impatient to get into dry clothes. Was there coffee? *Yes. A fresh pot. You're welcome.* She looked for his head and shoulders plowing forward and disturbing the surface. Everywhere it was flat and clear. At its closest point, the opposite shore of the lake was still far enough away that the trees blurred together. Swimming there and back might take a half an hour or more, assuming he'd stop on the far beach for a rest. He was nowhere in sight. His shoes and towel were at the water's edge. There was no one on the lake – no boats, nothing. She wanted to shout, but was held still by the thought that he must be nearby and she was simply missing seeing him somehow. If he were around, he'd be annoyed if she started yelling his name. She wasn't sure she could get the sound out of her throat, anyway. She waited. A cold feeling went through her as she tried to work out exactly how long it'd been since she'd gotten up, made the coffee, and walked out of the cottage in the ridiculous raincoat, which she now threw off in fear and embarrassment.

The phone was in the car. The keys were in Kyle's grey jeans. The jeans were in the cottage, somewhere in the bedroom – too many steps, and to begin working through them was to acknowledge that things had reached a point at which calling someone was necessary. She winced at the thought of sirens. Sirens would let everyone know how bad things were.

The keys weren't in Kyle's pants, after all. After a frantic search, during which she came close to deciding she would have to put a rock through the window of the car, she found them under the bed. She almost knocked over one of the dragons as she ran outside and up the path, then fought with the passenger-side door until she realized she had not yet unlocked it. Her phone was on the passenger seat. There were messages and texts waiting for her, but she skipped past those to find Jeremy's name. She couldn't think of who else to call.

"Please tell me you didn't burn the place down."

He sounded half-asleep. She had to swallow before she could speak.

"I can't find Kyle. He went for a swim, I think, and I can't find him."

"What do you mean?"

"I can't find him. I'm worried."

Jeremy's voice dropped and seemed to press into her ear: "You can't see him anywhere? He's not out in the water? Could he have gone to town for a second, or for a walk?"

All his stuff was there. His clothes and his shoes were all still there. His wallet. His phone. She was scared.

"Okay, nothing has happened. He's probably just swimming somewhere and you can't see him. Or he went for a walk or something. Have you gone to one of the other cottages?"

"Jeremy, his shoes are still here. Everything's still here except for his swimming trunks. He went for a swim and I can't see him anywhere."

"And he was gone when you woke up?"

Charlene felt a premature wave of grief come over her at the word *gone*. Farther along the road, near the hump of stone Jeremy had warned them to avoid as they were driving in, she could see a pair of small birds fluttering around in the dirt. She couldn't tell if they were mating or fighting. One would fly straight at the other, then both would flap their wings hard enough to kick up dust. Each bird looked small enough to fit in her pocket. As she stared at them, her mind leapt ahead in time to when there'd be police cars and an ambulance surrounding the Honda Civic. People from neighbouring cottages would be standing in groups, with looks of concern on their faces. Kids would be tearing in and out of the crowd, dimly aware that something bad had happened but energized by the presence of police officers with actual loaded guns on their hips, and by the flashing lights on the cars. They might even get the chance to see a dead body. The kids would pass that information among themselves, so that all of them knew, and all of them were ready: a dead body was coming. All they had to do was wait, and pray that their parents didn't make them go back inside. The older kids would be watching the faces of the adults for signs of wavering, and for clues about the state this body was in. Had it been hit by a boat? Was it all bloated? Would the eyes be open? Would it be naked?

Charlene had to put her hand against the car.

"I'm really scared."

She had the sensation of being drawn forward, as if the car had begun to roll down the hill toward the water. The lake was a big magnet, drawing in all life and smothering it in its cold depths, down with the lost sunglasses, fish hooks, pop cans, and weeds.

"Jeremy?"

"Yes. I'm here."

"I think he's dead."

"He's not. He's going to show up, I know it. Any minute now. He's just gone off somewhere and didn't tell you. Everything is going to be fine. It will."

"I didn't tell him what happened."

"What happened? Tell him what?"

"You and me. I didn't tell him. He didn't know."

Jeremy was quiet for a moment. "Look, everything is going to be okay."

"I don't know why I did it. I don't know why it happened. It wasn't your fault, but now Kyle's dead. Oh my God."

"Charlene, you have to hold it together. Everything will be fine."

"Jeremy . . ."

"Yes."

"It's not going to be fine, I know it."

"I'm just getting dressed. I'm coming out there. Everything will be okay."

"I don't think I'm going to be here."

"Why?"

Before she could reply, a loud honking made her drop the phone: a dark blue SUV was navigating the last corner on the road and rolling slowly toward her. At the wheel was a big man with a white beard and sunglasses who waved at Charlene. In the passenger seat she could see Kyle, wrapped in a beach towel. The man with the beard got out of the SUV and walked around to open the passenger-side door, as if Kyle were elderly or infirm. When Kyle stepped down onto the pine needles, his knees buckled slightly. The beach towel had Justin Bieber's face spread across the entire length of it. There was another towel on the seat. She ran over to take his weight on her own shoulder.

"Whoa, easy," the man said as Kyle nearly toppled over sideways. "We caught a big one this morning!" He was friendly and firm in his actions, and she couldn't help think how he reminded her of the host of a show she sometimes watched, the one about home renovations. He introduced himself as Steve, and said he had a cottage directly across the lake.

"If you guys weren't so far back from the water, I'd be able to see your place from my dock."

He'd been standing outside having a coffee and spotted Kyle having a hard time of it. It happened a couple of times a summer, he said: someone misjudged the distance and got into trouble. Kyle was lucky, because there weren't a lot of boaters on the lake that day. Steve himself was supposed to have gone home the day before. His kids made him stay another night.

"Which is lucky, eh?"

"Oh my God, thank you."

"This is what you do."

Steve said he would come by later to retrieve the Bieber towel. Normally he would just say to keep it, they had lots at their place, but his youngest daughter would throw herself under the wheels of the truck if they went home without it. "That smiling idiot has come in handy, for once. You okay there, guy?"

Kyle raised his arm in thanks.

Steve gave another friendly honk as he drove off, after refusing her offer of a coffee.

Inside the cottage, Kyle sat in the living room with a coffee in his hands. He seemed to have slipped out of himself, or somehow become his own adult twin:

recognizable but fundamentally strange. His eyes were red and tired. He looked helpless and confused. She'd never seen him that way. Even at his worst moments, he was always fundamentally Kyle. Not now.

She sat across from him, on the couch. She wondered if she should sit closer – that would've been the more loving thing to do, the more caring thing to do. She couldn't. Something had happened when she saw Kyle in the SUV, something had passed between them – some understanding that after more than a decade together, new and important information was being added to the profile of their relationship. They'd received a critical update. He had looked angry, but also beaten and drained. In an instant, all the fear she'd had vanished, replaced by a strange, stony feeling.

He was alive, and she was both glad and relieved, but she couldn't feel anything beyond that. The look on his face had cancelled something. She felt no interest in taking on his anger, in letting its barbed point enter her chest and start to work itself through her. She wanted nothing to do with it. He gave her the slightest angry look, and she rejected it. She simply refused, and he knew it. All in the space of a split second – even before she had helped him out of the truck, they both knew something had ended, a lid had been closed. He had been fished out of the lake, only to be thrown back by his own wife.

"Can we go home?" His voice was quiet, deferential. He seemed to understand that she held the balance of power now. "Early? Can we go today?"

She let him sit and finish his coffee while she packed their bags. She drove the Civic, and he didn't object. If they got stopped she was prepared to explain to the officer that her husband had nearly drowned that morning and was in no shape to drive, so what they were doing was actually the safer option, despite her lack of a licence. They drove in silence. Kyle was wearing long pants and a grey hoodie, though the day had gotten warm enough for Charlene to roll up the windows and put the air conditioning on in the car.

"Speed," Kyle said.

Charlene glanced at the dash: she was cruising along way over the limit. She drew her foot back off the gas and nodded without looking at him. It was the first word he'd said in an hour. She wondered if there were more to come.

As she drove on, it slowly dawned on her that he had not made her pregnant. No new connection had been made, no tiny, blooming truth. She was sure of it: a process so important could not have started up within her undetected. Maybe the whole upheaval of the morning had killed whatever chance they'd had. The sperm that had been nuzzling its head into the egg had died of shock from all the fear going through her, and the egg went black. Or she had killed it by sheer force of will. Or maybe no sperm had even made it there.

Maybe his little guys just aren't swimmers, she thought.

She refused to tell Kyle why she was laughing, and he pouted silently for the rest of the way home.

A few weeks later, when a store-bought test added its semi-official authority to what she already knew intuitively – that there was nothing Kyle-like growing inside her – she wrapped the dipstick in toilet paper and hid it at the bottom of the bathroom garbage can, regretting the $20 she'd wasted on the test.

"DISAPPOINTMENTS ARE ARROWS, NOT STOP SIGNS."
– *Grow for It*, Theo Hendra

There began a season of calamities and minor fuck-ups. Jeremy, like an animal that sensed changes in the air pressure and took shelter before a storm, could usually tell when these kinds of things were on their way, but this time they completely blindsided him. He had been walking around with such a glow for so long that it was even more of a shock to discover, yet again, that the universe didn't give a shit about his mood.

First, one of the younger Tactix players got hit by a car while crossing the street to get to the Shack for a game. The car clipped him as he stepped off the curb, sending him back into a mailbox and shattering his leg and hip. Jeremy had been sitting and dozing at the cottage when it all happened.

When he got back, he had the accident recounted to him by customers who had turned to look out the front window just as the poor kid got lifted and thrown aside.

"He honestly looked like he jumped on a trampoline," one told him.

The next time Donnie came into the bar, Jeremy told him the games were over, they'd need to find a new location. "I really feel terrible about what happened, but maybe it's bad luck having you here." He offered him a free Diet Coke and said again that he was sorry.

Donnie would not accept the drink. "There's nowhere else we can go. We get booted out of everywhere. Even McDonald's."

"Well, maybe that's the world trying to tell you something, dude. People get too old for games."

The next thing was a fire in the pharmacy next door that could've easily reduced the entire block to a pile of charred timber and bricks. The old pharmacist had fallen asleep in the back with a lit cigarette in his hands after locking everything up and almost torched the place with him inside. Everyone at the Shack stood in the parking lot and watched as the firefighters dragged hoses through the front door. In the end, the idiot only ended up scorching his arm and blackening the back half of the pharmacy.

"That fucker should've gone up like a twig," Jeremy told people. "Imagine smoking in there."

Less than two weeks later, the company that owned the building sent out a letter saying they were very sorry to have heard what happened, and were glad that everyone was fine and that the damage was minimal. It did mean, however, that insurance rates would be going up across the board, and that an entirely new sprinkler system would have to be installed – no exceptions. They couldn't afford to have one weak link in the chain. The company, of course, owned the sprinkler systems, and would be selling them directly to each tenant.

"That miserable old shit falls asleep with an Export A in his mouth, and I get fucked for it. How does that work?"

Glenn said it was exactly how things worked. "When something like that happens, the smart people know how to use it to their advantage, while all the dummies like you and me are out on bucket brigade. Classic shock doctrine."

"But we're all struggling as it is. They must have bigger people to go after."

"It's easier to steal one piece of candy from a hundred babies than to steal a hundred pieces from a candy store. All predatory animals go for the easy kill."

"Are they really predators, though?" Phil asked. "Even if they're just trying to protect their business?"

Glenn laughed and put a hand on Phil's shoulder. "Spoken like an easy kill!"

And then, on a quiet afternoon when Jeremy was thinking he might slip away from the bar and head out of town for a night or two in order to escape the swirl of chaos happening around him, Tyler nearly cut off the fingers of his left hand while chopping vegetables. The knife, the one he'd bought himself and brought home each night wrapped in a heavy cloth, came down hard, and within seconds, the entire area was covered in blood. The dishwasher stared at the mess in disbelief. Patty grabbed a nearby towel and wrapped it tight around the injured hand, while Jeremy ran to his Jeep and brought it around to the kitchen entrance. He got Tyler to the hospital in less than five minutes, speeding the entire way and telling him repeatedly not to drip blood on the car seat. By the time they arrived at the emergency room doors, the towel around his hand looked like a rose in full bloom.

"Does it hurt?"

Tyler nodded yes, and Jeremy asked the nurse if there were painkillers he could have while he was waiting to be seen. The nurse refused at first, and Jeremy argued loudly with her until she gave in – as much to shut him up as to help the wounded cook. Jeremy bought him a bottle of water from the machine so he could swallow the pills. They sat and watched a man in the waiting area take apart a newspaper page by page, separating each sheet from the rest and folding it neatly like a handkerchief. He did this until the entire paper was reduced to stack of tightly folded pages. Then he picked up the stack of paper, walked over to a recycling bin, and dropped it all in.

"I once knew a guy who took the tips of his fingers off," Jeremy said. "Got a chunk of money for it and spent his time off learning how to wire a house. He does that now, full-time. So he did alright."

———

At the next meeting with Brian and Stuart, they let Jeremy know right away that they'd heard about the fire and the insurance rates going up and about Tyler's accident, and wanted to know what he was doing about it all, what plans he had made to cover the extra expenses and the lost cook.

"You left out the kid who got run over," he said. They froze. He laughed and reassured them. "Don't worry: that one's not my fault. None of this is my fault, actually. Just shitty luck."

After Jeremy explained what had happened, Stuart said

he'd never understood why the gamers had been allowed to do their thing in the bar in the first place.

Jeremy shrugged. "They sort of became part of the place. I was sad to give them the boot to be honest. It kept a little bit of money coming in during the day, anyway."

"The bar's brand and its image and the future: *these* are the things we need you to be thinking about, Jer, not turning the place into the Island of Misfit Toys. The goal is long-term growth, not short-term survival. Otherwise there's no point in Brian and I even being here, is there? Okay?"

Brian, looking down at his phone, nodded along.

"I'm just trying to stay alive here," Jeremy said.

"Staying alive is the easy part," Stuart said. "We need you to do the hard part, which is bringing the place to the next level, which means being a little more selective and more strategic. We need you to be *smarter* about everything, Jer. I know you built this place, and that's great, okay, but we're looking *forward* now."

"I'm looking forward, too!" Jeremy said. He knew he sounded like a little kid trying to get in on a big-kid game, but he couldn't just sit there in silence.

"Are you?" Stuart asked, and he got up from the table and walked over to the bar. Patty was standing there wiping pint glasses and watched him approach with an expression of suspicion she made no effort to conceal. Jeremy wondered how much she had overheard. His own face was burning; he tried to think when anyone had talked to him like this since he was a teenager. "Look at this," Stuart said, pointing at the Zombie Gallery of party photos. "Some of these look like they've been stuck here for a decade. I don't even see any new ones. *Are* there any new ones?"

"There's new ones on the website," Jeremy muttered. Though even those, he knew, were likely years out of date.

"The *website*," Stuart said, and smiled carnivorously as he came back to the table. Brian looked at Jeremy over his phone.

"When's the last time you went to the Shack's site, Jer?" the lawyer asked him.

"Honestly? I couldn't tell you. Why?"

"Well, if you went there right now – as in today, right now – you probably wouldn't notice anything different from the last time you went, whenever that was. Do you monitor the amount of traffic the site gets, by the way? Never mind, that's for another day. Anyway, it's fine now, but if you'd gone there maybe three weeks ago, you would have found that the whole thing was an ad for Japanese Viagra."

Jeremy laughed, though he wasn't quite sure what the joke was.

"What do you mean?"

"I mean the site was all pictures of Japanese boner pills."

Jeremy reached over to open the bar's laptop. Stuart said not to bother.

"The registration must have lapsed," Brian explained. "You must've let it lapse, or someone forgot to renew it. Did you get an email telling you to renew at some point?"

"An email? No, I don't think so." Jeremy was trying to understand what he was being told, but nothing was clicking. "So the website is . . . gone?"

Stuart gave a deep sigh that seemed to come up through his entire body.

"Jeremy, look: the website thing was embarrassing, but it's fixed now, we got the registration back. It helps to be a lawyer. The real point here is how unprofessional we look when that kind of thing happens. And if we look unprofessional, it makes it that much harder to convince outside people we have a valuable brand here."

"What outside people?"

"I sometimes talk to people I think might be useful in building the business. Nothing formal, not lunches or anything, but if I run into someone, I tell them about the place, feel them out a bit. That's part of my job as a partner in this."

"So you're what, telling people to book retirement parties here? I do that all the time, too."

Stuart said there was more to it than that. It was about long-term planning. He asked if Jeremy knew a Susan Toller. Tall, with red hair. Jeremy said he did, though it'd been years since he'd heard her name. The sound of it made it feel as though someone were cranking his ribcage tight around his lungs. Susan Toller scouted new locations for Crane's, and was responsible for bringing more than half a dozen places into the fold. By the time Jeremy left, she had become an almost mythical figure: if she began to show interest in your business, it was like seeing Death standing in the corner of the room. The threat may pass by as silently as it came, or else you only had a matter of months left. Either way, to see her pull up in your parking lot in her bright red compact car was a bad omen.

"She still at Crane's?"

Stuart nodded. "Her territory is most of Southern Ontario now. It's amazing that she still does it, driving all around. She says she won't sit down behind a desk until she's just about ready to retire." He smiled. "She's a little like you!" Stuart said that he knew her a bit from some business his firm had done for Crane's a few years back.

"Long story short," he said, "I ran into her a while ago, and told her a little bit about what we've got going here. She sounded pretty excited and said she would drop in at some point to say hi."

"I'll need to get the holy water ready, then."

"What do you mean?"

Jeremy made the sign of the cross with his index fingers.

Stuart gave a tolerant smile. "Let me say this: I understand why you would feel that way. I really do. Okay. But we need to keep all our options open."

"Even options that aren't an option?"

"Okay, wrong word. Let's say we should always be trying to make friends. Friends are better than enemies."

"Oh, I don't know about that – enemies can be useful."

Stuart laughed, having decided he'd made all the points he'd needed to make. "You may be right about that. You may be totally right. But don't slash her tires if she comes around. Try to be nice."

Trying to catch one of the last few warm nights of the year, Jeremy sat out in front of the cottage, unable to relax. The water was too cold for swimming, and most of the other places on the lake were dark. Thin, woollen strands of smoke came from the year-rounders. The only activity on the water was a line of imperious-looking ducks seeking shelter for the night. The last time Patty and Shawn had come out, they'd installed solar lights all along the edge of the woods, and these began to blink into life. They had also left him a bottle of bourbon, which he had open next to him. After accidentally dropping his glass in the sand, he began to take sips straight from the bottle.

Before coming up, he'd picked up a copy of *Power Talk*, the latest from Theo Hendra. It was a collection of interviews with Hendra himself, for which Hendra wrote an introduction in which he claimed to have learned as much from his interviewers as they did from him. Jeremy was in the middle of a long one on the subject of failure. Hendra said he rejected the idea that such a thing truly existed. "Our lives are driven by perception," he said. "That is our genius and power as human beings, but it can also be our weakness. If we perceive ourselves to have failed, then we have failed. The subjective thought becomes objective reality. And that's a real bummer!" Better, he said, to adjust our perception so that what we believed to be failure could be seen as merely the equivalent of one negative result in a series of experiments ultimately leading to success.

Jeremy kept getting up from his chair and going inside to check his phone, though on principle he would not bring it outside with him – he was there to disconnect. A bartender left a voice mail about a late keg delivery, and Jeremy called him back to shout at him that he had bigger things to worry about, and why was it so important to let him know the kegs were late, since they were there now, and everything was fine? Fuck's sake. An hour later, he called the bartender back to apologize.

"Too much caffeine," he said.

His sister sent him a text, saying she wanted to get together to talk about some money issues regarding their parents. He replied that he would be stupid-busy for the next few weeks doing renovations.

He sent Tyler a text, asking him how his hand was, and got no reply, which he found somehow reassuring.

. While he was at the LCBO in town, a large man had walked up to him and introduced himself as Steve, Kyle's rescuer. He said he recognized the Jeep: he had driven around to Jeremy's cottage a few weeks before and saw the car was there, but no one was around when he knocked.

"My wife was bugging me to make sure everything was okay with your daughter."

"My daughter? Yeah, no – she's fine now, thanks."

"She was pretty upset when I drove up. Not that I blame her at all."

"Well, thanks for being there to grab the poor bastard."

"Oh, Christ – it was no problem at all, no problem at all. I have to say, though: that guy didn't seem all that happy about the whole thing. I could be totally wrong about this, but it was like he was *pissed* with me for grabbing him, which is weird. I had a real fuck of a time getting him in the boat. I figured he was exhausted and scared shitless about almost drowning, but just before we got around to your place he said something really snippy to me. I didn't think much of it, but I wasn't expecting it, that's for sure."

"He was probably in shock," Jeremy offered.

"Could be, could be. You may be right about that. Anyways, I'm just glad I was there when I was there. And tell your daughter she can keep the towel, after all. My girls have dropped that little Bieber asshole like a hot rock. They're all into this other guy now – can't remember the name."

Jeremy stood for an hour at the edge of the water, looking out into the darkness and trying to shift his perception by sheer force of will. Then he finished the bourbon and fell asleep in the chair outside, only waking up when the fire was completely out and the cold began to eat into his clothes.

When Jeremy told Charlene that he had run into Steve, she showed no curiosity about the meeting, and barely seemed to recognize the name.

"He said he didn't need his towel back." He smiled.

"I already threw it away."

He tried a few times to talk to her about everything that was going on, but she always seemed distracted, and would have to admit, after he'd spent a whole five minutes unburdening himself, that she hadn't really been listening. Her nerves, too, seemed always exposed and crackling like a downed wire. One time, he came up behind her as she was filling salt shakers and touched her lightly on the back. He'd only wanted to say that she could leave early that day if she wanted to – he could clean up and get everything ready for the evening. She jerked her arm away in surprise and yelled "Fuck!" the moment he touched her, sending a spray of salt across the surface of the bar. The unfilled shaker clattered into the sink. Instead of laughing off her jumpiness or letting him apologize for startling her, she walked away quickly without looking at him and disappeared downstairs. Even over the music he heard the door to the women's washroom swing violently open and closed.

Things began to slip whenever she was on the floor. He started hearing more complaints about her – not just from customers whose orders she screwed up or forgot to put through to the kitchen, but from other staffers, who said she'd always been the best in terms of leaving things clean, stocked, and ready for the next person to take over. Lately, however, there'd been half-empty fridges, orange juice jugs with nothing but dried pulp, and dirty bar towels in the sink. She sometimes went off the floor without giving her last tables their checks. When the other servers complained, wanting to know why he was not setting her straight, Jeremy did his best to calm them down.

"Everyone gets to be the goat," he said. "It'll be your turn again soon enough."

She stayed late at the bar most nights, even when she hadn't worked that day. She didn't sit with Jeremy, but would find strangers to talk to, or sit on her own. When she'd had a few drinks, she liked to badger the bartender into putting on a particular song, often something that Jeremy had never heard before. There was one she asked for almost every night called "Love Will Tear Us Apart."

"Who is that?" he asked her. It definitely wasn't his thing, but there was something relentless about it, something tense and urgent.

"Joy Division!" she shouted back. Her eyes were closed, and she was swaying awkwardly to the beat.

Glenn, in the middle of an argument with someone nearby, perked up like a dog at the name. He turned to her and asked, "This band is called Joy Division? For real? *Joy Division?*"

"That's right."

He grinned like a detective whose target had just given herself away in the stupidest way possible. "Do you even know what that means?"

"Nazi whores."

She kept dancing in her seat.

"Pretty much," he muttered, then turned back to his argument.

Another night, she came in after dinner and was still there when Jeremy was getting ready to go home, a little before closing time. As he was leaving, he went over to remind her she was on schedule for the next day, and to suggest she maybe call it a night. She was in the middle of trying to convince Phil of the fatal sexism of the Harry Potter books – something about how the girl wizard gets pushed aside all the time, despite being the only character who has her shit together. Though Phil seemed amenable, her voice kept getting louder and angrier, as if he were dismissing the idea outright. Jeremy put his hand on her shoulder in hopes of getting her to cool down a little.

"Oh, fuck *off*," she shouted at him.

The bartender's eyes went wide. Jeremy just smiled, shrugged, and walked away, too shocked to say more.

The next morning, she called nearly an hour after she was supposed to have started her shift and left a message saying she would not be coming in, that she was sorry about the night before, and that she was done working at the Shack. He called her three times that day; she didn't answer, except to send a text asking if he could drop her final paycheque in her mailbox.

The next time Jeremy's birthday came around, he had to be reminded of it by Phil, who asked if they'd been doing their three-way thing with Glenn again.

"Don't call it that," Jeremy said. "But sure, of course."

And so the three of them sat at the far corner of the bar, enjoying a bottle of expensive scotch that Jeremy brought up especially for the occasion. Even Glenn, who was normally reluctant to abandon beer, said it was a treat. He made a point of thanking Jeremy for the booze and for the free dinner he'd been treated to, as well.

"I swear to God you're getting mellower with age, buddy," Jeremy said.

"It happens."

"This is the first year that I haven't been distracted by any of the female students in my classes," Phil said.

"That's *too* mellow."

The three of them laughed like sad old gods.

"SOMETIMES LIFE IS JUST TOO MUCH."

– *Congratulations on Everything*, Theo Hendra

Right in the middle of interviewing new wait staff, Jeremy got a call telling him that Patty's husband had died. It was a complete shock. It was also, as far as Jeremy was concerned, the absolute worst time for something like that to happen. Not that he blamed anyone: he made very clear, over and over, that he didn't.

"This is really sad. I feel terrible for Patty. What utterly shitty timing, though."

Worse, it had happened at the cottage. Patty and Shawn were there for a belated wedding anniversary, and on their very first night, when she came back from a short walk along the road – it was too cold for swimming – she found him dead on the ground, a few steps from the front door, roses scattered everywhere like blood. He still had two or three flowers in his hand. At first, she thought he'd tripped and banged his head against one of the dragons, but after the ambulance arrived and his body got swarmed by paramedics, it was quickly determined that he'd had a sudden and very severe heart attack, and was likely dead before he hit the ground. The paramedic who told her this was relatively inexperienced when it came to death, and thought the information would make her feel better.

It was Patty's sister Rebecca who called Jeremy with the news. She called again the next day to say that Patty was feeling bad about missing her shifts.

"Tell her to not think about it for another second. How is she?"

Rebecca let out a long sigh. "We'll get through it. It's all been such a shock. I know *I* won't sleep tonight. I've been on my feet since I first got the call. You must be used to that, because of where you work, being on your feet all day, but not me."

She seemed to enjoy talking on the phone, even to a relative stranger, and told Jeremy about how her own husband had died over a decade earlier from a cold he'd picked up in Mexico that turned into pneumonia. He'd barely been sniffing on the flight home. Within two weeks, he was gone.

"It feels like a thousand years ago now. Isn't that strange? Something big like that, and now it's so far off? I remember, though, that I had nobody helping me at all. I'm just glad I can be here for Patty so she doesn't have to do what I did."

"Listen, tell Patty that if there's anything I can do, that any of us can do . . ."

"She's sleeping right now," she said tersely, as if Jeremy had demanded she go right away and shout the offer in her ear.

Jeremy got the staff together at the end of the night to tell them what had happened. He made everyone put their drinks down and turn off their phones for a moment of silence. They all looked at the floor as they took in the news. The dishwasher kept asking people around him who Shawn was.

"Losing someone you've spent your life with," Jeremy said, "that's just about the biggest boot to the balls there is."

Maybe because of the details about the wedding anniversary and the roses, the story of Shawn's death got around. It made the local paper. People kept telling Jeremy they'd heard about it from someone else, with slightly different details. Some heard that he'd drowned, that he'd taken Patty out for a romantic canoe ride and gone over the side. His parents left a message, saying how awful they felt when they heard the news.

Marie heard about it, too, and she called him at the bar.

"Is that the Patty who was always very chatty?"

"That's her. We're trying to give her some space right now."

"Brian says he heard it was at some kind of staff retreat. That doesn't make sense."

"There's a lot of nonsense flying around. I don't even know why it's such a big story, to be honest. Is there nothing else going on in people's lives?"

Stuart called to say his office would be sending flowers.

"Is there anything else we need to do around this? Is the bar doing anything that I need to know about?"

"Not that I know of. Not yet, anyway. We'll probably

have something here after the funeral, but I haven't heard any details about that yet."

"Where did it happen? At a cabin somewhere?"

"Something like that. I haven't spoken to Patty yet. What an awful thing, though, eh?"

Within a day or two, the truth about the cottage came out, and Jeremy started getting calls from Stuart, all of which he ignored. Having figured out that the place existed, Stuart quickly worked out how it had been paid for. The bookkeeper called him to say the lawyer had been on the phone with her for an hour, demanding that she send him, right away, the bar's complete and authentic financial details, including all of the details concerning the purchase of the cottage, and that failure to do so would result in him putting in motion charges of professional fraud. As it was, he told her, she was fired, effective immediately.

"We'll see about that," Jeremy said, though he knew there was not much he could do about it at that point. "He's not the boss, whatever he thinks."

She was in tears, and barely able to speak, though she mustered enough anger to call Stuart a *goddamned queer*.

Jeremy sighed. "Come on, now. There's enough trouble going on here without you bringing more ugliness into it."

She began screaming at him over the phone, calling him a drunk and an asshole and suggesting he was probably a goddamned queer, too. With some relief over the fact that she had provided him with the perfect excuse for not trying to save her job, he hung up on her shouting voice.

He got a few angry calls from his father, and ignored those, too. The voice mails gave him the gist: Gord wanted all of the money they had ever put into the bar returned to them immediately. All of it. He could hear his mother yelling in the background. He decided to wait a few days before calling back – he figured that once they'd calmed down a little, he could probably convince them to accept a part-ownership in the cottage, instead of cash. After all, land up there would ultimately be worth more in the end, and in the meantime, they'd have a place to go in the summer whenever they felt like it, free of charge. If he could just wait out their anger, he was sure he could work everything out so that everyone benefitted. There was no point in going into panic mode.

Marie and Brian were trickier. His sister called him to demand the same thing: the immediate return of all the money that had been put into the bar. She *knew* he could not be trusted, she said. She knew it, and now Brian knew it, too.

"I can't believe you two were pulling this shit behind my back. I'm actually shaking. That money isn't yours. This is theft, pure and simple."

If he did not return the money, she said, Stuart had already offered to buy out their share of the bar. In fact, she might just go ahead and let him do that – she honestly didn't want to have anything to do with Jeremy for a while.

"Oh, and by the way, we're finally having someone come in – someone who actually knows what he's doing – to fix some of the mess made by your good friend Benny, that pig."

She said she felt like making Jeremy pay for the work, too, since he'd been the one who recommended the dirty old creep in the first place.

Right away, he sent her a series of texts saying that he was preparing an invoice for all of the free meals and free drinks she and her fucking husband had enjoyed at the bar, and for the wages of the floor staff who'd spent countless fucking hours scraping clean their tables after they'd been smeared and scratched by her fucking kids. They'd need to pay *that* before she could expect one penny from him. In addition, he wrote, since Brian clearly had the balls of a lamb, she probably should've gone ahead and fucked Benny when she had the chance. Might've been a learning experience.

He could not think of single scenario where sending the messages made things better, but he felt happy for having done so.

The first thing he did was go to the bank to talk to one of the account managers. They couldn't quite understand what it was he was asking: he wanted to change, not the account, but the account *number*? Same details as before, just a new account, technically at least? "And only I have access to it," he said. To him, it was as simple as switching the number on a door. The account manager didn't see it that way, and brought in *her* manager, a short man who asked Jeremy to explain it all to him again.

"Are you trying to hide the account?" the account manager's manager asked. "This is a business account?"

Not *hide* it, Jeremy explained. Just make it so only he had access again, just like it had been when he'd first opened the account. It wasn't hiding if he'd done nothing wrong. The manager's manager did not agree. And so Jeremy left, saying he'd be shutting down the account altogether, in that case – not right away, because he didn't have the goddamned time, but soon.

The next thing he did was send his mother an email with a photo of the cottage in the fall, surrounded by painted leaves and with the late sun hitting it like it'd been placed there by the photographer. At the very least, they'd have to acknowledge what a beautiful spot it was.

"The rats are circling," he told Glenn that night at the bar, and raised his glass.

"They always are."

Jeremy bought Glenn a beer, then gave him a quick overview of some of the bar's current business troubles, omitting the details about the money that had been intended for his parents and the fact that the cottage was in the Shack's name. Then he came to the point: he needed people who knew and loved the place to come in with some support, and the first person he'd thought of was Glenn. They could work out the details in terms of partnerships or co-ownerships or whatever they chose to call it – these things were all just words, convenient labels – but the basic idea would be for Glenn to put a little skin in the game.

"Think about it this way: you'll drink for free here from now on."

Glenn said he liked that part, but there was no way he could do it. He was already having to tread water as hard as he could to keep his own business afloat, he wasn't about to take on another one. Not to mention – and this was really the deciding factor – he'd discovered long ago that mixing business and pleasure was exactly as bad a plan as people always said.

"You believe that?"

"Some things are a cliché for a reason."

Jeremy said he understood, and told the bartender to give Glenn another beer on the house. Then he went back into the kitchen, and almost gave the dishwasher a heart attack by kicking a box of industrial detergent across the room, rupturing the jugs inside.

Patty appeared in the bar a few days later. Jeremy had to will himself not to react to the way she looked. She had lost weight, her skin sagged over her skeleton. She wore jeans and a black sweatshirt, and her face was devoid of make-up. Her hair was everywhere. As soon as she walked in, he got up from where he was sitting, going through overdue invoices. He gave her a long hug, directed her to a table, and brought her coffee and a glass of water.

"I feel like all I do now is thank people," she said. "There's been so much going on, I can barely put two thoughts together. When I got in the car just now, it took me a moment to remember where everything was. Seat belt, steering wheel, gas pedal, brake, turn signal – okay, got it. Now how do I actually start the darned thing?"

"I bet you drove like a champ."

"My sister wanted to drive me here herself. Actually, she didn't want me to come at all, but I can't sit at home anymore. I keep waking up in the morning and wondering where Shawn is. I'll think, *What's he doing up so early?* And then I remember, and I have to get up and out of the bed right away."

She sounded cheerful, as though she were only relating how she'd fared during a power outage. She looked undeniably older. It wasn't just her hair or her skin: she seemed disconnected from the present. One eye was trained on some invisible past. Jeremy had watched this happen with his grandmother a decade earlier, just before she died. Eventually, both eyes became focused on the invisible, and it was almost impossible to talk to her. Then it was over.

"I feel like I haven't been here for months," she said. "I

miss this place! I really do. Has Charlene come back? I was hoping to see her."

"She pulled the cord for good, I think. She'll be fine, though, whatever she does. I left her a message to tell her what happened."

"I worry about her."

"She'll be fine. You worry about yourself."

Patty became frustrated, and sadness began to seep out through her face. "That's all I've been doing, Jeremy!" She recovered quickly, and smiled at him. "I'm so sorry. You must think I'm such a mess. I should get going before I fall apart completely like some old crazy lady."

"Don't even think about it. Seriously. To be honest, I should be the one apologizing."

"What for?"

"Because . . . the cottage. The whole thing."

She slapped his hand. "Jeremy! Absolutely not! Letting us go out there was one of the nicest things anyone has done for us. We felt just wonderful whenever we went. My Shawn is about as good at relaxing as he is at speaking Chinese, but when he gets out there, he's a different person. He bought me flowers – he never buys me flowers."

"I bet that's not true."

"Oh, what was he thinking sneaking around in the dark getting roses? He must've hidden them in the car. I had no idea! You know what I was thinking the other day? I was thinking that I should've grabbed one of those roses – they all got trampled and left behind, the poor dears. If I'd only thought to grab one and take it with me. Just one. I could've put it in a vase at home."

"I'm imagining you riding in the ambulance, holding a rose."

"Oh, true. I would've looked completely bonkers."

Before she left, she insisted on ducking into the kitchen to say hello to Tyler. They found him chopping celery furiously enough to make them both recoil a little at the sight of the bright blade coming down so close to his bandaged hand. He stopped when he saw Patty, then disappeared into the back of the kitchen. When he returned, he was carrying a heavy uncooked lasagna in a glass casserole dish.

"You just have to put it in the oven," he said, and held it out for Patty, who broke down and was unable to speak. Jeremy took the dish and led her to the back door of the kitchen and around to the parking lot. By the time she got to the car, she had recovered, and asked him to thank Tyler for her, and to apologize for being so rude as to not do so herself.

"He picks his moments, doesn't he?" Jeremy said.

"I feel so stupid."

"Then you're in the right place."

"He must think I've gone crazy," she said brightly as she wiped her eyes. "I think I have, too, almost. There's been so much running around, so many people coming and going – I know this sounds wrong, but it's almost like planning a wedding. Isn't that crazy? It won't be as expensive as one, at least."

She laughed, and Jeremy made himself laugh, too, though he began to wonder if finding her husband dead on the ground had cracked something inside her. He put the lasagna on the back seat of the car, and covered it with a jacket that was sitting there.

"Listen, if you need any money, or if things get tight, just let me know. There were a few people here talking about raising some money to help you get through the next little while or pay for anything that comes up."

She shook her head. "Tell everyone thank you, but I would feel terrible taking money for something like this, especially when there's the insurance. It's worth quite a bit, apparently. That's according to Rebecca, anyway. Knock on wood. My Shawn always made sure he had everything covered, and that I would be taken care of."

"That's really good news," Jeremy said. "Thank God for Shawn, eh? So there's a lot coming? From the insurance?"

"I haven't had a chance to really think about it yet. But Rebecca thinks there will be. We'll see."

"Very glad to hear it. Don't spend it all in one place. In the meantime, you let us know how we can help."

Patty nodded. She stared at the Shack with a slight smile on her face, as if she were seeing the place for the first time in decades.

"I used to get so *upset* when things went wrong here," she said. "It's been nice to be somewhere where nothing matters."

———————

Shawn's funeral was held at a church on a leafy street in Patty's neighbourhood. Jeremy had trouble parking, and had to wedge the Jeep in between two SUVs. He hit the curb faster than he'd intended, spooking two old people walking slow and wearing black. The minister welcomed everyone and read a short prayer that most people mumbled along to. Then Shawn's brother, a man who looked like he'd been bred solely for the purpose of heavy lifting, got up and made a short speech that made Jeremy think the two men hadn't had much contact since childhood. Aside from a small joke about them sharing beds as kids whenever cousins came to stay, there was almost nothing to suggest they'd spent any significant time in the same room. Shawn's mother, who looked as though she ate only spider webs and milkweed pods, was walked onto the stage by Shawn's brother and an usher, but didn't say anything. She just stared down at the front pews with a slight smile, as if it were her birthday and she were waiting for cake.

From his seat at the back of the church, Jeremy could see a few people from the Shack scattered around the church, a couple of servers and at least one bartender. There were some regulars in the crowd, too: Phil was sitting in the same back-row pew, though at the opposite end of it from Jeremy. The dishwasher was there, which surprised him. The rest were all grey-haired men and women. He couldn't see Charlene anywhere. He had texted her the details, but heard nothing back.

A man with a red face stood up at the front holding a few sheets of paper. He was mostly bald, and so tall that it seemed like he had shot up and broken through the fringe of hair around his ears. After getting his papers in the right order, and mouthing a few things to a group of teenage boys who'd been sitting next to him – his kids, Jeremy assumed – he introduced himself as Patty and Shawn's son.

"Shakespeare," he began, but then faltered: something his boys were doing had distracted him, and he gave them a helpless glare. "The great writer William Shakespeare said that it is a wise father who knows his own child. My father knew me, I think. I've had a lot of challenges in my life, and have had to make a lot of adjustments, but I think I was able to do this because he was an example to me. I am proud to be his son. I thank our Lord for making my father a wise man. And I thank Him for helping me face the many challenges I have. I think I'm a different kind of father than my father was, but that doesn't mean I'm better, or that he's worse. Just different."

The son asked for everyone in the room to join him in a moment of quiet prayer. The minister sitting behind him seemed surprised by this and stood quickly, as if insisting on jurisdiction. He even began, "Thank you, oh Lord . . ." before remembering that the prayer requested was a silent one.

A teenager with an acoustic guitar sang something, and there was tentative applause after he finished, no one being sure if it was okay to clap at a funeral. The boy then accompanied two younger girls in flouncy dresses who sang a duet that Jeremy couldn't make out a single word of, because both mumbled into the fronts of their dresses. That got more applause in the end, which Jeremy thought was unfair: the boy had been better on his own. He assumed Patty would not say anything. How could anyone keep it together under those circumstances? What person could stand and speak about their dead husband or wife while the heavy evidence of their passing lay right there in front of them? But after the singing and a few more words from the minister, Rebecca stood and helped her sister to the microphone.

"Oh well," Patty said, looking around the room. She looked even more detached and colourless than when she'd come to the Shack. She seemed to be aging a year for each day she went without her husband. Jeremy looked down the row at Phil, who was staring up at her with a broad smile as if she were his own mother.

"It was lovely to hear all this singing. Shawn always said he couldn't carry a tune, but every once in a while, if he was in a good mood, he'd start in with that 'Just a Gigolo' song."

A couple of people nodded in recognition.

"Imagine my Shawn as a gigolo – he wouldn't have made much money, that's for sure."

People laughed.

"He drove me crazy sometimes with that song. I always said, *I don't remember marrying a gigolo. I'd know if I did!* Imagine Shawn as a gigolo! He wouldn't have made much money at it, that's for sure."

There was less laughter the second time. Someone ahead of Jeremy made a sympathetic noise. Patty looked down at the body of her husband for the first time since she'd started speaking. The awkward smile she had on shivered a little and dissolved as she looked at the lifeless face that had been her companion for decades. Rebecca seemed ready to bring her sister back to her seat, but she quickly recovered.

"I was a teacher for almost 40 years, and if there's one thing I learned, it's that you have to roll with whatever gets thrown at you. You never know what kind of nonsense you're going to have to deal with on Monday morning, so just take a deep breath, wear a smile, and make sure you have some white wine in the fridge at home."

A small group of women, likely peers from Patty's teaching days, gave a communal chuckle. Someone clapped.

"Losing my Shawn like this, it's the worst possible thing, but I am just going to have to roll with it, like everything else. What else can I do?"

The question didn't sound rhetorical: she wanted an answer, and the silence that followed seemed to demand one. She leaned away from the microphone instead of stepping back, so Rebecca put her hands on her sister's shoulders and guided her to her seat. A few other people spoke, but only briefly. A man who'd worked in Shawn's office told a story about the two of them attending a conference in Montreal decades before, getting lost, and going AWOL for half the day. He said it was one of the most fun days of his life. Someone else, a family friend, spoke about how Shawn took up hiking late in life, and how everyone was surprised at how dedicated he was to it. Shawn never made a big thing out of whatever he was doing, the friend said. He wasn't the type who showed off his new car, or forced you to look at pictures of his grandkids all the time. "Most people didn't even know he *had* grandkids." Jeremy saw Patty's son bow his head a little at this. "Shawn didn't brag, but you knew he was proud of all these things, anyway. And the thing he was proudest of was his marriage to Patty. A lot of people have trouble with their marriages here and there, everybody, but he and Patty were always just so solid. It was an inspiration."

There was some applause. The minister said something, and people began moving in the aisles.

"That was pretty painless," Jeremy said to Phil after the coffin had been carried out, with Patty and her sister and everyone else drawn up the aisle in its wake. People were milling around in the lobby, not sure what to do next. "I'm impressed she got through it all in one piece."

Phil shook his head in awe. "I don't think I've ever seen anyone handle herself so well. She's so strong."

"Cheers to that. Let's see what they've got for coffee."

The basement of the church was warm and dry, everything was carpeted, and the food and drinks laid out on a group of long tables looked half-decent. Jeremy bypassed the sandwiches, not wanting to eat in such close proximity to death, and poured himself a coffee, which was – happily, surprisingly – hot and fresh. Stern-looking elderly ladies stood nearby to replenish the trays and refill the pots.

One noticed the basket of creams was nearly empty, and disappeared to find more without a word. "I should get them working for me," Jeremy said to no one in particular. There was swing music coming from somewhere. It felt like intermission at a concert or a school play. He looked around to see where Patty was, and spotted her standing near the entrance with a large knot of people around her, as if she were a visiting celebrity. Right next to her was Phil, standing close enough to link arms.

Jeremy wandered through the crowd, smiling and nodding at all the old folks in black, few of whom smiled back. He introduced himself to Rebecca, and thanked her for letting him know what had happened. She was standing a little ways away from the crowd around her sister.

"I feel like I am at one of these every month now," she said. "I don't even put my black dress away. I'm seeing people here that I only ever see at funerals, and it's like we're friends. When my husband died, we were all still young enough that we didn't know what to do. It's like it's become a part-time job now. We're professionals."

"It's good, though, being able to say goodbye all together like this."

"I didn't say it was bad."

"Let me get you a coffee. On the house."

He brought her a cup, and she said she was sorry she had not yet visited the Shack – her sister was always going on about it, and she'd always meant to. He promised her a tour of the kitchen. "I've always been curious about what goes on back there," she said. "Do I want to know?"

"It's like a Wilderness Safari tour: you have to keep the windows up and your hands inside the car."

He said hello to the staffers who had stuck around,

including the dishwasher, whose name Jeremy struggled in vain to remember. After he had crossed the room twice, he found himself back near the crowd around Patty, waiting for an opportunity to pay his respects – he kept hoping she might spot him there and break out of the pack herself. Someone touched him on the elbow, and he turned to find Charlene standing next to him and smiling. Just behind her was Kyle, looking far less happy. Before he could say anything, she moved in to give him a hug. It was the closest they'd been to each other since the night of his birthday, more than a year ago. The smell of her hair was instantly familiar. He told her he was glad to see her.

"I wasn't sure you would be," she said.

He shrugged this off and reached around her to shake Kyle's hand.

"How're you holding up, buddy?"

"What does that mean?" Kyle shot back.

"Nothing at all. Hey: the coffee's not bad here, considering. You should try it."

He hoped Kyle would move off to sample the food tables for a while, leaving them alone to talk. Instead, he rooted himself in place like a bodyguard, arms folded and scanning the room with suspicious eyes, looking for potential trouble.

"This is so sad," Charlene said.

"It could be worse – the food looks good. People seem to be enjoying it."

"I mean about Patty."

"Oh no, that's awful. Just unbelievable. It happened out at the cottage, too – did you hear that? I'm starting to regret buying it. It's like it's cursed or something." He looked at Kyle when he said it.

"How is everybody?" Charlene asked quickly. "How's Tyler? Is he here?"

"Tyler is Tyler – you know. He's back at work, at least. With a damaged wing."

Kyle shifted around, looking uncomfortable. "We should get going," he said to Charlene.

She ignored him. "Have you talked to Patty yet? I tried, but there were a lot of people."

"She was in last week, and was asking about you. She's a tough one, isn't she? Why don't you come by the Shack tonight? We're having a sort of informal wake. Nothing depressing, just a few people coming by for a drink. You should come."

"You're going to the bar?" Kyle asked Charlene. His voice was tense.

"You're welcome too, there, buddy. The more the merrier."

"I don't know," Charlene said. "I might."

"There's a chill room now, if that helps."

Charlene smiled. "Are you serious? You finally did it?"

"Are you crazy? It's *all* a chill room, as far as I'm concerned."

"Charlene," Kyle said.

"Come for one drink, at least. On the house. Seriously."

"I don't know about tonight," Kyle said.

"Why not?" Jeremy asked, unable to hide his annoyance. "Someone we know died, we're at a funeral, maybe it would be nice to relax a little after. It's not like this happens every week. I promise there'll be no *swimming* involved."

Kyle's body visibly tightened. He announced that he was leaving, then turned and moved quickly through the room. As he was about to go through the door, a woman from the church stopped him to let him know there was plenty of food left if he was hungry. The response she got seemed to surprise and confuse her.

Jeremy apologized to Charlene. "I'm sorry, that was me being shitty. Was he your ride?"

"It's fine. We're not together," she said. There was a note of finality in her voice.

"What do you mean? How did you get here?"

"I mean, we're not *together*-together. I've been staying with my mother."

She told him she'd moved out of their apartment weeks ago. She and Kyle had been fighting so much lately, which was not that unusual, except that they had begun to say things to each other that were so toxic and harmful, it felt like a mere technicality that they were not physically assaulting each other. She convinced him they needed a break, and so she moved into her mother's apartment, and had been sleeping on a fold-out couch – her old room was now the TV room, and had no room left in it for a bed. She had asked Kyle to come with her to the funeral because she didn't want to be alone and wasn't sure if anyone from the Shack would talk to her, but other than that, they'd hardly seen each other.

"Yikes, a fold-out couch."

"Have you seen that documentary about the killer whale that goes crazy and kills its trainer? There's this whole thing about the tiny pens they keep them in. That's me right now."

Jeremy wondered if he should invite her to stay at his house, but had no idea how such an invitation would be received.

"So, a break? That's it?"

Reluctantly, she admitted it was maybe more. "He keeps saying he wants to work on things, but all I can think about when I'm with him now is how good it would be to hit him really hard. Like, in the face." She burst out laughing. "Sorry. I was just picturing it."

Jeremy made a shocked noise.

"I've been feeling so shitty since I heard about Shawn," she said. "I wanted to call Patty, or at least call you, but I thought you'd all be mad at me."

"Not a chance."

She smiled. "That's a lie. You always lie to make people feel better. I didn't even really notice it until after I left."

"I don't think I lie."

"It's not a criticism, I'm just saying you do. It's sort of sweet, in a weird way. Anyway, I know I was a total bitch to you, leaving like that. I'm sorry."

He dismissed her apology with a wave of his hand. "Everyone goes into the ditch once in a while."

"You're lying again."

"No, that one's true. You can set your clock by it. Some people go in and never come out."

They stood and watched Patty smiling and chatting with the people surrounding her. They all seemed more sombre than the widow. Jeremy laughed when the dishwasher finally broke through the crowd to shake Patty's hand. She smiled and accepted his presumably kind words, and only let her confusion show after he'd moved off.

"There was something else," Charlene said, not looking at Jeremy. "It's really embarrassing, but I want you to know. You know the day I quit? When I called in so late?"

"You don't have to say sorry for that. Water under the bridge."

"That's not what I was going to say." She stopped and looked through the crowd in the direction in which Kyle had disappeared. "I was late because I wasn't calling from home."

"Where were you calling from?"

"Someone else's home."

She watched his face and waited for the meaning of her words to sink in. It finally did.

"It was someone I'd known a long time ago, and ran into totally by accident. His name's Jesse."

"Jesse. Okay."

"Kyle knows. I don't actually feel bad about it. I felt rotten at the time, but I think I was just embarrassed."

"It happens. Obviously."

"I wasn't embarrassed about that," she said. "Or not exactly." She screwed up her face. "It's because I slept in. *We* slept in. He told me we had to get up early, but we slept in. And then I had to hide in the bedroom while he got his daughter ready for daycare. She didn't know I was there, and he didn't want her to know. So I had to hide until he left with her. I've never felt so . . . gross. Like I was this dirty thing that could not be seen."

"Interesting."

She laughed. "*Interesting?*"

"I opened my mouth and said a word. That was the one that came out." He paused. "Come tonight. You should be there."

"I'll try. I need to go home first."

"Home?"

"My mother's."

"Right. Try to come."

He was about to say something else when a huge crash

made them both jump. There was chaos and devastation at the food table: one of the elderly church volunteers had burned her arm on the big coffee pot and knocked it over, shattering it and spilling it contents. A steaming brown slick was spreading quickly across the floor in all directions. Another volunteer was trying to get her upright, and in her efforts managed to knock over another pot, instantly ruining two trays of sandwiches. The men and women standing nearby weren't sure what to do with themselves – the service had made them passive and reflective. They backed away from the spreading lake of coffee, while a few of the smaller kids edged up right to it, daring the mess to spoil their good shoes. The injured woman, who looked like she was about to pass out, was guided across the room to the exit and out to the ladies' room. Right away, Jeremy walked through the crowd to the centre of the mess and asked where the mop was. He told the one church volunteer who was left to gather together the unspoiled sandwiches on a single tray, like survivors of a flood. She went slowly, trying to put like with like – egg salad with egg salad, tuna with tuna. As he sloshed the mop through the lake of coffee, Charlene brought out a fresh pot.

Patty walked up to the table just as they were putting everything right. She had Phil in tow, though the rest of the well-wishers had finally exhausted themselves and scattered. She smiled at Jeremy, and reached out to touch his shoulder. "I'm so lucky to know you," she said. Her voice was rough.

"*I'm* the lucky one," he said. "No joke."

"These are really good," Phil said, holding up a half-eaten blueberry muffin. "Pat?"

Patty looked down and seemed surprised to see trays

of food there. She had the impassive expression of a judge at a county fair. She rested her finger on the corner of one tray as if activating a display. The sandwiches – egg salad – stirred something in her mind, and she smiled. "My Shawn is allergic to eggs," she said. "That's what he always tells me, anyway. I used to always make him scrambled eggs when we first got married. I made him scrambled eggs with brown toast, which was a new thing. Then at some point, he announced he was allergic."

She looked at Jeremy, Charlene, and the church volunteer in turn, as if waiting for them to process the story thus far.

"These are good, too, Pat," Phil said through a mouthful of carrot muffin.

"I think what it was, was he was out late with some of his work friends and woke up feeling sick. It wasn't the eggs, it was the beer. But you know him, he won't ever admit to that."

Patty tapped on the edge of the tray. It rattled slightly, and a few of the sandwich wedges tipped over. The volunteer looked concerned, but didn't move to right them.

"It was just pride. Stupid pride. Like when he drove us into a ditch that time – I didn't see any raccoon, but he swears there was one. He would never admit he had fallen asleep. And my poor little boy in the back – he was scared to go in the car for a long time. I always told him I never blamed him, but I don't think he believed me. He said it was a raccoon." She looked straight at the volunteer, who seemed too shocked to even breathe. "It would've been wonderful to have a little girl."

A man in a black suit shuffled up to the food tables and began to inspect the trays. He didn't appear to notice Patty. "There's muffins now," he said.

That night, Jeremy went behind the bar himself, and started pouring drinks for the small group huddled around. It took him a while to find the right music, and finally settled on Johnny Cash, which turned out to be a stroke of genius. They all sang along to the tunes they knew. Some knew more than others. Jeremy was happy to see people enjoying themselves. Phil arrived after a while, saying that he'd gone back to Patty's house, where there'd been a small, informal dinner for the family and a few close friends. He left after he realized there was only wine, and on the way out knocked over a tray of sandwiches that had been brought from the church. They spilled all over the living room carpet.

Jeremy said, "That's good, you giving her something else to think about today."

He felt as though bees were swarming in his head, and took two long sips from his glass to settle them down. There was a moment, pouring out house white for someone, when he almost lost his grip on the bottle, and wine spilled across the bar – he got a towel on the spill before it spread too far. They all sang "Ring of Fire" together, while Jeremy played an invisible guitar. Tyler appeared, and Jeremy insisted he sit at the bar and accept a pint of Guinness, the cook's favourite. "Just don't tell me I'm pouring it wrong or I swear to God I'll break the glass over your head."

He came out from behind the bar to check his phone, which had been buzzing periodically throughout the night. There were new messages from Stuart, telling him he was meeting with Brian and Marie the next day at his law office. His parents would be there, too. He told Jeremy that this was a private meeting, and that he would fill him in later on what they all decided. Stuart also sent an email, saying he would be meeting with Susan Toller in the next few days, and that the two of them would be visiting the Shack. He would let Jeremy know the date and time as soon as they were able to firm it up. Obviously, he said, he could not prevent Jeremy from being there when they visited, but he was sure he would agree that it might be less awkward for everyone if he wasn't. Jeremy said "fuck you" into his phone as the message ended, and dropped the device behind the bar, feeling nothing but disgust for the way some people, at a moment of grief and tragedy, revealed themselves to be nothing more than cheap little assholes.

There was a moment of weirdness, as things were getting late, when a man appeared, wearing a green track jacket and looking rough. He only came a few steps into the bar, and stood near the front door, staring at the group. Jeremy didn't even notice him at first, until someone pointed him out. "Private event, buddy! Private event!" Jeremy shouted, and moved to come out from behind the bar. As soon as he did, the man turned and went back through the doors without acknowledging he'd been spoken to. "Was that the Ghost of Christmas Past?" Jeremy asked. Within a minute, the buzz of conversation resumed, smoothing over and obliterating the intrusion like a wave on a beach.

Jeremy got two beers and two vodka shots from the bartender and brought them over to where Phil was sitting. They both downed the shots, followed by long gulps of beer.

Jeremy raised his empty shot glass, and Phil did the same.

"To Patty and Shawn!"

"To Patty. Aren't you supposed to do a toast *before* you drink?"

Jeremy fingered Phil's collar. "We're both in suits, we can do whatever we want."

He asked how Patty had seemed after the funeral, and Phil told him she'd run around saying hello to everyone and making sure they all got food. There was a lot of food in her house, but no one was in the mood to eat it, except him – he took every sandwich he got offered. Her sister finally got her to put down the trays, but she kept moving from room to room, determined to give everyone an equal and generous share of her attention. He said he thought it maybe hadn't all hit Patty yet, that she was running on autopilot.

"She's got all these distractions right now, but they'll go away," Jeremy said. "What she needs is to keep focused on new things. I was actually going to talk to her, once everything settled down, to suggest she maybe stash some of that insurance cash away where the tax people can't find it."

"Away where?"

Jeremy pointed around the room. "The Ice Shack Savings & Loan."

While Phil puzzled over this, Jeremy talked about all the ways that money could be kept safe and even grow in a business like his. There were a thousand ways, millions. And investing in the bar might be exactly the kind of thing she needed to get involved with right now. After all, she had a kind of family at the Shack, not to mention her final hours with her husband had been at a cottage that was technically owned by the bar, which he had been letting them use whenever they wanted.

"I'm not saying she *owes* me anything – she doesn't, not one dollar. I'm only saying this could be good for her, and that there's already a strong connection here. And maybe, after reaping all the rewards of working here, maybe it's time to give a little back. Just a thought. I'll see what she says. Anyways."

"Sure, but . . ." Phil struggled for the right words. "She's having a pretty rough time of it right now. I don't know if that's something she's going to want to get involved with."

"Pretty sure I said it could wait until the dust settles. Maybe *dust* is the wrong word. What's that song? 'Dust in the Wind'?"

He began to sing it.

Phil gripped his glass tighter as if to root himself in place. "You can't ask her for money. Her husband just died."

"Yes? And?" Jeremy took a breath and tried to sound conciliatory. "Look, if you don't think she'd be into it, that's fine. I'm just trying to help. What are you, her business manager, buddy? She can always say no."

"It's not that she wouldn't give it to you. She probably would."

"How do you know that?"

Phil, looking embarrassed, admitted that Patty had offered to loan him some of the insurance money to get a place of his own, so his daughter could stay over more. She said she never liked the idea of his poor daughter sleeping on a cot in some basement. She would loan him the money for as long as he needed it.

Jeremy laughed and slapped the bar. He reached over to clink glasses.

"Jesus, you move fast!" He'd been wondering whether he should ask her to throw a little insurance cash at the bar, and here was Phil looking to get *adopted*.

"I told her *no*."

"You did? Well then you're a fucking idiot, and you deserve to live in your sister's basement. Christ's sake."

Jeremy got up and went back behind the bar to select some more music. He put on a novelty rap song from the '80s and threatened to breakdance right there behind the bar while people laughed and yelled for him to change it. He finally switched it to Elvis Presley singing "Suspicious Minds." As the music played, he wrung his hands and stared hard at a grinning troll doll with wild hair that'd been placed among the booze behind the bar years ago and never removed. He fingered the keys on his belt. The bartender said something about a keg sending up nothing but beer-flavoured foam. Here it was again: it was his job to fix everything, to keep the ship afloat, to be Very Zen, and when the time came to give back a little, *boom*: everyone disappeared. He grabbed the troll doll by the throat and dropped it in the garbage, then killed the music and climbed up onto a full case of beer that was on the floor. He demanded quiet, and waited until his request was fulfilled.

"I know that Shawn, of all people, would appreciate all this joking around, given the occasion. Patty would, too. I'm sure of it. Those of you who were not there today really missed something. She was up there, and she was not about to get knocked down – she took the hardest hit you can possibly take, and still had the strength to laugh about it. I knew Patty was tough, but what I saw made me think there's probably not a lot you could throw at her that she couldn't handle. What a pro."

A few people said, "*Here, here.*"

"I wish she were here so I could tell her this to her face, but I wanted also to say that it's been a personal honour to have had Patty here as one of the team, one of the family. As far as the future goes, she may even be involved in other ways, who knows. Door's always open. If anyone sees her before I do, tell her that: the door's always open. Actually, I should lock it before that creep in the green jacket comes in again." There was laughter. "Seriously, though, watching her tough her way through what is probably the worst time of her life just reminds me what *this* place is all about." He got quiet and began to speak more slowly and deliberately. "We've had a few tragedies here, we lost some good friends, and *almost* lost some others. We will probably lose some more so-called friends for one reason or another, but whatever, good riddance. Seriously. There are a few people running around pissing their pants right now because they're not really part of the family and don't get how we do things here. That's fine. Whatever. The Shack has been through some real shit, *I've* been through some real shit, and I don't sit around feeling sorry for myself. Winners focus on winning because losing takes care of itself. I really believe that, because I'm not a fucking loser. Not like some people I could mention, but I won't."

He raised his glass and nearly drank before quickly adding: "And to Patty, because we love her and wish her the best right now." He stepped down from the beer case, twisting his ankle a little as he did. He decided to ignore the pain and pour himself another generous drink.

A few people came out to the darkened patio to say goodnight to Jeremy, but most just left soon after his speech. The bartender said he would shut everything down, but Jeremy said not to bother.

"Just do your cash-out and leave the rest," he said. "I'll take care of it."

The river below was dark. Corpses could've been floating

by, just under the surface, and he wouldn't have known. He felt like swimming, and wished it were warm enough to go to the cottage. He thought about Shawn face down on the ground, and about Kyle struggling as he was pulled into the boat, and about the kid who'd jumped from the bridge. He had a manic urge to embrace them all, to tell them everything would be fine, to forgive them. Everything that had ever happened at the bar was forgivable. People always shit on him, and he always forgave them. He forgave Glenn for being a cheap, opinionated asshole. He forgave Phil for being Phil. He forgave Benny for some of the half-assed repairs he'd done and for running his mouth. He forgave Tyler for being a sullen little shit. He forgave his parents for overreacting – they were being fed bad information, after all. He could not forgive Brian and his sister, or Stuart, but maybe one day he would. Everything at the Shack was working just fine at the moment. Nothing had gone wrong in weeks. The equipment was humming along without a clank or a rattle. The washrooms got used without complaint. He'd been checking all the mouse traps and rat traps: not a whisker. Even the new fire-alarm system, which he had cursed and tried so hard to prevent coming in, had earned his respect for not going off screaming if the room got too full, as the old one sometimes did. There were reasons for gratitude all around. You just had to look for them. Losing Charlene had been tough – and the fact that she hadn't shown up that night told him she was gone for good – but there were new people coming to the bar all the time. He was always seeing new faces. The crowd would keep turning over and over, they'd get into the weeds and get right back out, better than ever and grateful for the experience. It was all a matter of shifting one's perception.

And he would be fine, he decided. He'd come out of all this a winner, no matter what. He broke off a nearby branch and held it out in front of him like a sword, then flung it out into space as hard as he could. He didn't hear it land over the sound of the river, but for a second, it looked to him as though the water had suddenly frozen, stopped dead.

When Jeremy came back through the patio doors, he discovered a man standing behind the bar: the same man in the green jacket he'd chased out earlier. The man made no move to leave. The way he was standing, he'd clearly heard Jeremy coming, and had let himself be discovered there. His hair was reddish and cut brutally short, like he'd been burned or deloused, and hadn't shaved in a while. He looked to be about the same height as Jeremy, but skinnier. Jeremy worked to commit these details to memory. The green jacket had a stain running from the left shoulder right down to the end of the sleeve, which Jeremy worried was blood. He hoped it wasn't, as that would therefore mean he was dealing with someone who was either crazy or badly hurt, or both. Where the man was standing was the same spot where the floor staff sometimes gathered on busy nights to do a celebratory shot or to gather themselves for a moment before heading back out into the rush.

"I think you need to get moving there, buddy," Jeremy said, trying to make it sound like friendly advice. "We're all closed up."

Without looking, the man reached over and plucked an unopened bottle of vodka from the shelf behind the bar. He put it in his left hand, then reached and grabbed another bottle, again without looking. A fancy mint liqueur. Jeremy nearly told him to pick again: he didn't want the guy coming back later, angry, wanting to exchange it. He

– 275 –

must've known from the shape of the bottle, the feel of the glass neck, that he'd chosen wrong. He looked down at the liqueur as though he'd been handed a baby. The liqueur got replaced, and he reached for another. Rye this time: much better. He tucked the rye under his left arm, then picked up a steak knife from the surface of the bar and held it up to show Jeremy. He held it with the toothy blade pointing at the ceiling – not threatening, just making clear the nature of their current relationship. *This*, the knife declared, *is the difference between you and me at the moment*. The knife didn't look like one of the Shack's; he must've brought it with him.

"You can take those, I won't call the cops," Jeremy said. "Take those, and that'll be the end of it."

In his mind he was willing the man not to notice the security camera in the corner of the ceiling. He was also trying to remember if it was turned on.

"This doesn't have to get ugly, nobody has to get in trouble. I get that things are probably not good right now, and I totally understand. I've got shit going on, too."

The man gave no reaction.

"All I'm trying to say here is that we have options. We've got a choice, and I think we'll make the right choice, right? The right choice isn't easy and it isn't obvious, but we almost always know it when we see it. If you want to take the bottles, you can. I don't give a shit. But if we wait too long right now, though, the alarm is going to go off, and I don't want that to happen."

The man started shifting around and getting nervous, and Jeremy knew immediately that he'd fucked up by mentioning the alarm. Especially since it was a lie – he hadn't activated the alarm.

"Just take the bottle and go. Take two bottles, I can buy more. No harm, no foul."

This is new, Jeremy thought. After decades of working in bars and restaurants, he'd never encountered this exact situation before, and had no basis on which to decide how to respond. He was in entirely new territory. It was a strange comfort, and the very kind of thing he tried in vain to make people understand: boredom was an impossibility when you did what he did. There were no ruts to get stuck in. A place like the Shack would always find ways to pull the rug out from under you. It was only certain kinds of people, like Jeremy and a few others, who knew how to keep their balance when that happened. And that's all he had to do: keep his balance.

"Look," he said, taking a step forward, "a friend of mine died last week, and today was the funeral. I'm a little shook-up, so I promise that if you go now, I won't report it or call the cops."

Wanting to make sure that the cash-out from the previous few nights was in a black zippered bag behind the bar where the bartender would have left it for him, Jeremy took another step toward the man.

"Fucking *back up*."

"Okay, I'm staying right here. I promise I will not take another step if you go right now. You are in the position of power here. Seriously: take the bottles, take more if you want. I'm not moving. You've got the power, I have none. This is my place, I'm the owner, I built it, but you switched it around with one move, and now you're in charge – one hundred percent. No one else is here. You can walk out and I will never see you again, swear to God. Just take the bottles."

Instead of a bottle, the man reached over and picked up

something else from behind the bar: the cash-out bag. He'd probably known it was there the whole time. Or else Jeremy had given himself away by trying to get at it. It was heavy with three nights' worth of credit card receipts and cash – losing it would mean the bar was truly fucked.

Carrying the bag and the bottles, and still pointing the tip of the knife at Jeremy, the man began to cross the floor toward the exit. He was wearing construction boots that were too large for his feet and made a resounding clomp like Frankenstein's monster. As the man passed in front of him, Jeremy lunged forward and made a grab for the bag, thinking he could get it and run into the kitchen and out the back before the creep had a chance to react. Instead, the man took a surprised step back, dropped everything except the knife, and pushed the blade hard into Jeremy's outstretched hand. Before he even had time to scream at the lightning bolt of pain that came shooting up his arm, Jeremy's foot came down on the rolling vodka bottle, and he spun in the air. He saw the ceiling slide past his vision, and the doors to the patio, which were still open, before dropping back down and cracking his head hard on the floor. Something large and pointed dug hard into his hip: a clump of wild keys, splayed out like an anemone. The man grabbed at one of the bottles, but left everything else and clomped out the front doors. Jeremy held out his hand in front of his face, trying to take in the fact of the knife wedged in so deep that the blade, now blackened with blood, stood proud in the centre of his palm. He fought to get his lungs to accept air, his heart to unblur.

———————————

Two ambulance attendants stood just outside the emergency room doors, leaning against the unoccupied stretcher and talking about something that one of them found disturbing, the other amusing. Nearby, a police officer stood looking at his phone with confusion. Inside, Jeremy sat next to Charlene on the hard plastic chairs at the far end of the room, away from the triage nurses who, when they were not dealing with new patients or with doctors, were exchanging stories of difficult pregnancies. It had been Jeremy's idea to move to the corner: the nurses' voices were making his headache worse. Above their heads, the TV had been muted after repeated requests from Jeremy and was replaying scenes from an earlier basketball game in which one of the players, viciously fouled by an opponent, had fallen sideways and snapped his oversized ankle. They kept zooming in on his agonized face while the other players stood around him like sheep baffled by a wolf attack. The two police officers who had already interviewed Jeremy twice that evening were standing near the bathrooms, talking to a nurse who, as far as Jeremy could tell, had nothing whatsoever to do with what was going on. He was still wearing his suit, which was awash in blood. His hand was lost in bandages.

Charlene had shown up at the Shack as they were loading him into the ambulance. She'd gone to her mother's apartment after the funeral and immediately taken off her heavy dress and the rest of her clothes and climbed into her mother's bed. She slept for three hours straight. Her mother woke her up when she got home from work. Charlene lay there and listened as the older woman moved around the apartment, picking up her daughter's clothes and exclaiming at the state of the bathroom. Later, the two of them sat on a small couch in what had once been her childhood bedroom and they ate dinner while watching a show about women who'd had too much plastic surgery. Her mother tsked at the sight of these women and their fright-mask faces, and said she could not understand why anyone would do such a thing. Charlene understood: these were people who hated themselves, and who thought the only way to find happiness was to keep carving themselves up, as if joy lurked somewhere beneath their old cheekbones and their old noses and had to be dug out. She left her mother to watch the rest of the show, while she did the dishes. Kyle had left a series of new messages on her phone; she gave up after the third and deleted the rest without listening to them. As she put away the dishes, she remembered that she had once watched the same show with him, and had told him her theory that addiction to plastic surgery was the result of deep self-loathing. He only said that it had more to do with being so rich you lose all sense of perspective.

Hating yourself was not a matter of perspective, she'd said.

She got dressed and went out, telling her mother not to wait up. There was a bus that would take her past the Shack, but she decided to walk – she didn't feel like being thrown around inside a bus, and felt even less like waiting for it. Seeing the flashing lights outside the bar, she'd run the last two blocks. She saw the dark smear of blood and the chairs and tables that had been knocked over. There was a lone bottle of rye in the middle of the bar floor. One of the police officers gave her a ride to the hospital. They followed the ambulance in silence, never using the siren.

"What a fucking mess," Jeremy said. He didn't even know where his phone was.

Charlene held out an unopened can of Diet Coke she'd bought from the snack machine. She had already offered it twice already.

The ambulance attendants broke the blade of the steak knife and unstuck the handle from the back of his hand. Once they determined that nothing serious had been severed – he could still wiggle his fingers, and the rush of blood had been stopped – it was as though he'd done nothing more serious than cut himself shaving. They hadn't even taken him straight into the room beyond the triage station, but told him to wait. One of the attendants asked if he wanted to keep the broken knife.

"A few dozen stitches and you'll be fine. No concussion, either. You're lucky."

"Luck has nothing to do with it," Jeremy told them.

He wished the display in the corner of the TV were not so diligent at letting him know the time: he wanted to forget how late it was. On the screen was the fouled basketball player again, the ankle, the look of unbelievable pain. His own leg was sore, and he could feel a lump the size of an avocado pit on the back of his head. His keys were gone – the attendants had stripped them off him before lifting him into the ambulance. The adrenaline was draining out of him, and he worried he might pass out – that, at least, might get the nurses and the doctors to move a little faster. How many steak knife injuries were they dealing with that night?

He sat down again on the other side of Charlene so he could not see the TV. She looked exhausted, too. He liked the outfit she was wearing, which wasn't the same one she had on at the funeral.

"I must've done something really shitty in a past life," he said.

"You don't deserve any of this."

"I don't know if *deserve* has anything to do with it. I think I'm just always in the wrong place, wrong time, wrong life. Sorry, I'm whining."

"I think you have a good excuse."

She reached over and held his uninjured hand.

"There was a guy I worked for, when I was maybe 20 or 21," he said after a while. "It was at this place that just could not seem to make money, no matter what the poor fucker did. He was a nice guy, he was trying, but something about where it was, or the look of the place – I don't know. He did all kinds of shit: changed the menu every few weeks, brought in bands, did all these dumb contests that never worked. I was working bar." He winced at the throb that had started again in his hand. The painkillers were evaporating from his system, and soon he'd have to ask for more. "So people started to leave, all these people who'd been there from the start – gone, one after another. He kept asking me if I was planning to quit. Sometimes it was like he was begging me not to, sometimes he was mad and seemed like he was ready to fire me on the spot."

"Did you quit finally?"

"I never got the chance. I came in one morning to get my paycheque, before the place opened, and there was nobody there. I had keys, so I let myself in and went behind the bar to get a coffee. I'm standing there, and I hear this moaning – scared the absolute shit out of me. I don't even believe in ghosts, but hearing that made me jump. So I go look, and there's my boss at the bottom of the stairs. He'd been in there all night by himself, drinking his face off, and then fell down the stairs. There was blood coming out of his ears."

"Oh my God."

"I know. So I call an ambulance, and I'm down there trying to keep him awake, talking about whatever shit comes into my head – I think I started telling him about *Ghostbusters*, because I'd just seen the movie. I'm like, *There's these three guys who fight ghosts. They have these packs on their backs, and laser guns, and they hire a black guy and drive a cool, old car.* I think he actually got interested at one point. Who knows what he was thinking."

Charlene had to push her fist into her teeth to keep herself from laughing. "I think you told me this one."

"I probably did. So that was it, my last day. The crazy thing is, which I didn't remember until just now – honestly, just as I'm sitting here – is that when I asked him how he fell, he told me he didn't. He said he *jumped*. He was trying to break his neck, and he almost did it. I don't know, I must've blocked that in my mind."

They sat in silence for nearly a minute. Someone turned the volume back up on the TV, and from it came the cry of the fouled basketball player.

"I remembered to hide the cash-out bag, at least," he said. "That would've been perfect, losing that."

She squeezed his hand.

"I never jumped. Congratulate me."

She did.

"APOLOGIZE FOR WHAT?"

– Theo Hendra, quoted in *USA Today*

In the middle of a cold snap, Jeremy got a call from an OPP officer saying his cottage had been broken into. Of course it had. He nearly laughed. The officer told him he'd been doing a regular patrol along the lake roads when he spotted boot prints in the snow, then broken glass and discarded bottles. The front door had been forced open, and there was mud all over the floor inside, cupboard doors almost snapped right off their hinges, cigarette burns on the counter. This kind of thing happened every once in a while, he assured Jeremy: kids drove out looking for televisions, stereos, and liquor. Some places got nailed two years in a row. If they didn't find anything, they partied and smashed the place up. Once he'd found a kayak out on the ice. Jeremy realized later the officer had been trying to make him feel better. He wondered if the dragons were still intact. The officer didn't mention them, which was strange. You would mention something like a pair of plaster dragons.

They arranged a time to meet to inspect the damage, the officer assuring Jeremy that no one would be going inside the cottage before they got there. It was sealed up with police tape, and he was personally doing a drive-by each morning.

The news came as Jeremy was arranging to sell a bunch of the bar equipment in his garage – replacement parts for draft systems and that kind of thing. Someone came out to take away all of it. As he was handing over the cash, he spotted a box full of Theo Hendra books. Jeremy said they belonged to an old girlfriend.

"The guy makes a few good points, actually, if you ignore the wackier stuff. You know anyone who might want them?"

"Not anymore!" the man said, and laughed.

Jeremy nodded. It had come out a while ago that Theo Hendra had been having a long-term affair with his children's nanny. There were rumours of a child that had been kept out of sight and paid for through a secret slush fund of millions that Hendra's accountants had established somewhere. There were further rumours about Hendra forcing his nanny to have multiple abortions, and about whether their relationship had been completely consensual. Hendra's wife, the same Dominique to whom so many of his books were dedicated, was suing him for millions in child support and a generous share of the business. She gave multiple interviews in which she claimed that he'd been an absent father and a neglectful husband, and had furthermore suffered from impotence for most of the past decade. Jeremy saw, read, and heard all of it, and what he didn't see, read, or hear, he was told about by people he knew, who were only too happy to pass it along. His sister kept sending him links to stories. It was all he ever got from her, other than lawyer's letters.

He ended up promising the Theo Hendra books to the woman working the front desk at Stuart's law firm. He was there for a meeting – one of many – and had spotted one of his books on her desk. It looked new. She said she knew about all the shit he'd been up to, but had been thinking for a while about opening her own business one day, and was curious to see if he had any good advice.

"I know there's a lot of tax-type stuff you have to figure out."

"It's about more than that," Jeremy said. He opened his arms, trying to think of a way to explain the breadth of ideas Hendra had to offer, and found he had no words. So he let his arms drop and offered to give her the entire box of books, no charge.

Stuart met with him in the firm's boardroom. It had one long window and a dry-erase board mounted on the wall at the far end. On the opposite wall was a flat-screen TV. The sky outside the window was bright and innocent and blue. On the dry-erase board someone had written the word *capture* in capital letters, plus a bunch of random numbers. There was a framed cartoon on the wall with a smiling man in a suit and a caption that said: "*Being a lawyer is as easy as one, two, fee.*" Stuart offered Jeremy coffee.

"How's the hand?"

"Fine. A little sore, but fine." He forced a smile. "They're calling me Half-Jesus."

He rubbed at the scar. Somehow the blade had gone

clean through without cutting a tendon or chipping a bone, so it healed clean. But it hadn't stopped hurting. The throb woke him up in the night; he would lie awake, riding it out.

"I'm sorry, Jeremy, this has all been so crazy. This isn't how I wanted things to turn out. Nobody did."

"It's fine," he said again, not knowing what else to say.

Stuart talked for a while about how he, like the others, had been mad at first, but eventually he calmed down and came to see it from Jeremy's perspective, at least a little. Not to say that they weren't right to be angry – it had been more than a little underhanded, what he'd pulled, and beyond murky, as far as the law goes – but in the end, it wasn't like he had pocketed the money and run off.

"Or at least," Stuart said, smiling, "you didn't run very far. Brian and I went out to see the cottage, by the way."

"And?"

"And, it's a nice spot. I can see why you picked it. Brian thought it was a little too buggy and rustic, but I kinda liked it. Reminded me of the place my parents rented as a kid."

"Glad to hear it. So what's happening with the bar?"

Stuart's smile disappeared, and he explained there was an offer on the table, but that it wasn't even worth talking about just yet. Once they really got into it, he'd be able to make them go higher.

"Let me see it."

"It's just an opening offer. It's barely even formal. I just wanted to let you know that we are going ahead with this, and that I plan to get as much as we can. For everyone's sake."

"I want to see it."

Stuart reluctantly pulled a sheet of paper out of the folder he had in front of him and handed it over. Jeremy took the paper and held his breath before reading the number. The sheet was a printout of an email exchange between Susan Toller and Stuart. There were all kinds of friendly jokes and references to things that had nothing to do with the Shack. It was almost flirty. And there it was: even lower than the worst-case scenario he'd imagined. Not just a boot to the balls, but a total boot-focused castration.

He handed the paper back across the table. Stuart gestured that he could keep it. It was left orphaned between them.

"I'm honestly a little shocked she would even send this to me," Stuart said. "They know they'll have to go up."

"Tell them yes."

Stuart seemed to relax a little. He'd obviously been expecting a fight. "Well, I've already said we're interested, *in theory*," he said. "I had to, to get them to make an offer at all."

Jeremy reached out and lightly tapped the paper sitting between them. "Accept the offer. This one. Email Susan and say we'll take it. Or I will tell her."

Stuart's smile faltered. "You're serious? Sorry, that's . . . we haven't really started, yet."

"Yes, we have. And we're finishing. Say yes to this and get the money."

The lawyer stiffened, and sat up straight. He pointed at the paper. "This won't cover what I'm owed. I was prepared to get a little burned on this, it's the nature of the business, but I'm not losing it all just because you don't feel like waiting."

"Okay then, get them to offer enough to cover whatever you need, then accept it. I don't want a penny. Brian and Marie have their money back. My parents have their money back. Get these assholes to come up with enough so that you come out even, then pull the plug."

"You're serious."

"Absolutely."

"You want nothing."

Jeremy thought about it. "I want the bar," he finally said.

Stuart's smile came back, more sad and indulgent. "I totally get it, Jeremy. Fuck, this has been a real pain in the ass for me, too, so I can't even imagine what it's been like for you. You built that place, and you gave it your best shot. And the last few months have been . . . It's hard to let go."

"I just want the bar. I want to take it out before we hand it over."

"You mean the actual bar? The wood and everything?"

"Exactly. I want it taken out."

"That kinda comes with the deal. They get everything inside the place."

Jeremy shook his head. "They'll just tear it out to make space for more tables. They'll put in a tiny stand-up bar, the exact same as in their millions of other locations. The one in the Shack is *mine*, I made it. I want to take it out of there before they can scrap it."

"I'll see if they go for it. I'll try. Is that it?"

There was one more thing. Jeremy took a deep breath and made the request.

———————————

A day or two after the call from the OPP, Jeremy turned off the highway and onto the dirt road leading to his cottage, already feeling the dampness and cold in the tips of his fingers and his toes. He was half an hour early for the meeting with the officer. Here and there, he spotted ghostly kites of smoke hovering over hidden cabins in the trees. There were people around. A few dozen people on the lake were there all year. They had special tires on their trucks and ATVs in case the snow situation got really hairy. It was something Jeremy had once thought about doing: winterizing the cottage and spending the whole year out there, waking up to the sight of the lake frozen over and the sound of distant snowmobiles, testing the will of the Jeep on an unplowed road. He'd discussed the idea with Benny a few times, who only said that they'd probably have to dismantle the existing structure and build a new one from scratch.

"Why can't we do it with the old building?"

"Same reason your first wife can't fuck like your second: too old, no good."

Cresting the final hill before his cottage, Jeremy drove over the dull tip of an enormous boulder embedded in the ground in the middle of the road. The rain and run-off had exposed more of it than usual, which he noticed too late to steer around it. It gave the back bumper of the Jeep a final smack that almost sounded angry. He used to try and guess how big it was whenever he was out for a walk. No one he asked seemed to know. There was always talk of dynamiting it. Jeremy had once been a staunch dynamite supporter. Lately, however, he had changed his mind. The stone had likely been left there by retreating glaciers, dropped off as a parting gift by the same dying walls of ice that had scooped out the lake. He was taking the long view lately, about everything. He could look at anything now – a tree, a building, an old person – and he would see them as artifacts, with whole long stretches of time behind them, shaping them, forming them, harming them. As he walked down the path to the cottage, he didn't see the broken glass and the beer cans, he saw a ridge of land shaped over centuries by water, wind, time, and weather.

Taking the long view also made it easier to accept what had happened to the Chinese dragons: both had been reduced to sprays of broken plaster on either side of the front door, which was closed and sealed with yellow police tape. The dragons had only ever been temporary, artificial recreations of something ancient. Nothing fake lasted, no replicas endured. The missing dragons were a lesson in shattered plaster. He was hit with something that might've been grief when he saw the mess, but was able to choke it down. He had seen worse, and forgotten worse.

He stepped carefully down to the water's edge, using the dock – which he had dutifully remembered to pull out of the water before the freeze-up – as a handrail. There were more empty bottles on the ice near the shore, along with what looked like a used condom. With the toe of his boot, he broke the crusty edge of the ice that had been pushed up and out of the lake. As he did so, he worked his way through a mental inventory of everything that had been inside the cottage, trying to come up with anything that would be irreplaceable. There was nothing, except for the arrowhead stone, which he had left sitting on the TV. Chances were it had simply dropped to the floor, unnoticed, while the TV itself got smashed or stolen. That was the hope, anyway. He decided he ought to retrieve it before the officer arrived.

Way out on the lake was a thin, grey hut. Someone was fishing.

"THERE IS NO POWER IN THE WORLD GREATER THAN FORGIVENESS."
— *Awesome Love, Awesome Life*, Theo and Dominique Hendra

Charlene stood outside the coffee shop, hidden from the view of anyone sitting inside, for as long as she could stand it. It was only when she began to worry about passersby thinking she might be in trouble or having some kind of episode that she finally stepped out from behind the corner. She had also recently hit that stage, one of the many she'd been warned about, in which standing still for extended periods of time made her feel as though someone were hooking heavier and heavier weights into the flesh behind her bellybutton. She sometimes felt as though she were collapsing inside, the way stars did in dramatic computer simulations of celestial death. She'd thought she would feel like she was pushing out, ready to pop, and though there were days when she felt stretched, dangerous, and vulnerable, it was mostly this black-hole sensation, an overabundance of gravity. And she really had to pee. Again.

The windows of the shop reflected the brightness of the day. She couldn't see inside, couldn't make out the faces of any customers. She knew Kyle was in there, though. Not a chance he'd be late, even by one minute, and it was more than a quarter of an hour past the time they'd agreed to meet. It wasn't intentional, though he would likely assume that. She told herself to let him assume whatever he wanted, to allow him that moment of judgment, of superiority. But it wasn't true that she had intended to leave him waiting. It was tougher to get around now, and she still wasn't used to having to allow for extra time.

As she approached the doors, someone pushed through from inside carrying a cardboard tray that, strangely, only held one tall cup. She worried for a moment that it might be Kyle, but it was a man built like a cinder block. He held the door open for her with his free hand. She thanked him, but still put out her own hand to ensure the door stayed put. She'd had a few scares where people, thinking she was already clear and not bumbling along like a fat old lady, let go of the door too soon. She wasn't used to being so protective of herself. She used to take stairs two at a time, not in haste but out of childish sloppiness and greed. Now she stepped down slowly, one at a time, aware of each measured drop and careful not to put her entire weight on the lower foot until she was sure it had landed square in the middle of the stair. She stood on escalators like a toddler treating the moving staircase like a ride and wanting to make it last. She let commuters run up or down past her. She was more aware of things in her immediate vicinity, the corners of tables and the hard handles of doors.

Her doctor had commended her for her carefulness, but said it wasn't entirely necessary: that wasn't a jug of nitroglycerine she was carrying. Women in much more precarious circumstances had been managing this vulnerable period for thousands of years, and it usually worked out okay. He knew a few women who'd been in car accidents even further on than she was. There was one who'd been in an actual plane crash – not the fiery kind where two jets tackled each other in mid-air, but a still-scary situation where one of the landing gear buckled, sending the plane sparking and sliding along the runway. No harm done. Mother and baby were fine.

None of that mattered to Charlene or helped to overcome her fears. She stayed vigilant. It had been weeks since she'd gotten up too quickly out of a chair and been hit with a storm of dizziness and faintness. She came up slowly and carefully each time now, like a diver avoiding the bends. Her body had become a project, a building site she was sworn to protect. Way up at the top of that body, her mind still watched herself do these things, take these extra cautions. She watched herself shuffle around like an old dog and wanted to laugh and throw herself into a pile of leaves. If she were ever genuinely tempted to do just that, however, the thought would be quickly overruled. She had a job to do, simple as that. And that was to not be so stupid. Not like she had been for so long.

Kyle was sitting in a corner at a table against the wall with a coffee in front of him and a plate with a tiny Danish in front of the empty seat. He was on his phone typing something fast, but didn't seem angry. He smiled like a relative at a funeral when he saw her and rose from his seat to greet her.

"I just have to use the girls' room, sorry," she said, halting him as he moved toward her.

The women's washroom was at the other end of the room. It was the kind with a lock on the door and room for just one person at a time, which she was thankful for. She hated dashing into a stall to the indulgent smiles of women checking their hair and reapplying lipstick. There was an overhead fan making a lot of noise, which made her feel even more safe and comfortable.

Had Kyle really been about to hug her? After everything? Would he want to come into contact with the literally growing evidence of her total departure from his life? She doubted it, but the only other explanation was that he was getting ready to kick her in the stomach, which she doubted even more. So it must've been a hug. She'd heard, through mutual friends, the ones who were still talking to her, that he'd been in some kind of therapy, something he'd had to be talked into at first, but which he had apparently embraced with single-minded fervor, as if eager to prove he was not afraid of it, and was genuinely willing to change, if necessary. He looked as though he'd gained weight, though that might've been an illusion created in part by the thick beard he now sported. It made her smile: Kyle had always resisted facial hair. Even slightly shaggy sideburns were hateful. She wondered if he had a girlfriend who was telling him to grow it. There was an expected pang at the thought of it, but she still hoped it were true. For one thing, it would make talking to him so much easier if he were truly moving on with someone else.

When she unfriended him on Facebook, he sent her a text demanding to know why, and accusing her of doing so as part of her efforts to make him feel as low as possible. So she deleted her Facebook account entirely, which was no loss: she could not effectively curate the visible evidence of her life. For so long she'd had no status to provide an update for, and now that she did, she had no interest in sharing it, in putting it out to be loudly approved of or silently criticized. She got enough of that in real life. Her last two posts, eight months apart, had been: "Rainy day – what happened to the sun?" which a few friends had liked and commented on, and then simply "Ugh," which only her mother commented on, asking her if everything was okay. She never replied to Kyle's text. She didn't reply to any of his angry messages, only to strictly practical questions or requests. Had she spoken to a lawyer? Yes, she had; he would be in contact soon. Was she really planning to sign the document? Yes, she was. She didn't bother asking him if he would, too – there was no way that he would not, even if everything inside him was against the idea. He would never let her get ahead of him like that.

It had been nearly two years since they'd even seen each other face to face. That was a disaster, the memory of which prompted her to let out a small groan that was covered up by the bathroom fan. People had been urging her to do it, to not let the lawyers take over where it had once been just the two of them, two humans. Even her mother, who had spent those first few months in a heightened state of confusion – smug that she had seen through to the unworkable nature of the relationship, yet scornful of her daughter for finding herself in the middle of this mess – had come around to the idea that Charlene owed Kyle an explanation. She told her that if Kyle wanted to meet, away from lawyers or anyone else, she would have to agree to it.

"You said exactly the opposite before," Charlene said.

"Don't try to make this about me – you can't blame me for this."

No, she couldn't. She couldn't blame Kyle, either. The whole process was pointless, irrelevant, a waste of energy. She tried to convince Kyle of this at their first meeting. They met in a secluded corner of the park down the street from their apartment. His apartment. Meeting there had been his idea, and she had not said a word of protest, though she knew he had picked the spot so that strangers could not witness the two of them together. She felt like a co-conspirator. They were plotting the end of their marriage. It didn't matter how this all happened, she told him. They should both focus on not making things harder and more painful than they already were. The damage was done, etc.

He had not been ready to accept that kind of no-fault approach. In fact, the question of where the fault lay was the very one he'd been most interested in exploring, and he did so, at the top of his lungs, until she had no choice but to walk away from him, with tears falling all over the front of her coat. He stayed where he was and did not follow. Angry texts took over from his voice before she reached the park entrance.

Since then, all of their communication had been done through the lawyers. And then, about a month ago, he had sent her a message, saying he'd heard the news. She ignored it for a day or two, and then he sent another, saying he was happy for her and hoped she was okay. It had been her idea to meet. She could meet him on whatever weekend day worked for him – she finally had her driver's licence, she told him. Shocking, no? She was still working through the week, and always felt like shit at the end of the day and too tired to go anywhere. Once she finally got inside their place on a weekday evening, she would not budge. Their condo was on the eighth floor, and although there was an elevator, you had to walk up a half-flight of stairs to get to it. The building had been erected a half-century ago, before anyone gave a shit about pregnant ladies or people in wheelchairs. From the living room couch, she could see the CN Tower pointing brightly into the sky. Jesse liked to turn out the lights in the apartment whenever the tower was blinking red and blue. He called it the cheapest show in the city. They would sit there and stare at it until his little girl – who still couldn't pronounce Charlene's name properly and hadn't worked out exactly how she fit into her and her dad's life – began to complain about the dark.

"I pee like a dog now – every 10 minutes," Charlene said when she came back from the washroom. Kyle nodded. Lowering herself into the empty seat, she tried not to call attention to the state of herself, but it was impossible even for a non-pregnant person to get in and out of those hard chairs with any kind of grace or dignity.

"You're okay?"

"I think so. I'm not sick all the time anymore, which is nice. My feet have been hurting more, and I have to sleep on my back now because of this ol' thing."

She put a hand on her belly, then regretted doing so. She was being too casual, as if she were talking to a friend from work. She wished she hadn't mentioned anything about how she slept, too, as it would only serve to remind him that she wasn't doing it alone.

"Sorry, is that too much information? Bottom line is I'm okay. Thanks for asking."

"No problem."

It may have been partly an effect of the beard, which she found always made men's faces seem more haggard and toughened, but it seemed there were dark lines under Kyle's eyes. She wondered if he was sleeping properly. Having talked about her own sleep problems, she had a perfect segue to asking him about his, but couldn't bring herself to do it. She had to admit: she didn't want to think about who else might be in the bed with him, either. That realization reinforced the decision she'd made to accept whatever anger he was planning to throw at her. Not *accept*, that was too passive: she would simply not try and match it. She didn't want to have come all that way, only to end up screaming across a Tim Hortons table. He was wearing what looked like a new shirt, buttoned right to the top. She decided that was a sign of hope: if he'd been planning to let fly the full force of his righteous anger and hurt, he likely wouldn't have gotten dressed up. Unless he was working right after their meeting. Maybe she was going to get yelled at, anyway. Maybe there was simply no way to avoid it. She'd just have to sit there and wait until the fire died down inside him a little.

"How's Woody?"

"He's okay. Older."

"I'm sorry I couldn't take him – his daughter is super-allergic to cats."

"Whose daughter? Oh."

"I like that shirt, it looks good on you."

He looked down to see what he was wearing, and pinched lightly at the material.

"This is for work," he said, partly to deny ownership, and partly to dismiss her interest.

"Well, I like it."

"Sure."

Aha, she thought: she was going to get yelled at, after all. Now that she knew, she could prepare herself. It's not as though she'd left him with many other options. Throughout everything, he had merely been himself. He was damningly consistent. She, on the other hand, had brought in something new, had slashed at their life together in ways he couldn't have predicted. *She* was the villain – not as much as some people would like to believe, and not to the extent that she ought to spend her life wracked with guilt, which she had no intention of doing, but a villain, all the same.

"So, how long?"

She was confused for a moment, thinking he wanted to know how long their meeting would last. She only clued in when his eyes dropped down to her belly.

"Oh, three more months. More like two and a half. I'm at the point where I'm starting to wish I could get it over with." Kyle made a puzzled and slightly shocked expression, which she quickly tried to counter: "To have it, I mean. To get over the finish line. At first, you don't even think that you're going to have to actually deliver this thing. You just get told it's in there and growing, and everybody's all happy about it. But then the truth starts to kick in: this is gonna *hurt*. Ha."

She was babbling. She made herself pry off a corner of the Danish on the plate in front of her and put it in her mouth. She hadn't planned on eating anything, though she was starving.

"Thanks," she said through a mouth of crumbs.

"Did you get my note about the books?"

"I did, thanks. You can throw them all out, or recycle them. There's only one I want: that picture book that was in the bedroom."

"*Bunny Talk.*"

She smiled. It had been a gift from her father, sent to her for her third birthday. Her mother had always hated the sight of it, but its cloud-blue colours were an occasional reminder that her existence extended beyond whatever four walls she was penned in by at the moment. Lately, she'd been wondering if she were a shithead like her father, and had been all along: one of those leering foxes that pops its head up out of the bushes every time a chatty bunny gets curious about the darker parts of the woods.

"That's the one."

"It's not in the bedroom, anymore."

"Oh. Okay."

He touched the side of his coffee cup but didn't pick it up, as if quietly checking off one order of business.

"There's also a box of your makeup and things like that. I put it all with the books."

"That's okay, I don't need any of it." She didn't have room for anything from her old life, anyway. She was living in an apartment with a man and a small child in it, and was determined not to infect it with the germs of her old life anymore than she had to.

"There's not a lot."

"Kyle, I really don't need any of it. You can throw everything out. Honestly. I just want that one book. You can send it to my work – I'll give you the address."

He went quiet. After a while, he said, "I guess you and Jeremy got most of it when you came over."

"Yes, we did. Whatever I could grab." She was annoyed, and didn't try to spare his feelings. The meeting could not become a hostage negotiation, because the hostages were already dead. She had made sure of it.

Kyle stared at the table between them, seeming to memorize the whorls of the fake wood.

"Have you seen Jeremy lately?"

It wasn't a question she was expecting. "No. Not in a long time. Have you?"

The question came out before she could stop it. She'd only been trying to make conversation. She braced herself for a flash of anger, but instead he told her he had.

"A few months ago. Someone from work was leaving, and the going-away party was at Crane's. The one that had been . . ."

"I know which one you mean."

Kyle seemed almost apologetic. "Right. Anyway, so we went there, and there was some problem with the reservation. We'd booked the private room they have there now, but another group was already in it. Jeremy came out and got us all to sit at the bar while he cleared the other group out."

"And he recognized you?"

"Not at first, I guess because of the –" Kyle reached up and touched the tip of his beard, smiling guiltily like a little boy. "He did eventually, though. Because I saw him looking at me when we all went in. Honestly, I was thinking I might just go home. I got up at some point to use the washroom, and on my way back, he came up to me and said hi."

"He said *hi*." Charlene had to stop herself from laughing. It was the craziest thing she'd ever heard. As if two warring gods, who'd been hurling stones and planets and fire bolts at each other throughout eternity, finally met in line at a movie. According to Kyle, Jeremy asked if everything was going alright with his group. Kyle said it was, and then Jeremy apologized for the mix-up. He said they had some new staff on the floor that night, and were operating in a state of barely controlled chaos.

Charlene smiled: at the Shack, new staff members were inevitably the source of all trouble and problems, even when no such staff existed.

That was it for most of the night, Kyle said. He went back to the going-away party. At the end of the night, when they were leaving, Jeremy was there by the door saying goodbye to everyone. When Kyle, who'd gone back to find his gloves and scarf, finally came out, Jeremy was standing there, waiting for him. He asked again if everything had gone alright with the party, and Kyle told him yes. Jeremy said he was glad, and told him to tell the rest of the group they were welcome back anytime.

"You're sure he recognized you?" It all sounded so strange.

"He did. He asked me about you. I was getting my scarf on and he asked if I'd heard from you, and how you were doing."

Charlene's breath started to come faster, and she felt a prickle of sweat break out on her back and on her neck.

"What did you say?"

Kyle looked at her, briefly regaining the upper hand he'd lost so utterly when he came home to their apartment that night to find most of her things gone, and the front door still ajar. She guessed that the door was probably the worst part for him: for a while he must have believed she'd left it like that to make clear how little she valued the things she was leaving behind, the life she was leaving behind. She didn't care if anything got stolen. It was one of the things he accused her of when they had met in the park that time.

She could see the sense of victory going out of him in an instant. "I said I hadn't seen you for a long time, but that we'd emailed each other, and you sounded okay. Which was true."

"Okay."

"You haven't talked to him at all?"

"No. I figured he was mad at me. Everybody's mad at me."

She looked at him, hoping he would smile.

"I gave him your email address," he said.

"He already has it."

"He said he didn't."

"He does."

She hadn't replied to any of Jeremy's emails. Many times, she had written a long message that tried to explain what had happened, why she had acted the way she did, why she had suddenly left, why she had lied to him. She deleted them all unsent. There were no explanations to be made.

"I'll send him a message," she said. Kyle nodded, clearly not all that interested in what she planned to do with regard to that part of her life. For most of their meeting, he had kept himself open and had not locked up with anger – it was something he must have trained himself to do. He had mentioned in one of his messages that he was seeing someone new; learning to not lock up could very well have been one of the conditions of them continuing to see each other. But anger was like eczema: it would be with him forever. Seeing his ex-wife across the table from him, with her enormous belly glowing sickly between them, was clearly too much.

"So everything is good for you now?" he asked her. It sounded like an accusation.

Charlene could tell what was happening; she could see the stoniness creeping into his face.

"I'm a mess, but yeah, things are going okay."

"Well, that's good. That's great that things are okay for you."

"Kyle."

"They're not okay for me, but thanks for asking."

"I'm sorry – how are you?"

"No, *I'm* sorry. Sorry for not being interesting enough for you. I know it's really boring to be around someone who goes to school and has a career and doesn't cheat on people and doesn't have kids with people and leave them."

"Please, Kyle. I really don't want to fight. I can't do this anymore."

He sat back in his chair. "Oh okay. *My apologies*. You're going to be a mom, and so everything is forgiven."

"I'm not asking you to forgive me," she said quietly.

"Good, because I don't."

"I know."

"I don't forgive you and I don't care that you're having a baby. I really don't. I know the whole world's supposed to be all happy for you, but I'm not. I think it's the biggest cop-out in the world: you can't get your shit together, so you go and get pregnant, and then you're suddenly not responsible for anything anymore. You don't have to figure anything out, because now it's all about being the best mom in the world."

She put her head down. "I didn't plan this."

"No, because you can't plan anything. You can't plan for shit. You worked in a bar because you can't plan for shit." Some of the people behind the counter were looking over, so he brought his voice down until he was almost hissing at her. "Don't you see what a cop-out this is? You fuck me around, you fuck your boss around, but now I'm supposed to act like you're a saint because you have a baby. As if that's some big accomplishment. Am I supposed to congratulate you for getting knocked up? Oh, *congratulations* on doing the easiest thing in the world! Congratulations on solving all your problems by having a kid! Congratulations on being a total cliché! And I get to look like the asshole because I knew what I was doing and I took care of shit. And I never fucked around on you. Never. Not once."

"Stop it, Kyle. I didn't want to hurt you."

"Oh, fuck off – yes, you did. You wanted to hurt me and you did."

She knew right away that he was right. It wasn't enough to get away from him, it wasn't enough to break apart what they had built, as pathetic as it was. She had to crush him in the process. She'd wanted to humiliate him as revenge for how humiliated she had felt for so long. It didn't even matter that it wasn't his fault she felt that way – or not entirely his fault. She needed to cut him. Lying in her new bed, in her new home, in the middle of her new life, unable to sleep because of the new life shifting around painfully within her, she burned at the memory of having wished, more than once, that he had drowned in that lake.

Kyle stood up, not looking at her, and put his coat on. He stood still for a moment, looking down at the table between them, then spoke in the voice of someone merely passing on some neutral information.

"You're a coward and a liar, and you better hope your new guy doesn't figure that out."

After Kyle left, Charlene sat and cried for so long that one of the counter clerks got sent over by the shift manager to see if she needed help. She told him she was fine, which came as a relief to the clerk, it being too late in his shift to get involved in any pregnant-woman-crying drama. She tried to pull herself together. There was almost no one left in the place, and she was aware of having become, by default, the most visibly troubled customer – not a good category to be at the top of. The pastry Kyle had bought her was still half-eaten on the plate, and she made herself swallow a few more flaky bites. Her back was hurting from sitting so long in that hard chair, and she felt utterly drained.

She'd lied to Kyle: she *had* seen Jeremy, less than a month ago. Though he had not seen her. She was in the condo, stretched out on the couch and watching TV. No one else was home, and she couldn't make herself do any more baby proofing. The whole morning had been spent putting guards on cupboard doors and sealing unused electrical outlets with hard plastic caps. There were still many, many ways for the baby to die there, and no way to eliminate them all. So she lay herself out on the couch and turned to the all-day news station, the only thing her ravaged attention span could absorb. A story came on about a contest held by a car dealership in North York in which six people vied for a brand new minivan by sitting together inside it for an entire hot weekend. One by one, contestants dropped out until it was down to two men – one was a retired soldier who said he planned to give the van to his daughter, and the other was Jeremy. Charlene felt something shift within her at the sight of him, and was not sure if it was the baby or her own stomach. There he was, wearing a Crane's golf T-shirt soaked to a dark maroon with sweat and a pair of cargo shorts with pockets the size of saddlebags.

"Oh my God," Charlene said out loud, and laughed. "Oh my God!"

He had come in second, taking home five years of free oil changes. But he looked happy. That was the first thing Charlene noticed, once the initial shock wore off: he was beaming. He looked thinner, too. Climbing out of the van with the help of two models who wore the dealership's logo on their T-shirts, he smiled weakly and gave the thumbs-up to the cheering from the crowd in the parking lot, like an astronaut returning from a long stay on the International Space Station or a miner freed from a collapsed pit. Jeremy was handed a large bottle of water and a towel, and a man with a big Red Cross symbol on his hat gave him a quick checkup and asked him some questions she could not hear. She could see new lines on his face, new damage. For a moment, he looked a decade older, and the exhaustion he must've been feeling seemed to creep over him like a poison. She worried he might collapse right as they were filming, but the camera cut away to the van again, where the victor – looking as red as raw beef – was emerging, triumphant. He stumbled a little stepping down, and needed more substantial aid than the models in the tight T-shirts were able to offer, so two other men in Red Cross caps ran up to grab his elbows and walk him into the first-aid tent, where more people in caps were ready with melon slices and water and a list of questions designed to determine just how badly his brain had been baked while sweating it out inside the van for the past 48 hours.

When the camera turned back to Jeremy, he was smiling again, and a pretty young woman with a microphone was with him. He seemed renewed. He had the towel around his shoulders, and looked as though he'd done nothing more strenuous than an hour of hot yoga. It took her a moment to realize he was wearing a fresh Crane's shirt – someone must've had one at the ready.

The woman with the microphone asked how he was feeling.

"There were moments there when things got a little hairy, for sure, but I'm totally fine now. I'm used to some pretty tough situations."

He waved at the crowd again, and she briefly caught sight of the purple welt in the centre of his palm.

"It must be a little disappointing to have stuck it out this long and not win the van, though," the interviewer said.

He set his face in an earnest expression and told her that he was not disappointed, not at all.

"Obviously, a brand new van would be great, but it sounds like my new friend is planning to give it to his daughter, which is amazing. Good for him. He deserves it, a hundred percent. I'm not disappointed because I didn't really do this for a van, or even to win a prize. Seriously. I'll take the oil changes, but I did this because I wanted to test myself, to see if I could find my limits and push past them. I really think you need to do that every once in a while, just so you know you still have room to grow and learn. If you don't push yourself, you never know what you're capable of. I took a shot, and second is pretty close to first."

"Wow. I think if I did something like this, I'd give up after an hour. How did you do it?"

Jeremy smiled and reached up to touch his temple. As he did so, the surge of adrenaline that had been sustaining him eventually subsided, his face collapsed into confusion, and he slumped sideways. Hands reached out to steady him and draw him off-screen as the woman with the microphone threw back to the woman in the newsroom. They both agreed they would not say no to a free minivan, but could never have stuck it out that long. The next story was about a dog in Etobicoke that had befriended a duck.

In the Tim Hortons, Charlene prepared herself for the ordeal of standing up and walking the two blocks back to where she'd parked. She checked the time on her phone: she'd told her mother she'd come by for a visit. There was a voice mail message waiting, which she hoped was from Jesse. She sometimes got nervous when her phone buzzed, and would right away start worrying that something bad had happened to his little girl. The worst, most gruesome scenarios filled her head, images that would not dissipate until she heard his voice, and he reassured her.

She had never worried about that kind of thing before.

She took this as a good sign.

From *Power Tools: The Expanded Edition* by Theo Hendra

"My friends in Canada don't wait for spring to go fishing: they will drag a little shack onto a frozen lake, and put it on top of a hole they've drilled right through the ice. I've been lucky enough to do it with them, and it's amazing. Does it get cold? It sure does! Especially for a kid from California like me. But when a fish finally tugs at your line, you instantly forget how cold you are. You want to jump up and down and yell, but that would scare all the other fish away, and it would ruin the fishing for the people who were nice enough to bring you along. So you quietly put your fish in the cooler, bait your hook again, drop your line back through the hole, and wait. Only this time, you know that you will catch another fish. Because you used your Hard Work Tool, your Social Tool, and your Patience Tool, you have reached a Success Stage and are filled with Power. *Congratulations*."

ACKNOWLEDGEMENTS

Many, many thanks: Michael Holmes and everyone at ECW Press, Martha Webb, Anne McDermid, and everyone at McDermid Ltd., the incomparable Gary Taxali, Emily Schultz, Rachel Heinrichs, Emily Donaldson, the Ontario Arts Council, Wolsak & Wynn, Tightrope Books, everyone at *Quill & Quire*, Eileen DeCourcy, Vera Beletzan, Antanas Sileika, Andrew Pyper, Priscila Uppal, Alex Lukashevsky, Paul and Mary Lou Strimas, Ken and Verlie Whitlock. Rest in peace, Bates Strimas.

All my love and everything else: Iago, Olive, and Lou.

© Iago McEvenue

NATHAN WHITLOCK's award-winning fiction and non-fiction has appeared in *The Globe and Mail*, *Toronto Star*, *National Post*, *Toronto Life*, *Report on Business*, *Flare*, *Fashion*, *Geist*, *Maisonneuve*, and *Best Canadian Essays*. He is a contributing editor for *Quill & Quire*. He lives in Toronto with his wife and children.

Published by ECW Press
665 Gerrard Street East
Toronto, ON M4M 1Y2
416-694-3348 | info@ecwpress.com

Whitlock, Nathan, author
Congratulations on everything / Nathan Whitlock.

Issued in print and electronic formats.
ISBN 978-1-77041-290-3 (paperback)
ISBN 978-1-77090-857-4 (pdf) – ISBN 978-1-77090-858-1 (ePub)

I. Title.

PS8645.H566C65 2016   C813'.6   C2015-907295-6
C2015-907296-4

Editor for the press: Michael Holmes | a misFit book
Cover illustration and design: Gary Taxali
Author photo: Iago McEvenue

The publication of *Congratulations On Everything* has been generously supported by the Canada
Council for the Arts which last year invested $153 million to bring the arts to Canadians throughout
the country, and by the Government of Canada through the Canada Book Fund. *Nous remercions le
Conseil des arts du Canada de son soutien. L'an dernier, le Conseil a investi 153 millions de dollars pour mettre de
l'art dans la vie des Canadiennes et des Canadiens de tout le pays. Ce livre est financé en partie par le gouvernement
du Canada.* We also acknowledge the Ontario Arts Council (OAC), an agency of the Government of
Ontario, which last year funded 1,709 individual artists and 1,078 organizations in 204 communities
across Ontario, for a total of $52.1 million, and the contribution of the Government of Ontario
through the Ontario Book Publishing Tax Credit and the Ontario Media Development Corporation.

Printed and bound in Canada by Friesens   5   4   3   2   1